VOID CORPORATION

BLAKE BUTLER

T0282006

PRAISE FOR VOID CORPORATION

"There's an exceptional amount of intention and control on display in the telling of this story... Don't expect a conventional reading experience. [*Void Corporation*] is a meditation on art and perception whose form seems to serve as both a meta-comment on the function of the novel, and a challenge to the expectations that a reader should bring to one. It's rare for me to enjoy and value a book on those terms, but this one worked for me. And even more to the point, I respected it for insisting that I rise to its challenge."
—*THE NEW YORK TIMES BOOK REVIEW*

"[*Void Corporation*] signals Blake Butler as our most imaginative writer."
—*THE BELIEVER*

"Butler is a master of the American dystopic, language-driven novel, and here returns with his penchant for mining the unsettling national psyche, delving so deeply into its unconscious that the resulting delirium is uncannily close to truth."
—*THE MILLIONS*

"A remarkable accomplishment ... [Butler's] constant worrying at what's genuinely personal, struggling to detach it from the endless play of light across wall and screen, strikes me as an undeniably contemporary project."
—*LOS ANGELES REVIEW OF BOOKS*

Published in the United States by:
Archway Editions,
a division of powerHouse Cultural Entertainment, Inc.
32 Adams Street, Brooklyn, NY 11201

First published as *Alice Knott* by Riverhead Books, an imprint and division of
Penguin Random House LLC

www.archwayeditions.us

Daniel Power, CEO
Chris Molnar, Editorial Director
Nicodemus Nicoludis, Managing Editor
Naomi Falk, Senior Editor
Mia Risher, Publicist

Edited by Chris Molnar
Proofread by Sylvana Widman

Library of Congress Control Number: 2024940585

ISBN 978-1-64823-078-3

Printed by Toppan Leefung

Cover art: Seymour Rosofsky, *The Inspector*, 1968, oil on canvas, 50 x 60 in.
Author photo: Molly Brodak

First edition, 2024

10 9 8 7 6 5 4 3 2 1

Printed and bound in China

VOID CORPORATION

BLAKE BUTLER

ARCHWAY EDITIONS / BROOKLYN / NY

FOREWORD

In the summer of 2007, I sent an email to myself, just six words: "Corporation that buys and destroys art." No way I could have known I'd spent the next decade writing and rewriting from scratch at least three totally different novels trying to find my way into the world behind the idea.

The original version, at the time titled *Void Corporation, or The Obliterations*, opens with a nameless man who is invited to a private party at a mansion where after signing NDAs, the guests are made witnesses to the incineration of a Rothko, no explanation. In the weeks thereafter, the man becomes obsessed with the event, eventually absorbing himself in an ever-deepening wild goose chase, seeking answers from loose threads strung among a civilization falling to pieces under dementia, terrorism, mob violence, and collective decay.

The last time we see the man—at the end of the first chapter—he returns incensed to the site of the incineration only to find it has been stripped bare, or so it seems. After further examination and nearing his wit's end, he discovers that the entire mansion, once considered historically significant, is only makeshift, comprised of sequentially numbered tags for easy breakdown, like paint by number. Furthermore, the digits on the tags aren't merely static; he finds they shift beneath him as he moves:

> Whereas before I clearly remembered the digits on the latticed tiles in the front room had been numbered between 800000 and 810000, now I found ones

marked in the mid-750000s and below. And while once again moving clockwise led me over tiles of steadily descending aspect, moving counterclockwise caused the same effect. That is, no matter which direction I went in the rooms from one to the other, the digits on the tiles once I had left them out of sight continued dipping in range to lower and lower registers. So that when once again I'd completed a full route in crouched position through the connected chain of empty rooms the house contained, I found myself again there in the front room on tiles clearly marked differently than they'd been the first time that I touched them.

Not long after this discovery, he disappears. The bulk of the rest of the draft, in retrospect, reads like a dozen novels crammed into one, stacking subplot onto subplot—including a massive immersive Winchester Mystery House/Tower of Babel-like installation made entirely of dead artists' workspaces and homes; a viral livestreamed program titled "Reality One" that anyone who wishes can volunteer to appear on, at their own risk; a rapidly approaching celestial object that appears to be an exact copy of the Earth; a child prodigy—who will later become President—whose inexplicably high-concept artwork causes viral illness, madness, and loss of consciousness in its audiences; massive plots of black sand spreading so rapidly they threaten to cover every remaining inch of navigable land, leading to the discovery of a direct portal to hell in California—until there's nowhere left to turn.

Much like this nameless man—who I imagine must have at least in part been based on *me*—very little of the text of that original version made it over into the novel as it exists today. Immediately after finishing that first draft, I filed it away and started from scratch, having realized all I'd really done was dig a bottomless pit. It all felt a little too conceptual or implausible, lacking a heart to hold together—traits I normally wouldn't mind about a text, but that this time felt like a beginning, not an end.

Most of my writing during this period happened at my parents' house, where every morning I would drive and set up shop in the same childhood bedroom where I'd first learned to masturbate, peering out through purple curtains onto the yard where I'd spent endless preteen afternoons pretending to be the leader of a private rebel organization whose only mission was to defend our family home from unseen foes. Since then, my dad had fallen deep into dementia and required constant supervision, a task my mom had taken upon herself to see through in their home. The terrain of my writing, then, became pervaded with a fog of ambient illogic and disillusion, often interrupted by Dad speaking and acting in non-sequitur, alongside my mother's struggle to stay sane herself amidst the loss.

When not assisting with caretaking, I'd put on headphones and blast heavy records to blot the world out and provide consistent space where I could think—most frequently Tim Hecker's *An Imaginary Country* and *Ravedeath, 1972*, Miles Davis's *Bitches Brew*, The Necks's *Body* and *Drive By*, Growing's *Color Wheel*, Earth's *Hex (Or Printing in the Infernal Method)*, Fennesz's "A Year in a Minute" played on loop. It wouldn't be until years later, after Dad passed away from complications of Alzheimer's and I fell in love and moved out of my loft into a house with proper office doors I could close, that I would find my way back into the project yet again, destined to spend the next several years on continued serial expansion and revision before I finally landed on what would become *Alice Knott*.

Unlike the original, packed full of loose threads and dead ends, my goal headlining the final reboot was to try to write a novel someone could read the way they might working a maze. I took as my primary model *The Crying of Lot 49*—a consistent third person limited omniscient voice focusing primarily on one protagonist—inspired by reading somewhere that Pynchon had said he only wrote his thinnest book and biggest hit so he could attain the necessary cultural cache to publish his behemoth, *Gravity's Rainbow*. Finally, the perfect way to frame wanting to be understood for once, I thought, unlike how for so long I'd mostly thrown myself blind into abyss after abyss, no looking back.

Even still, I wasn't sure where I was aiming, unwilling to be trapped by making outlines and the like—easy paths to courting tedium in my opinion at the time, preferring instead to work by trial and error, more like a sculptor or a coder than an author. I'm sure I couldn't see it then, but I believe the skeleton key I'd eventually need to lead me past where I'd already gotten lost so far came through my mother, who after Dad died entered a dementia of her own. Having always been a bit of a mama's boy, I felt a much different experience of intensifying confusion and depression through her undoing than I just had with my dad's, madness that threatened to dismantle not only our realities, but the potential life of the soul, my will to be. I'd learned to think imaginatively, both as a writer and a reader, first from Mom—a retired high school art teacher and lifelong quilter, whose process prized exploration over illustration, process over format; soon enough, though, just as my dad had, I knew she wouldn't remember my first name, or then my face, or then her own. I suppose in a way it makes strange sense now that she didn't survive to get to read it, despite having read everything I'd let her since day one.

"Did you read that new book by Alice?" Mom asked me one day out of the blue early on in her disease, before we knew. I had to smile. "Alice Who, Mom? Munro? Notley? *Alice in Wonderland*?" I watched her think about it for a second, reaching to remember. "Oh, anything by anyone named Alice is probably good," she concluded finally, blushing a little as she laughed. Not long after that, Alice showed up in my novel, already as disoriented in her own mind as Mom would come to be eventually, as if the shifting plates I'd described in my first draft had somehow appeared beneath our feet.

Over time, witnessing the dissolution of her capabilities came to feel as real to me, or even more real, than any house or stretch of land or work of art. The more alone I felt trying to negotiate my way through the devolution of the mind of the woman who'd created me—not to mention the maddening tedium of bureaucratic corporate health care, the widening morass of social media and targeted ads backed by fake news, the worldwide rise of autocratic government alongside suicide, the fakeass feelgood mindsuck of what many still insisted upon calling the Golden Age of TV—the more it seemed to me, glued to my desktop in despair, as if reality itself was the real death trap, and the only imaginable salve, at least for me, should be discovered by boring a hole *through*, rather than *into*, the darkened heart of the American mirage.

Today, nearly four years after its original release early on in the COVID-19 pandemic, under a stand-in title I didn't choose—apparently the marketing dept. at Riverhead thought *Alice Knott* a better draw—*Void Corporation* feels in my mind less like a novel, or even a narrative, and more like some kind of subterranean catacomb hidden in plain sight; full of booby hatches, false floors, red herrings, two-way mirrors, and other intentionally deceptive slights of hand, psycho-coded much like dreamwork, and designed to shift its apparent shape with *you* inside it as you read, much like reality. More so than a moral or meaning, *Void Corporation* might be meant to work much like a map without a legend, or a key without a lock. If that sounds like hyperbole, may I suggest you reconsider your in-line thinking about language—the most uncanny and prismatic form of technology we'll ever have, continuously auto-updating its own core functions whether we'd prefer it to or not.

I suppose there should be something more to say about the ways the world since this was written has turned out to reflect it as reality— including the current trend of utilizing theatrical violence against art to corral attention, the rising rates of dementia and Alzheimer's, the monocorporatization of absolutely everything and our semi-conscious public fear of death, the discontinuous ubiquity of surveillance and tokenization of consumers, the for-profit mass media and its despotic mind war against the imagination of the soul. Such tropes were always written on the cave walls, though—mere piecemeal features of a space-time we all must learn to find our way through in search of sense, a clearer calling that might finally override the noise. In the end—or *In the beginning*, if you wish—the real story, like any story, only exists among its many shifting shadows, obscured in plain sight as if in spite of itself, begging the question: *What are you going to do about it?*

If only we didn't think we already knew the answer…

Baltimore, MD
3/18/24

for Barbara

0001

The video begins with an establishing shot of a famous painting, hanging alone on a wall of white. The camera is clearly handheld, a feature divulged by its framing's subtle waver, rather informal given the context of the forthcoming act. And though the footage bears no titles, no credits, many will immediately recognize its featured image as *Woman III*, a work of oil on canvas composed by Willem de Kooning, according to records, in 1953.

In the painting, a sprawl of subdued color—gray, gold, blue—forms an abstract female figure shown head-on: breasts like blunted pyramids, braced beneath shoulders so broad no ambulant human could hold them upright. Mangled, muddy hips bracket the focus of her crudely rendered crotch, outsized in turn by massive, jagged hands hanging to her knees. Atop it all, the woman's diminutive face, a landscape of moon dirt, leers slyly toward the viewer, as if aware of something inevitable none among us might wish to know.

The original version of the video, unlike the truncated one eventually most widely shared by news media, allows one full minute elapsed in silence, a last glimpse of the object without suggestion of its fate. In later edits, this buildup will be cut, plunging the viewer headlong into action without preamble, for there is little time to waste.

Likewise, not until after the video has been shared online more than seven million times—a reach accrued in less than three nights following its debut—will any major news source link the painting's fate to a related story several weeks prior, wherein said work had been reported stolen from the primary residence of its last known owner, an aging heiress by the name of Alice Knott.

Regardless of preamble, in any version of the video, a pair of masked figures eventually appears, coming in on each side of the painting from offscreen. They are dressed identically, in stark white hooded work suits that obscure their hands and faces. Together they lift the painting off the wall, turn it over flat, and hold it still, yielding no sound but the low, ambient buzz of a hot mic recording nothing.

The camera tracks the figures as they carry the painting across the room, revealing the edges of a much wider empty space, buttressed on its far end by a small formal audience seated together on silver bleachers: six men and six women, each dressed in stately fashion; the men in tuxedos, the women in gowns, the cloth of their garments as stark white as the walls are in surrounding, as if they've meant to blend into the space. These spectators' faces have each been digitally obscured, leaving only a warble of busy pixels where their features might have named them. Together they look on, calm as lambs, as the painting is placed faceup before them upon a small raised platform, like a patient, of no nature to do anything but wait—a condition matching ours, the viewers', as what we are seeing is in the past, already happened, including all as yet to come.

The camera pans then to assume the perspective of the attendees, divorcing their physical image altogether out of the shot, taking again as its primary focus the fate of the painting. There is a lingering beat, poised upon the object, in which it seems this point of pause could last forever, fill the duration of our lives with its soft looming, though, then, why exactly are we here? What are we meant to be receiving? The drift between each question and its answer spans the absence until, startlingly, against the silence, the soundtrack lurches to life: a high-treble, jarring pink noise, like a blister splitting over and over, emitting a monotone barrage of high-end squall that overrides all other possible audio in full, so much like the wide white walls that fill the space, as if to press the monotonicity of surfaces surrounding the painting through the speakers of the spectators at home.

And then, again, this time from behind and to the left of the camera, a human figure appears onscreen. This one, though, unlike the others, is wearing a chrome-lined pack strapped to its back, from which a long slim chrome nozzle extends to be wielded by the wearer, and then, from that, the bright eye of a blue node of focused flame. The figure moves to stand over the painting at its head. It adjusts a setting on the device, causing the bud of light to grow almost a foot long, the corresponding aural furor likewise intensifying, as if to permeate the viewers' concentration.

The figure proceeds to apply then the ember of the burning to the work.

The incineration begins along the canvas's upper left-hand edge, instantaneously eating into and through the paint wherever it is made to touch; such that during the interface the image becomes obliterated—each mark undone from its original instatement at the hand of the artist, himself expired and cremated; each inch of the creation that had survived him rendered unto ashes as the steadfast neon eye continues across its face without relent, quadrant by quadrant, stroke by stroke.

The rest is simple math, an eventuality rather than a wonder. The bright and rising buds of fire suggest some wilder version of the painting, unlock from within it some charisma of a kind that could once have been borne from a culture's total fear of its creator. The flame is thin and wide and asks no questions. The total annihilation requires little time—the image turned to absence without so much as a whimper, any word, nothing to restrict its path to full annulment, leaving behind only loose cinder and a disseminating smoke that curls and rises from the focal point of its destruction, into thin air, as we all breathe.

At no point is any distinctive feature of the obliterator made apparent seen onscreen; only the assured, surgical attention of a person performing an assigned chore, with the same poise as one might have washing a window, digging a hole.

The destruction is beautiful itself, too, some viewers will argue, in its own way; how the flat, detached tone of the recording stands so firmly apart from its reality's steep expense—that is, not only the $137.5 million *Woman III* had once commanded at auction, setting a record for the contemporary era, then breaking its own mark again a decade later in reselling to the Knott estate for an even more ungodly sum; not just that, but the elimination of the work from all existence forever. We can already hardly remember what the painting resembled beyond fragments, many will soon find, even amid the countless replications of its likeness in archive left behind; no single feature strong enough to override our fresh perception of the char that's been impressed upon our senses as the recording ends and we remain outside it, and there is only then the screen, at once and suddenly blank.

What did we just witness? Why had it happened? Who would have sponsored such a thing? There are, of course, no direct answers, at least none made public, and the absence results in a sprawl of theory and debate, sprung from fact into philosophy, unto exhaustion on all sides. Perhaps the video is no more than some strange hoax, some posit, a camera trick designed to stir reaction, mass attention—if so, in fact, a job well done. But to what end, and for whom? What even can be said to have been forfeited, others will ask, beyond dollars and cents; how much different, without one such image among innumerable others, could our world yet really be?

What's not debated is how within two weeks of its original appearance online—uploaded by an anonymous user under the handle oedipaoapideo, thereafter shared and copied countless times—the video of the obliteration of *Woman III* amasses more than thirty-seven million views. Attempts to ban the video from being hosted at various sites by the request of certain legal and preservation-focused entities, citing terms-of-service violation on the eventually discounted grounds of *copyright infringement* and even *explicit content*, do little more than incite further growth, as its replicating presence looms and winds, spurred forward by countless outlets responding in tones ranging from curiosity to horror, from deep regret to uncanny joy—a discursive heat within which there very quickly seems no center, like a snuff film, an act carried out against the state of human aspiration in and of itself; as what had we lived for, some conversation's final word might yet project, if not for evidence of something sacred allowed among us, let alone within us, in pursuit of which we so often go nowhere but in circles.

Alice Knott, unlike so much else, is not at all difficult to find. She hasn't left her house in years, a fact she offers freely, loudly, to the cameras gathered at her door, seeking comment from the destroyed painting's final owner. She had even been home during the night of the theft, or so she claims. The spoils of that night, according to the official police report, included not only the now apparently vanquished de Kooning but several other works possessed by her estate. She's lucky just to be alive, she might imagine; had they killed her during the job, she wouldn't be standing here, sweating and swaying, left anticipating some other future way to die.

Alice knows, of course, that cameras are rolling, hence the morbid inspiration. It was she who had called the cops and the reporters in herself, amid the escalating rhythm of would-be scandal; she alone who stood out on the front step of her house to meet and greet them in waning daylight on a Tuesday, waving around a tumbler most would assume is filled with booze, given her demeanor, though Alice hasn't had a drink in years—not that she doesn't still feel drunk most days, half asleep and half dissolved. She can feel the onlookers' probing eyes assessing hers, so self-aware she can't quit blinking and licking her lips as she forces an answer to every question that must be asked, for the record, the fast, involuntary tics that have persisted all her life, though only in front of strangers.

She is aware, too, that she's a suspect—perhaps the only suspect, as it stands—in a case without clear legal repercussion as much as moral, as far as she can tell; rights to the pilfered work remains hers, after all, or so the law states, and therefore the right to destroy or display it as she sees fit, all subsequent provenance notwithstanding. It is her choice to change her world, so she believes, no matter who or what else it might affect; each and every act, no matter how small or opened up, must suffice unto and within itself alone, now and forever.

Not that she'd done it, the destruction, or had anything to do with it: Alice hadn't done a thing. The true invaders of her home, whoever they were, had taken eight works, a fact she'd discovered under the same shade of disbelief as anybody else. She'd entered down into the vault beneath her house that morning on a whim, having for the most part come to treat the secured space as if it didn't exist, despite—or perhaps in light of—how for years now she'd housed there the bulk of what had once been her family's substantial financial worth, the product of a period of her life in which she'd begun converting all liquid assets into aesthetic objects, things no one on Earth but her alone could own. Whatever logic had inspired such a pastime no longer survived in Alice as it stood—some kind of semi-self-destructive process, she imagined, somewhere amid the wake of ongoing mourning and her innate abhorrence of the unasked responsibility of wealth. Simply nothing else but spending all the money had made sense to her at that time, as far as she could remember from the distance of what seemed by now another life, an urge she often wished she'd spent on traveling the world, giving cash away to those who could use it better; instead, though, she'd filled a basement with glorified antiques, each now a reminder of all she could have been or done and yet had not. Even the vault itself, as she saw it now, had been installed as a private practice site for the ongoing conceptual emotional torture only she could comprehend; no sooner had the installation been completed than she recognized it as another ill-starred misstep in the fulfillment of her stint, another reason to never quite forgive herself for being who she'd become, not really.

Which was fine, as Alice saw it, not so much different years later than a day. It seemed impossible, no matter how confident one's aim, to hit the mark of even our most immediate intentions, to know exactly what and where the target is and how it might echo upon impact, much less to carry that faith forward in daily confidence, unto death. It was so difficult even to remember what one was doing as you were still doing it, was it not? For instance: Who were all these people on her lawn? Where had they come from, and to whom might they return? But yes, despite the continuous exception of all that, Alice concedes, she is the violated, not the violator, despite what other forms of abstract possibility her imagination might perform, what willingness she's felt throughout her life to let the others have their ways.

In fact, the sharpest sense so far of her experience in the present situation was not of fear or guilt, not even loss exactly, but of something more like the absence of the loss she should have felt—like not actually feeling wronged within the fact of being robbed—like feeling nothing, neither from the loss of property, nor from even the basic texture of what her home's spatial violation should have caused; and there within that, how acknowledging the inevitability of one's own death by now bore little dread, and on the worse days, loomed as relief; nor even, then, her recognition of the apparent gap between her own perception of self, how she carried forward, versus the expectation of any other, their unspoken demands, especially amid such spectacle as all this, the silent cameras and the nameless faces, the utility of public consternation and reframing. She is who and how she is, you shit; no more, no less. And there the world was, ever awaiting, in all directions, at all sides.

What had struck Alice more than anything about the crime was how all non-artistic objects in her archive had been ignored: drawers of high-dollar assets like necklaces and watches and rare coins and stamps and bonds and even deeds to land Alice had never herself stood on, stuff she'd stuffed her family's funds in before transitioning to art—everything besides the *singular works of human imagination* allowed to go on rotting in their cases, far from light. Whoever had broken in had done so in pursuit not of simple monetary value, but of the irreplaceable. And so it seemed they'd known exactly why they'd come; known what she had and where she had it, as well as exactly how to get in and out unseen, without a hitch—at least according to her private security provider. Not a single trigger, by their records, had alerted the system of an intrusion while she was being ransacked, nor did their surveillance mechanisms capture any fragment of a clue. The footage had simply *blanked out* during the incident, is how the reps had put it; that is, they hadn't stopped recording, but instead all present visibility had gone black, as if a lens cap had slid over every camera at the same time, though no other signals of interference or manipulation had been detected, suggesting that the perpetrators' technology had been beyond expected capability, and so beyond detection, as yet it stood.

Even more inexplicable than what they had or hadn't taken, at least to Alice, was what they'd left behind. A single mirror, forty-eight inches square, freshly hung in the display vault in the very position previously occupied by Robert Rauschenberg's *White Painting (one panel)* (1951), the first of all the artworks Alice had acquired: a square canvas covered in white house paint, a work the artist had referred to in interview as *a clock*, and within that a thing that "if one were sensitive enough that you could read it," so he had stated, "you would know how many people were in the room, what time it was, and what the weather was like outside." More so than all the other paintings she'd purchased through the years, Alice found, it was this infernal square that some nights she couldn't get out of her mind: how it seemed to be not only aware as she observed it, but capable of absorbing some of herself into itself. Some nights she felt as if she could feel it even through the walls, as if it were assuming other arcane forms while out of sight, melding back into white when she returned.

As such, it had been difficult at first to tell if the painting was really even missing, given how precisely the monotone shade of the piece matched the walls, embodying the same absence of all color, the studied silence. It was just a blank white canvas, after all, a work of concept over form, not remarkable unless *the thought of nothing* was, or perhaps the continuous nonpresence of the possibility of nothing; how the blank was never really blank.

But as she'd come to stand before the object that long morning, Alice noticed how now the surface of the image continued to coincide with her perspective as she moved: its empty texture shifting against the incandescent light between them, its coordinates intermingling before her eyes. The object appeared to recalculate and correct itself continuously in relation to where she was, or how she saw it, altering the intention of its refraction as she continued in approach, as if its surface were still wet from being painted; or as if it were not flat at all, but somehow open.

And then, there in the image, Alice was: her present living body, as she'd seen it, contained within the shining glare as it amassed. She could resolve herself there in its grain, seeing herself rendered standing in the white field as a reflection, of living flesh. The thieves had taken *White Painting* after all, she knew then, leaving in its place an unlike replication, one for one. The effect, to Alice, in the otherwise bare room, felt demonic; an object made even more aware in its replacement, given new purpose; dare she say it even felt somehow *alive*? If nothing else, that much more near to what it really wished to be, if not as well what it always was?

For some reason, one she could not decrypt to herself even now, she had not mentioned the mirror or the missing Rauschenberg to the authorities, who themselves had no record of what might be lost or gained beyond her word, the receipts she could submit to prove what she was worth. Instead she'd kept the detail private, a secret left to linger between her and the culprit, whoever it was, and how, and why; and anyway no one had asked. The police performed their responsibilities according to their contracted obligations alone, deferential only to what could be said for certain, in the present, *just the facts*. They seemed somehow not even to have been able to see the unfamiliar mirror hanging there amid the scene as they'd performed their investigation of what was lost, to the point that Alice had begun to wonder what else might be missing that she could not remember.

———

Alice watches herself from inside herself perform for the police and the reporters, the cameras, the vortex represented in each eye. She gives them exactly what they wish for—content—even if every question they offer, for once, has a clear answer: "I don't know." She could make it up, she thinks; then there'd actually be something to submit, though in the end there could only be more questions, more thirst for bandwidth. They were there not for evidence, not for information, but to be there being there, wielding their mics. They had to know that she knew only as much as they did, all on-the-record information already being filtered through their feeds. She'd seen the video of the erasure of the de Kooning only alongside their other millions, as much a spectator now herself as any, in effect, any claim to ownership separated from her own fate and into some other historical status entirely. Seeing a work with such personal resonance that way, and for the last time ever, apparently, even on a screen shared with so many, did at least push her toward a new sort of feeling, one not of fury or even wonder, but simply: *who?* Whose blurred faces were those seated as spectators to the destruction? Whose eye peered through the lens that led the camera, and who worked the blowtorch? Those people seemed to matter more than even whoever had come into her home, if they weren't in fact the same. What really was at stake here, and for whom?

She knew, simply from speaking to the two badge-bearing dolts who'd come looking for a way to paint her as more than just a victim, that local authorities weren't really interested in truth. They cared enough to act alongside one another, in a performance of protection, long enough that when they were done they could go home and drink beer splayed on the sofa to watch dickheads with strange equipment compete onscreen in the good name of their hometown. That was where the real cachet of culture lived and breathed, of course: in the veins of the athletes, each drawing salaries in the same register as many collectors paid for priceless art. All this blather about a painting blown to dust mattered to Joe J. Jones nowhere near as much as whether Joe J. Jones Jr. caught the orb and won his squad the title, as the crowds lurched around and scarfed the hot dogs and donned the copy jerseys and made applause.

"Anyway, it was really, in the scheme of everything, a minor work," Alice finds herself explaining to the cameras, off the cuff. "The goddamned de Kooning, I mean, in my opinion. It could have been more powerful, more unspeakable; could have worked harder to be nothing other than itself, to exist beyond the confines of its conditions; at the very least it could have been more beautiful. And the same goes for you and I. Minor works, each and every one of us, shits in a blender. Get it?"

Nobody seems to want the jokes, no matter how she shucks around or hams it up. She's only talking now to keep filling air, right? To get the sound out of her head. The heads bearing the microphones and booms and lights are staring openly at her now, as if at some other abstract gob they refuse to try to understand; and yet their perceived distance only further spurs her on. She's positively beaming by now, eating up the opportunity between spectacle and spectator, really flushing.

"Would you just get a load of your-all's face?" she scoffs, holding her glass like a weapon. "Like this is news now, actual news? Like you aren't all up all night every night trying to forget how you spent your day, all those sad hours chasing someone else's dreams?" At least two of those assembled are writing down her every word, she sees, or at least writing *something*, transcribing every passing moment into false form. Alice is no longer sure which of them are cops and which are pundits, or lackeys of pundits, or lackeys of other lackeys, and in the end it doesn't matter because none of them can really hear her for what she means. "I mean, they might as well have sawed my limbs off, mightn't they, whoever did the crime? Not that I really even need my arms that much at this point anyway—not as much as a quarterback or a seamstress or whatever important people do these days—nor do I even go on much in the pursuit of human pleasure. To all of you it would have felt only the same to see me murdered, no big shake between my flesh and some dickhead's imagination."

By now some of the camera people have started packing up, she sees, having vacuumed up enough sound to fill fifteen segments with the local color for what they imagine has occurred. The only people left now are the real rats, the fucking lesser web media maybe, onlookers wandered over from unknown corners to watch the roast. The whole of it has her by now a little lightheaded at the edges, disoriented after the mass of questions meant only to lead her on, to entrap her into answers that would remake her as spectacle in place of person; like a second shadow, taught to split.

"Either way, of course, I'll end up cold in the earth all on my own. *Alone*—you remember that word, right? You still get that feeling sometimes, when you're all done pumping at your pissholes? Not that there's anything to understand about it but the dark. Anyway, I plan to be cremated, same as the painting, same as, eventually, the ground beneath our feet. Which, by the way, aren't they still mine? I mean the painting's ashes? Once whichever of you are out there working to recover what was lost has done their job? I'll bet you've already locked down the rights to every square inch of future cinder, haven't you? Waiting to snort it like boutique blow. Well, that's fine. You all can have it. Just save a line or two to rub on the gums of my corpse."

Alice takes a big swill of her soda water, sucks her teeth. She's suddenly unsure of what she's said, all of it already on film. She can feel all through her skin and blood and bones how their devices have come in and taken possession of her person, filling out her visage with spectral residue of public sight, some numbing agent drawn up in preparation for pending broadcast to further masses, and for the future of her person, as she must be, in death and beyond before all the rest of us burn up, before the silent cells of all we've lost are no more than vibrant dirt over our heads, submerging under rubble everything there ever was and ever might be, every precinct and every soundstage in the same grist as our graves.

━━

That same poached feeling will spread beneath her through the remaining hours of the evening: in ghostly bloat of excess memories being worn away within the aging minds of every life, as if what Alice perceives is not actually there and never was and could not ever; as if she no longer owns all of herself; such that by the time she finds her body collapsed in front of the TV, already watching recaps of hours before, she can't remember having been there, can hardly recognize her flesh. Her depiction seems too overrun, her skin aggravated and inflamed, as if she had been pressed against a baking surface in her sleep. That couldn't be what she actually looks like to other people, could it? And yet there she is, clearly standing on the lawn of her own house, identified in strong font with what she believes to be her name and whatever implicating info: *Local heiress, Alice Knott, suspected of destroying multiple works of invaluable art.* So there she must be, yes; who else could so appear, wearing the same teeth and tongue still in her live mouth, though even still her voice on the recording doesn't sound like her voice as she knows it, nor are her answers to their questions words she remembers having said. *They edit these things so completely, I could have mumbled anything and it would still say I am fucked*, she thinks aloud, still in the performing voice she'd used onscreen, though by now she is well outside the sphere of influence on her own portrayal. Who she is or will be remains at the mercy of the public eye, pushed along its soft trajectory within the record as it stands.

For instance, this *act of terror* with which she is associated—the term now being applied to the destruction of her property as the story reaches wider scale—is presented tonight alongside advertisements, scores, and weather, all of them wearing our attention down, molding our position of confusion into a feed that we can nurse through our adult lives. And once one station has taken up the broadcast, unto tumult, every other channel in collaboration then also must, clustering dozens or hundreds of public personalities each bearing little to no actual interpretation around the single supposition of what had actually occurred, another thread in an immeasurable bulk prescribed to correspond with our reality as they've described, and thereby stitch by stitch becoming woven into the ongoing sprawl of all personae, who we are.

As it stands on record, regarding whether or not it is actually Alice there appearing as herself—it absolutely must be. It is in fact, in some ways, *all* she is, at least to most: a recent fragment of a life available to mostly no one beyond every long façade she never even recognized she carried on, the ground floor of a series of experiences so obscured she can't remember feeling the certain feeling she just felt, likely in immediate revulsion for her own aura, already loathing every other of her even from inside its pending shell—clear now onscreen as the distinctly lighted side of any moon, its other half there lurking just beside, flush in darkness, sharing her breathing, feeding her mind; and yet it is only she, who she is *right now*, who can choose to open or close her own eyes.

As if to contradict her introspection, then, her image there alone on the screen splits in half; or, rather, it is replaced by a side-by-side portrayal of two faces: a straight-on headshot of a younger version of herself, beside another person so much like her in complexion, a spitting image, the depiction of which she has no idea how they've procured; the image had long been buried amid her home's begotten junk as in her working memory. It's an image she has held in her own hands many times, though she remembers nothing of its moment of capture outside what the picture itself carried on, sourcing all extant perceptions not from real time, but from its rendition; much less how it could have become accessible within any kind of public network, never having been uploaded anywhere she knows of, or even scanned; and yet now here appear their faces, names together, in the same breath: she and her supposed sibling, *Former death row inmate Richard Smith.*

At once, in examining the original childhood image again, without the nametags, it would be hard to tell which child might actually be which, as if either could have been labeled with the name of the other; Alice herself can hardly even tell their heads apart beyond the sudden sinking feeling that gains hold of her on sight of him, his face so much like her own, both then and now, at least to her, despite the way the years had pushed them each through different changes, nose, forehead, mouth, cheeks, though time had not been kind to either. The longer she looks from one back to the other, in the blink before the screen shifts, the more she can discern the minor differences that had at some point singled them out: the way Richard clamped his lips closed tightly, covering his bad teeth; the way her eyelids in almost any picture went half closed; each only further distinguished then by the insert of an overlaying image, nearer the present, of each of the children as adults, Alice's visage paler, tighter, made of angles, while his is grizzled, bloated, sun-damaged; and in his eyes a kind of dead adrenaline, as from having nearly fallen from great height; though really, seen in just the right way, they still looked so much just the same.

What was the point of fleshing this out now, Alice wonders? What did their impression mean to say? Richard hadn't even come up with the cops, despite his not-so-unrecent appearance in the same news streams she finds herself conveyed within now, his from the proceedings that had surrounded his heavily divisive release just days prior to his scheduled execution, after which she'd hardly seen his name in print ever again. Alice had never understood by what means his return to freedom had been secured, how he could have been cleared after what seemed such definitive proof, even his own hellishly explicit testimony of his crimes. Back then she hadn't been able to bring herself to dwell upon it, what such a sudden shift in fate might mean; instead, she'd simply gone on as if he did not exist and never could have, as if he were no more significant to her ongoing life than any other stranger. They no longer shared even a last name; Alice had changed hers back to her birth father's as soon as she was able, as well as any other apparent legal linking or means of communication within her power, her relentless, recurring nightmares—even after she finally stopped drinking to drown them out—notwithstanding. She had simply no space for him inside her heart, her head, nor had she ever really, and yet through the years he'd remained somehow always just on the cusp of out of mind, sometimes even more so in her unwillingness to actually admit him.

Despite however long it had been between then and now, just to hear his name alongside hers in someone else's mouth made her feel as if he were somewhere behind her in the room, sharing her air, if always still hidden even in periphery regardless of how fast she moved her head. Suddenly everywhere she touched and had been touching felt inscribed with traces of him, his corporeal aura transmitted into not only her home but countless others, hub to hub, at once smothering out any sense of earned respite within the trauma, the code by which she'd learned to carry on, and therein finding little formal difference to the feeling beyond what might yet more definitively rise unseen, whether beyond her or within.

In truth, as she recalled it, Alice had existed in the span of her would-be brother's association for what felt like only half a life, though as she grew older her understanding of how it might once have been grew only fractionally more clear. The total time she'd spent in his actual physical presence once he'd been established, according to how she understood it now, had only really spanned several months, and even those mostly semantically: through walls, in pictures, by association of name. There were very few actual moments within their era when she could actually recall witnessing Richard's living, breathing body, alongside which she'd supposedly been born, not even counting the more recent spread of years she'd for the most part all blacked over. Thinking of it in the present, pushed by the mere indication of connection, Alice could hardly explicate how or when their *then* had ended—that is, the time she'd always thought of as the prior era of her being; childhood, some would call it, though by now it was more like a partition clipped from the mind of someone else; all auras and emotions more than anything concrete, beyond what others of her lineage had at some point determined as defining *how it was*.

She knew, at least, that she'd had a mother and father once, as must any person, though as the years passed she found more and more often that she could not recall so much about the way they were, as if she had intentionally forgone the context amid the many modes of open torment she associated with their presence. In the beginning, though, for certain, they were but three—mother, father, daughter—no pets or tenants and certainly no sibling, not even an imaginary friend, much less an actual friend whose shape withstood the imagination's long decay. The framework around their original nuclear unit obscured any world outside it to Alice as a child, as if they alone had been selected to exist as human life not only inside their home but amid the mass expanse of night, the rest of the world nothing more than a fantasy to young Alice, an expanse taking the form almost in full as one unknown. She had perhaps been much older than most kids before she went very far beyond their house's many walls, to see what else was or might be out there on all that land; and older still before she began to learn how there was no real center to even that world, much less her person. Once she'd begun to understand that, felt its insistence situate its face forever between her and who she ever felt that she could be, there began to come more potent interpolations in definition.

Such as how, one day, just like that, her father had disappeared; or, rather, the man who had so far been her father ceased to exist as she had known him, even in light of the shallow remains of the past Alice retained and called her own, in that following the dark transition she was the only one who seemed to recognize a change. He hadn't died, her father, at least not officially—there was no mourning and no funeral, nor had he officially announced himself out of the household going forward. Instead, the shift came without any form of friction at all, any blight beyond where Alice herself felt it—not her mother, no one else. The man had simply completely ceased appearing anywhere, as far as Alice knew, including in others' memory but hers, or any trace of evidence he'd ever been.

From room to room, on the first day after, Alice came into each space finding not only nothing left of him where it had always been before, but even amendments applied in the shaping of the places once all his. Such as: no set of hammers in the closet where he had kept his hammers, but instead board games she could never remember how to play; no freezer full of private beef, which he had hunted down himself and brought home and wrapped in plastic for some future meal that never seemed to come, but now branded frozen foodstuffs, from corporations. Their house itself appeared, as well, to Alice, to have been remodeled within the space of one night's sleep: the ceilings higher, the hallways longer; closets full of clothes she'd never seen (ones that would not have ever fit him or even close, from outdated eras, full of ruffles, awful colors). Even the ground around the yard beyond the windows where she had grown up playing by herself was nothing like it had been, if in only subtle ways: the private treasures she had buried for safekeeping no longer in the dirt where she had placed them, favorite paths in the forest leading not to secret hideouts or favorite landmarks but on to further paths to nowhere.

No matter how long It went on like this, that day and after, Alice remained the only one who bore the difference (except perhaps her father, though he was no longer there to say). Her mother, for instance, when asked where Dad was, refused to respond with anything pertinent: she would proceed instead as if she couldn't even hear her daughter's spoken words—not ignoring, or choosing to withhold reaction, but wholly unconscious of any reception of the man's name or any other acknowledgment of his residual presence in their timeline, as if some embedded editor were muting out all reference, leaving only enough overlapping continuity that she, as the now single head of household, could go on without having even sensed disruption, any ill tone. Her mother seemed concerned only with Alice's perception of concern itself, her sudden alarm, her manic anxiety, over not only the unnoted absence of her father, but also how nothing she could say to work it out; nothing too her mother could or would do to allay her child's fears but reiterate that everything was and always would be fine; but insist that Alice would calm down soon and see again what had once been and still was, what was actually actual, all okay. For many of those hours, during the rare early days when they were both home and awake at the same time, they would lie in bed together, mother petting her daughter's head and letting Alice wallow and sob until she exhausted herself so completely that she fell full bore into dreams, back then full of nothing else but gore and mirrors, no respite; and each day again awaking into a world that felt more and more as if it must hold someone else's life in her own stead, someone she couldn't peel away from or convince to calm down even from a remove, somewhere within. The same felt true each time she closed her eyes, the emotional coordinates of any moment scrambling and reconfiguring at any given opportunity, if only just enough that she could feel it and not name why.

The same perturbation of continuity was also true, if in a slightly less crucial way, of all other persons coming and going from their home during that period of transition, which for at least a summer was a lot: strange men and women in the late evenings, right at Alice's bedtime, often indecorously dressed, and most of whom acted as if it were not only Alice's father, but also Alice, who did not exist. Nearly every night for a while there: long parties that took their course for the most part throughout the hours Alice was supposed to have been asleep, and which her mother would often lock her door through, over into mornings and late into the next day, as Alice waited without food and drink. Often through long shafts of night she could hear nothing but screaming through the walls, afraid even to move or close her eyes, and in the mornings masses of bodies all passed out around various rooms of the house like corpses that eventually came alive and crawled out across the ground and left the house, only to return again the following evening, and repeat.

Of the men who sometimes stopped to speak to her, for once admitting she was there, many of them holding themselves close against her and grinning as if flooded with electricity, none seemed ever to have heard of her father either; they looked at her in pity when she explained with growing resignation what had happened, how everything was different now, wondering aloud when would it go back to how it was, until her mother came and hurried her away. Only Alice seemed to remember how much better off the house had felt during their prior lives; how much she missed the way they were then, and most of all just missed her father, the one person who loved her more than anyone, she knew and felt, even if she could remember nothing else about him even days after her awareness of his disappearance beyond a smell of moss or wink of eye; not even any face there in her remembrance, just the outline of a person.

In the end, what little she had held as real about her life before the shift could withstand only enough oncoming friction for her to grasp the difference for a short while after the fact, until it began to feel no longer really true but under review, confined in facts revised out of how the world had once been to any mind beyond her own.

———

It was around this time, age eleven, or was it nine, that Alice had begun to teach herself to drink, initially inspired after a few pulls on the dark bottles the passed-out people left all over their increasingly crowded home. No matter how many days she passed in the new condition, the glaring divergence between prior and present never itched her any less, nor did the fortitude of the alteration feel any less evidently everlasting, though the liquor, at least, made the overlap seem distant, increasingly transparent. Consumption made Alice's hours seem to blur both going forward and in reverse, giving time a graceless and yet transfixing texture held up against how it had begun to seem, inside of which she learned not only to disregard the trauma of dislocation, but to become it. The longer she spent inside the temporary corridors of medication, the more natural the relief seemed, as if no brain were ever meant to go untampered, in the name of taking reign over the illusion of one's life.

Once this door had been pulled open, it remained that way until there were no longer hinges or a jamb, even a wall at all, a prior world; her life even then at six or was it sixteen was soon as awash to her as any hour already past, semantically as much anyone else's going forward now as hers, or so she felt. Nothing could ever need to be the same. The older she became, the more there no longer seemed a math to how it went—no one true body or name actually embodying an identity belonging to their person, no past or future. Anyone could be only so much of a fraction of who they'd already been at any given time before, and any future balance could be revealed only as you became capable of its arbitrary fabrication, and, therefore, its impression of reality as fixed.

Not only did her father never appear again amid the strange light, nor eventually could she unremember how it had felt before, but as well there were each day new facts about the contiguous content of her life—presences that emerged out of the early hordes of partygoers and became constant, then the only—and then, one day, as if it'd never been another way; an ongoing reformat featuring, most prominently, another father, from out of nowhere, who at once held himself forth as her father for all time, confirmed as their home's ongoing and uncontested figurehead according to anyone who came around but Alice, who knew for sure this wasn't true, and nevertheless was expected then to treat the appearance of the new father in her life as if she felt the same way about him as he supposedly did her: that they were linked, that he had been there before even she had; that he in fact had given her existence, raised her up. There was no question, nor any contesting the conviction left allowed; there was only the way it was, and so now the way it had been, so they insisted.

And yet, despite whatever ways she tried to teach herself to go along, Alice could find no shred of tolerance for this new father's insertion over the old one; no matter what this small, bony blond man did or said or knew or showed her, whatever memories in common he could share, even all the ones predating his appearance in her understanding, predating her ability to remember anything at all, no foundation would be allowed Alice in accepting the man as anything but virtual, a human tick. Nor would even the conception of *stepfather* ever fit, as that still suggested some acceptance of the relation going forward on her part: that he had authority over her person in command. *Unfather* had been the only thing she could stand to call him or consider him, though rarely to his face, eventually, to avoid her getting smacked. Amid all of this she'd be continuously reminded, despite her mind's ulterior evidence, that not only did she wear his same last name, he also shared her image: the same round face, same pinned-back ears, same widow's peak and crooked teeth, even the same way of moving through a room or standing in one. Both he and her mother could spin a childhood's lifetime of reminiscence to ground the relation amid significant detail: places they'd all been together, catastrophes they'd weathered, food they'd shared, the long gone nights under one sky they'd all survived, one after another—not to mention the deeper relatives in common, so much kin long passed and buried in the very ground on which they walked, and for whom Alice was said to now carry on the torch, full of their blood.

As the new *way it was* took hold by span of accrued time alone, and its concurrent sovereignty extended, refusing to mutate in Alice into new loyalty by simple accrual but instead taking on a sort of sheen through which soon no word or wish felt really hers, gradually her mother's love and understanding—the only pins between her last life and the present—began to reoutfit themselves as well. The woman's initial patience with what she perceived in her young Alice as a kind of temporary dementia loosened into her own equivalent anxiety, then to frustration, and from there downhill into unabashed vehemence, almost spite. As weeks passed without the change becoming common to her daughter, even when secretly drunken, Alice's mother began to demonstrate increasing distaste as to why the child "suddenly refused" to accept her very own flesh, her gracious father who had only ever loved and supported Alice in all she wished for, without bounds.

If the distinction upset her unfather in the slightest, however, he had a funny way of coping. He would mostly refer to Alice's behavior as "fake forgetting," laughing it off; she would grow out of it, he insisted, would soon give up her ruse and settle into line once more mature; she was simply acting out, a reaction to the changes in her body, its desires, as he saw it, the most common form of insurrection in the world. He really even seemed to believe it, this total stranger standing alongside her mom above her during her bedtime as they had tucked her in so tight it was hard to move her arms; this adult man, not her father, full of some wholly other kind of means, looking down into her with an expression of what Alice could sense was his idea of mimicking concern, a performance she could see right through, without a doubt; and so no matter who asserted what or how they pleaded, promised, Alice refused to let him in, to occlude the heart of who she knew she really was, or at least had once been; to concede. If anything, his apparent passion for her just felt creepy, a malevolent trick his simple mind didn't even realize his spirit had taken up, executing it upon on her, her mother, and himself alike, if not the world.

It was likewise from out of nowhere, after just long enough to begin to seem to have worn away to achy lull, that the standing premise of their family again split, from out of nowhere, and only further in reverse of what Alice knew it once had been—not only was there an unfather, now, but an *unbrother*, whose appearance in her life felt even more unprecedented than the previous revision, without a base.

The child began to appear first in only pictures, like the one the news had broadcast, many often with Alice right there alongside; and whereas she and the unfather shared strong resemblance, she and Richard looked *identically alike.* They were twins, in fact, or so both her unfather and her mother claimed, over and over, rolling their eyes, even jeering at each other in shaming mimicry of her expressions when Alice would ask who that was beside her in the pictures. There was little about Richard that marked him as other from Alice but his supposed gender and his clothes, perhaps the strange look he seemed to always be emitting in the picture, as if he were trying to see through you; otherwise, even to her, it would be nearly impossible to tell them apart, a condition that in addition to Alice's lack of physical context for her brother in her life throughout those hours she would at various points begin to imagine was some cruel game, a manifestation agreed upon by everyone around her, designed to spin her world even further yet out of its course, even without clear motivation why anyone would wish to, what might be at stake in doing so besides to break her down.

In kinder moments, more and more rare the longer the condition persisted in her mind, one or both of her parents would sit her down and explain the whole configuration of their family once again as if from scratch, to an amnesiac, filling in the blank spaces in her heart and memory with language that made the bodies carry meaning, context, trajectory. *It had always been this way*, they'd say. And moreover: *It would never not be. When it came to family, you had no choice.* And so there could only be, so as they saw it, an eventual acceptance of whatever mental damage had been rendered in her ongoing understanding of supposed lineage, most of the damage in this case solely Alice's, to be held together by a system of ideas set in place long before her own appearance, full of questions no offered answer might assuage.

The truth was in her blood. She could not live without her blood, or so they told her.

———

And still the most confounding thing of all about the addition of the unbrother, which seemed to have happened longer ago each time the thought occurred, was how he never actually physically appeared. As at once within the era of his suggestion in the home among them as ambient presence, he was referred to openly and regularly only as "sick," and as such spent all hours prone in his bedroom recuperating, beyond all shared air and light of day. At no point in the present, beyond the applied memories she was expected to assume, was her supposed lifelong sibling not considered under quarantine, which meant as well, Alice discovered, that the door to his room, down the hall from hers on the same floor, was always locked; nor would it ever be opened in Alice's presence under the apparently dire premise that they didn't want her to be exposed—the comings and goings of their shared parents, supposedly, taking place only in secret, under cover, wearing masks.

When asked what was wrong about him, no one could say; her

mother would only turn her face and burst into weeping, both at the continuously injurious evocation of her child in pain, which at no point lessened in its drama, and at Alice's apparent willingness to press and pry into the family's open wounds, a tendency her mother read not as a cry for help but as mere cruelty, abandon. How could Alice refuse to acknowledge all the time she and her brother had spent together, always bent instead on testing and retesting the family bonds that should have grown only more meaningful—and so more powerful—with age? Did Alice feel the same lack of love toward her mother too, the woman demanded, clinging only more and more steadfastly to a brutal willingness to question what everyone else around her experienced as innate? This gap in their connection would be the last snapped straw of once-shared understanding as mother and daughter: as after the appearance of the supposed sibling, her mother regarded her at best then with shameful pity, tending further and further toward disgust, and only further fortified within the ongoing gravity of emotional engagement the male half of their burgeoning unfamily required, day in, day out.

Richard is in pain, the unfather might mumble from a corner of the room, unseen as Alice arrived again to petition her mother's prior understanding, fending her off through clenched teeth. *Leave our son alone. He needs his rest.* Her mother looking on beside her, saying nothing as the man's voice filled in over her own. *You know he's been through so much already. Why do you have to make it worse?*

Thus, the distressed gap in Alice slowly became a widening expanse, increasingly palpable between her and those with whom she slept in rooms beside, then turning only firmer as a rallying cause between them, at once walling Alice out and further confirming the distortion in who she'd once felt she was and who she seemingly could not discontinue in becoming. How much of life had gone on like this, without her favor, both unconscious and awake, leaving nothing to be desired but that there could ever be an end to the ordeal without having to start over? It seemed like every second, every hour; wherein all the times she'd felt most almost herself were as well the most completely swarming, clogged beyond her own influence, to the point that doing something like reading or writing became all but impossible under the anticipation of a last, unnegotiable deluge. Around every unseen corner, then, she sensed some sort of fall, an expanse so much wider than would ever actually reveal itself, allow conception; every wall only a wish and vice versa.

The resulting effect colored their open hours as a family unit with morbid weight. The days carried on, slow as silence, through whatever routines would make the seconds pass, until the mandatory family dinners through which the three able-bodied units hardly even spoke, allowing the world to go on around them gnawing in reflection, forced in the range of Alice's glare for only so long as they forced her to sit there, eating nothing, waiting once again to be released, which even then would be allowed only after Alice agreed to go and kiss the unfather on the cheek, his skin as slick and cold as a wax figure, full of loose fiber.

Throughout the night, though, alone and sleepless in her own room, Alice would swear she could hear the unbrother's breathing through the walls, a slow and paceless shrift that seemed to struggle to get a grip on any air. Such sound would permeate the edges of her shallow rest when it did happen, often enabled only by continued swallows from whatever bottle she had stolen from her parents, learning to understand and then to covet the thrumming of it, the measured burn. Sometimes she could even hear the child speaking aloud to himself in indistinguishable syntax, language that did not sound like hers, but full of words all sick themselves; syllables with which he'd never answer when she spoke back through the venting, or even when she went around the wall construed between them and knocked or banged; instead he would seem to go still, as if pretending not to be there, to wait for her to go away again and leave him be. It wasn't even that she wanted to see him in the flesh—she'd only tried the first time after deciding it was he who'd been coming into her room during the night, to stand above her in her sleep, to rummage through her stuff—though then the fact that he wouldn't answer made her want an answer even more, a burning question that grew more elongated with lack of pressure, wider, less impossible to phrase.

After a while, it became easier to allow the unquantifiable aspects of any given night to go on simply being, to act precisely as they wished; nor eventually did Alice even really feel the need to fight against such looming misrepresentations, an avoidant tendency that grew even truer with drink. It took not long at all before she slipped into a continuously developing resignation, feeling just lost enough inside the world to concern herself with only what she could discern directly through her own senses, however uncertain or predisposed anything seemed under the continuous smudging of her existence as it was, while at the same time, in her foremost mind, to more and more distinctly never accept anything in full, no matter how clear, for what it might purport itself to be.

———

What Alice began to experience then, around the base amendment of the configured people in her life, was a concurrent reshaping of the physical condition of their quarters. Where in her earliest memories the home they shared had been barely large enough for the three of them (her real father, her mother, and herself), now there always seemed to be new rooms, and different dimensions to the past ones:

higher ceilings, wider walls, different colors to the trim or furniture, and so on. Even familiar doors at times seemed not to lead to where they'd previously led, while others led to spaces that did not even seem part of their house.

For instance, where had this all-white sunroom come from, with the matching white grand piano in its corner facing a windowless wall? Since when did they have a greenhouse, full of so many vibrant plants it was difficult even to breathe, of hues she didn't know plants could turn, an overrun bouquet so rich it nearly knocked her out? Or how, parallel to her mother's prior bedroom, through a lockless door inside her closet you could only see while on your knees, a long, narrow archive full of videotapes—along which she had barely room to sidle along front to back, peering up at shelves that extended out of vision, all the spines unmarked or in a language she couldn't read—which would not be there when she came back.

Even the world beyond the house could not be trusted as such, she remembers, though mostly all she saw about the outside came by peering through the small diamond-shaped port-eye just low enough above her bed that she could stand on tiptoe and peek out. No matter when she'd looked through it back then, day or night, she could never see what she knew logically should be there, given her understanding of the layout of their property—the grass and trees of their own yard, the little woodshed with the weathervane on top that'd had the directions ripped off, now just a point. The shed had no windows of its own, and no key to its thick lock, though with her ear pressed against the door she could sometimes hear machinery: hammering or grinding, metal on metal; someone typing; even sometimes the sounds of people having sex. Yet when she looked through the window the woodshed was never there; nor was the forest framed behind it, obscuring all other land beyond. Most all she ever saw, then, beyond the glass from in her bedroom, was paved concrete far as the eye could see, unobstructed, and often covered up in massive darkness, even during daytime, a wide sky void of even stars, only sometimes a low, glowing moon that seemed so much larger through the window than in the world, its bright face burned into her vision long thereafter, floating front and center behind her eyes once closed for sleep, waiting to nod off again amid repeating prayers that *one day when I wake, the world will be so different I won't even recognize the past, and all of what's wrong will suddenly seem right again and always have been, a wound healed without a mark.*

Alice knew the unfather was very wealthy, or so he'd claimed; he was always wearing heavy jewelry and talking about plots of far-off commercial land, bizarre transactions handled by shady men who might appear inside the house at any given time—though in her prior understanding of how the family worked, it was her mother who'd been wealthy, heir to a vast estate passed down through generations, destined one day to be passed along to Alice. She didn't know what it was the unfather did, or how that credit for their fortune had become transferred into him as if it'd always been that way, all of this concurrent with how the house itself would not stop reassessing itself during her unconscious hours, appending and recompiling old partitions with prickly new ones, nearly right beneath her feet. Some days she couldn't even find where her mother or the unfather had gone, though she could hear them through the vents somehow still, laughing—at least it seemed like laughing—sometimes taking hours to figure out what space connected back to where. Alice never bothered to ask what on Earth was going on, even when their paths again did cross; she already knew they would in some way say nothing had changed; how, god, the jokes were getting old now, weren't they?

Could she grow up, please, and be a person, embrace life as it must be?

And still some days the house was all that Alice had, difference be damned; at least even as the walls were white, then yellow, then a paisley font that shifted as she moved; she could still reach out and touch them, feel their face. Many sections of the house now seemed derived from different eras, she began to notice: there would be a bedroom done up in Victorian décor, with fainting couches and ornate carving in the dressers, lace and diamonds every inch; then, adjoining, a room of brutal concrete, with only a dresser and a bed, of Depression-era manufacture; another still might have bright, thick plush blood-colored carpet and plaid wallpaper, neon lamps lining the ceiling around glinting lamps and pop-style prints. She had never been in this room in her whole life, she knew, nor again the next one, as the drift of consistency hurt her eyes, made her have to blink frequently to keep from blinding, her body moving faster even than her mind wished to allow. Whoever had selected the furnishings from room to room seemed to have paid no mind, it seemed, such that the house seemed hardly to understand itself, each range of influence flowing over and becoming eaten up by what came after. This feel, at least, in some way, fit with Alice's own internal discontinuity, making finally one aspect of the architecture seem spot-on; perhaps one day, she imagined, its evolution would land her somewhere else entirely, somewhere she could really feel herself inside herself, alive again.

Sometimes, within that paltry bud of future hope, having wandered hours alone from room to room in hush, she would get the sense that her untwin had been there with her for some time, just out of sight; he was behind her, perhaps, or even beside her, having at last appeared at some point out of his locked bedroom unannounced. She could sometimes even parse out how he looked in her periphery, before her head turned, beyond the pictures hung in so many of the rooms both new and old—how in person he seemed much different: short, stocky, nearly white-haired even as a preteen; deep marks in his face as if from acne, though he was never old enough; glinting braces; the strange, blank eyes. Each time, though, when she tried to move to look at him directly, there'd be nothing there—only the open room—yet this did not preclude the feeling of having interacted with him, if not fully face to face; at least as though at last they might exist in shared air, she thought, like actual people, not yet erased.

She even began to feel, in those moments of his presence, as she felt them open, and held on, that she could hear him speaking to her from inside her, as if his thoughts were in her thoughts—dim lobes like ideas split and flattened into sense, made up of fragments of a logic fleshed between the timelines, asking countless questions like her own: *What had become of the prior household*, for instance, and *What has been done to our real father, in whose name*; though rather than simply confirming her suspicions, projecting solace through shared belief, his suggestions always seemed to turn back quickly against her, framing himself as the real victim, resulting only in more grief: *How Alice had allowed this all to happen, all the changing—how she was as much complicit in their mutual loss as any else*—and worse, how now he *could see her resistance caving in, accepting the myth of their deformed reality as her own*, which then made him wonder *what else as a result might yet be dissolved, what other facts could insert themselves into the record, as fate subsumed them*. It was as if he could see straight through all the ways she'd learned to think about her world, now made his too, relentlessly reviving the codes of questions she'd already taught herself to bury in the name of staying sane, likewise *accepting their corruption*, the resulting damage *his* and *hers* alike, and thereafter only further enabling its belief, unto a fate already allowed so long unchecked there would soon be no going back. *It may have seemed a long time coming, where we're headed,* he would tell her, as in her own voice carried on, *but it won't be so much longer now.*

The morning after Alice's media debut, according to subsequent reports, at the Museum of Contemporary Art Chicago, a middle-aged man lifts up a screen displaying a looping presentation of Ann Hamilton's video *aleph* (1992–93) and throws it as hard as he can into Richard Tuttle's *Purple Octagonal* (1967), causing a large dent in the painting's pale pink canvas, while leaving the display screen relatively unharmed. The TV is reinstated by day's end, while Tuttle's piece, though capable of repair at a fully insured cost of $1.45 million, is reclaimed by the painting's donor and returned to private storage; it will never be the same. "Nor will the landscape of its milieu be spared, regardless of what methodical caregiving," some local critic writes, "as once compromised, stabbed in its face, and though it may be healed by all accounts, we still will know; and so will it."

Within the hour, it is reported, on the same floor, a local dentist, visiting some local art during her day off, will try to wrap her body in Jim Hodges's coal-black curtain sculpture, *The end from where you are* (1998), ripping the material down off its dowel; ruptures sustained in the fabric will require $520,000 worth of stitching, allowing new thread to be incorporated into the prior mass, inherently compromising the structure of the object, despite its relatively identical visage to any viewer.

And at the Menil in Houston, a high school senior, visiting to fulfill a class assignment, spends more than three unbroken hours standing before René Magritte's *An End to Contemplation* (1927), scribbling notes from which there will be derived no sense, before suddenly attacking it in silent frenzy, with her fingernails and fists, causing several long rips in the exterior layers and canvas, as well as a significant denting and flaking; later, the young lady will claim not even to remember her behavior, nor what had come over her, nor the art. She will plead guilty.

They will all plead guilty, and they will be found guilty.

"I can't say what it was," states Dina Horst, mother of two, who throws her body through an installation of Duchamp's *The Bride Stripped Bare by Her Bachelors, Even (The Large Glass)* (1915–23). "I don't even know why I decided to go to the museum today, except it was like there was this silence within me, coating my insides, in a way that made me want to do anything but be exactly what I am. It was as if my whole life had passed right underneath my nose, and it was blank." The glint of guilt in her eyes bears a mistakable correlation with what had in other walks been called *a passion*.

"Breaking shit is cool," says her teen son with a military crewcut, his cursing bleeped before it hits the air. "I don't like art, but I like shit that's been broken or might be broken later."

"I didn't do anything; I was just standing there," another middle-aged man insists, in the next segment, having taken down his pants and pissed directly into the mouth of the second largest figure in Louise Bourgeois's *Three Horizontals* (1998), thereafter kicking the entire display over, fragmenting the larger figure's skull. "Nothing actually ever even happened," the man says calmly. "I'm not here, and you aren't either."

Each and every station reports the unfolding actions and their subsequent social furor, one after another—casually termed *copycat damage* by the anchor on the screen in Alice's own home—and eventually replays a shortened video of the burning of the Rauschenberg over and over, citing its existence, and therefore Alice herself, as stimulus and central ember for the ongoing trauma, while at the same time reinforcing its web traffic with fresh vigor, a thriving network shared and reshared as if to cull all mortal eyes, so that what once had been might be again, construed in forced collaboration with a rising local pattern in our lives. Where at first had been one act of violence against an inert object, now there are many, and soon again more time has passed than we might claim, simultaneously filling out the burgeoning outline of our history at its loose end and provoking each subsequent future second's nature as only some form of ongoing response, unable to see itself, or yet to settle.

"I guess I just don't understand" [*air quotes*] "'art,'" the head of some ex-senator projects, part of an impromptu panel conducted live, "because when I first saw some of the pictures of the" [*air quotes*] "'masterpieces' under attack, I honestly couldn't really feel the fuss. You're telling me I have to believe this orange and red thing that looks like someone could have made it with their eyes closed is worth as much as all the cash my grandfather made for our family buying and selling oil for his whole life? What, can you take shelter inside it? Does it feed you? Can it mandate our country's laws? Of course I'm all in favor of eternal beauty and the like, but if it's all going to come off looking so, can I say, *arbitrary*, then what really is at stake?"

Alice holds her hands clasped in her lap in the corralled glow. She can't remember moving.

"I would say you *certainly* don't understand," says another face inlaid beside the first, the frontman of a once successful Top 40 band, whose current single—"When You Were In Me," the pundit pauses, then cites—has found new traction in the mass mind as the soundtrack to a contentious recent men's underwear commercial featuring chrome-plated AR-17s. He is wearing a beret and quite a bit more pancake makeup than any of the others. "But really, how could anyone expect you to?" the singer says. "You're a gifted man in your own right, bro, sir, to be sure, someone upon whose visionary morals and, like, vision of society, our entire nation—no, the whole world—has little choice but to depend on. But it is the mark of someone like myself, as bard, as shaman, one might even say, to plunge the depths of longing, *actual human pain*, bro, and excavate from there the, um, *inexplicable trueness* we all feel, as living people. . . . Well, like, I mean without my music, all of music I mean, and like all of art too, what good is legal living? Without *beauty*, man? How long can we keep getting out of bed and going to work and eating and crying and having fun, in like, an ineluctable," [*grins, straining to see the teleprompter*] "infinite cycle, without expression, such as in song? Consider my, our, next upcoming single, for instance—'Untitled (Beyond the Valley of Lust)'—in this work, we explore human anatomy through the metaphor of contemporary sensuality, but like, *seriously* this time, in search of, um, a finer understanding of, well, the continuous reseeding of our personal brands, which upon commingling, as flesh, and as creators too, we might recover our fleeting glory, not to mention our ongoing purpose, bro, to even exist. So for instance . . ."

"'Valley of Lust?'" the once-senator interrupts, his ruddy 4K face pushed up larger, louder in his confined quadrant of the screen. "You think glorifying sexual intimacy without shame, before God and country, is some kind of valuable service outside of those who'd seek to profit from mass fornication? The condom makers and vodka bottlers? Why, you're as corporate a shill as any of my past and future lawmakers, my friend; heck, you might be even worse, considering the package you've tamped yourself into as some kind of" [*also straining now to read the lines*] "grandiloquent bard. Tell me, Audio Rembrandt, what kind of *spiritual* message can be gained from taking in your work? What can your gift from God reveal to any of the rest of us about our own gifts, in our own living walks? And what the heck does that have to do, in the meantime, with some abstract painting that looks like my kid got sick on her shirt on the ride home from the all-you-care-to-eat buffet?"

The musician exaggerates a gag move, mimes cutely puking. "Art is forever, bro. Your kid is going to die one day. So am I, too. The difference is, I've written codes that millions of Americans had sung into their heads in repetition for years and years, to the point they can sing it without hearing. And I've been paid accordingly for my sacrifices, my exploration; yes, of course. But in return, our fans have, through the insight of my labor, become new people, faced experiences of worlds they could not have ever touched without me, been blessed anew. Same goes, you know, for paintings. For instance, that super old but super famous one, with the brunette just sort of smirking like *what up*? I remember the first time I saw that jaw-dropping work of light on Earth. I was on a three-day leg in gay Paris during our *Warriors of Witness* tour, and I got the chance to go by and check that rad thing out. You know they had to put it behind bulletproof glass, right? Can you imagine? So many people love it so much they want it gone?"

Alice can't blink, she finds, has not been blinking. Her heart, meanwhile, feels soft and strangled in her own chest; darker and thicker than it must just have been, pronounced with so many living layers of glaze it hardly still feels able to breathe. How many hours had it survived on its own dime, under the wear of why or where she was, immeasurably in pain, held under wraps. If she doesn't think about her passing feelings outright, with her eyes closed and breath held, she has no beat in there at all, feels *not actually alive* beyond the ongoing faculties she can't stop seeing, thinking, breathing under the thumb of, not a law but an inherent manifestation of human life that one day soon will cease to be, as where in any given instant there are so many knives and guns and ropes and pills, not to mention high story windows and long stairwells and bridges and canyons and cars to step out in front of and persons to piss off and wrong places to end up in at the right time. *Perhaps that is the difference between a painting and a person*, she thinks, *that I can kill myself whenever*, though once again, as felt so often, the voice seems not wholly hers, as if it too has been embedded and left pending, activated only upon the arrival of this exact emotional stimulus into her neural network and let to sprawl, its patient host.

Meanwhile, outside, unseen, the sun is razing down upon the open flatness.

———

Alice turns the machine off and stands. From here, the world is open wide; rooms as she recalls them now connect back into other rooms as long they should according to their architect's intent, in no way attendant to the emotional interpretation of a suddenly hyper-suspicious Alice, at this point in her life smashed no longer on gin and water but on her impression of the present as ongoing event, suspended between the conflicting impressions of isolation and surveillance at the same time, espoused as much by her ongoing presence in the news as her renewed awareness of the unseen network of security cameras she herself had ordered installed so long ago she can't remember when or even why, having never until the recent robbery seen a need: after years and years of tapes of uneventful footage fed into the upkeep of some corporate presence she'd hired to install and oversee, called with a name she can't remember from any other brand, and yet to whom she'd supplied all the necessary access and permissions to her life, as it were, based on a single advertisement that had somehow appeared on her radar amid so many. As if all you had to do was dial a 1-800 and sign a contract and you were theirs to have and hold, to keep up with and place faith in for no meager startup fee and the ongoing monthly premium. At very least it helped her feel not so secluded, so empirically vulnerable, living all by herself in this huge house, even if, especially in the early phases, the awareness of forever being monitored, even remotely, had in some way only redoubled her potential for paranoia: What could they see that they should not? Where might they have put cameras she doesn't know about, and what embarrassing proclivities might they somehow thereafter use against her? What did they know that she did not?

Under the thumb of such surveillance the whole shape of her every day was laced with a Schrödinger's cat–like question—Am I Being Watched Right Now or Am I Not—resulting in a conscious sense of suspended deviation that never fully left her, no matter how well she might have been able to pretend it didn't matter. She sometimes even found herself lurking longer amid known gray spots in the suggested setup of the cameras, remaining out of sight long enough that any conniving employee might move along, turn their sights to other clients, come back later, giving her rare precious time to act unseen. It became a game at times, hiding from nothing, a childish means of playing out the hours of a whole night, until at least she felt depleted enough to lie down and pretend to fall asleep, and eventually actually finally really nodding out, waking up the next day to begin all over again.

As for how much of any of this might or could be true, who really knew? Same as every joke had a hint of truth behind it, the second you stopped questioning the truth was when they really, fully had you. Better always to stay on top, to keep your mind peeled for infraction, for deceit. Perhaps it was the security company itself that had done the robbery, she's considered; who better else knew all the ins and outs, maybe even more than she could, their firm's contractors having kept certain susceptible dimensions about her home's design in their back pockets, to themselves. She had, of course, been assured and reassured, by both reps and longstanding reputation, of the company's core corporate philosophy, commitment to service, not to mention their continuously innovated and award-winning methods of encryption and confirmation, all of it so seamlessly incorporated into her daily life that the best that she could hope for in relief was to train herself to trust that if something was wrong she'd know about it, while still continuing to foot the bill and stay on board—because in the end, after all other apprehension, she simply wanted to feel safe in her own home, if not her flesh. How could a business have been around so long, after all, as Avoid Corp.—*that was their name*, yes, according to their site—if their service wasn't at heart established in good faith, all shades of conspiracy and organized underhandedness nothing more than paranoia, perhaps even some deep sense of misplaced guilt. Moreover, how could it be stopped now, long after she'd granted them access, contracted their work? It was so much easier to let what was meant to happen happen, Alice tried to convince herself, to get on with living and let the chips fall as they must.

As for the recent breach, though, specifically the recordings made as the robbery took place—that is, the only direct evidence, as it remained—all of that had been handled for her, transferred under her approval to the authorities for their investigation: a cooperative gesture, ill-advised from a legal standpoint despite the fact that she maintains nothing to hide. Even now she can feel the eyes of the authorities reviewing the surveilled footage on their own time, poring over the timecode of her life as it was captured sight unseen, perhaps even mapping out the surrounding hours leading up to what they might consider more significant acts, all of it rendered unalterably in the past, somewhere between known and not quite known.

Which, in review, made Alice wonder: Were they still recording even now? Were the cameras even still necessary, following the break-in? Or was there no longer any need, some unspoken new sense of downgraded vulnerability, of *Lightning won't strike twice*? What if the act of trespass was itself an inevitable product of the system's installation, the laying of the bait that finally lures the vermin, where once the trap had been triggered, the purpose of each was rendered complete?

Or else, Alice imagines, what if the first robbery was merely the impetus to let one's guard down, its certain trauma freeing the consumer to feel invincible, open to field? Perhaps it was actually *her* they were after, not her belongings, not that she could list a single reason why anyone would have designs on her uncertain life, beyond the apparently inherent thrill some derived in violation? Didn't the true criminal ultimately want nothing more than to be anticipated, pursued? She knew she shouldn't blame herself, and yet she couldn't stop thumbing the wound, wondering what was her surest way out of her apparent situation without fostering her own entanglement, legally or conceptually. How could she shut the whole rest of the world out, once and for all, without shutting her whole self down, giving in? Was there anywhere by now where the grid ended, any remaining mechanism of relief?

Either way, cameras or no cameras, Alice feels her every motion rendered fact, appended to the record in the slick mass of late evening, the air around her operating its condition in response to anywhere she lurked and breathed, and threading through in the unending sets of motions and emotions that line her hours, within which she finds herself newly inspired amid the apparent social tumult to return to the scene of the crime in her own house, if only to revel in its raw spot, feel it seethe. She's already halfway down the stairs by now, she realizes, having moved in muscle memory while still consumed in her own thought, the passage between one intention and another at such times as faint as bubbles trapped in ice, all eventually meant to melt again to liquid, to assume whatever shape it's asked to fill.

At least this is the only way down, as far as she knows, from ground level to the basement of the house, site of the vault she'd had installed by the same firm, in an effort to prevent the very acts that had eventually occurred. And the stairs come to an end, still, where they always had, on the white tile floor that spanned the space in full, blocked only by a wide steel door that spans the far end of the small landing alcove, still locked and armed post-breach despite its now-dubious effectiveness. There's nowhere else to go down here, though, without the passcode, its digits so well inscribed in Alice's memory she's never had to reach to call them up—those of the dates of her birth, as she recalls it, here entered doubled. She'd used some variation of that same string her whole life, for every bank account PIN and online password, with very little variation and no reset, despite the providers' safety warnings. How else might you remember any of them, one and all, in such a glut? And what good could any key be if you couldn't claim it; if you, the user, ended up locked out of your own life?

Inside, the vault is brightly lighted, all the walls the same blown white. Its newly naked layout seems less a safe than a singularity, Alice imagines, a condition around which the larger house said to contain it disappears. Its shape remains so still, so mute, that it might make an even better bedroom than an archive, rendered more neutral now with nothing on display.

Alice, though, can still make out exactly where the de Kooning once had hung—its absence now almost louder than any presence, a state only enabled by her understanding of what had once been. There are as well the vacant spaces where three other paintings in the first wing had previously appeared: Ellsworth Kelly's *Red Yellow Blue White and Black* (1953), a series of seven distinctly colored panels that had always stood in stark contrast with the abstraction of the de Kooning in her mind; while, once stationed beside it, Yayoi Kusama's *No. 2* (1959), had embodied an even more nuanced and innervating scale of concept, comprised solely from a deceptively sallow field of tiny dots, which to Alice had simulated reptilian skin, and then resembled more and more a shriveled outline of our cosmos as from some god's eye view the closer in you got; and, lastly, William-Adolphe Bouguereau's *The Nymphaeum* (1878), a relatively sober presence, if still fantastic, depicting thirteen lily-white nudes languishing within a menacingly darkened wood, all of them unaware or unconcerned about the gaze of two suspicious lurkers easily overlooked along the right edge of the frame.

For years those four works had hung together in perpetual display, each acquired in the throes of some distinct emotional disposition that passed through her like the money that changed hands, the works together eventually lending the space a certain sacred fixity of vision and corresponding physicality so concrete that even with her eyes closed she can almost still feel them pulling at her attention—like mirages marred into her vision, if inherently ruined by her own biases and inner sprawl, and only further decayed in passage since. She can recall, too, how perversely thrilling it had been to stand in the presence of objects others could only look at in print or sites online, with no one around to stop her from doing to them as she wished; each further replication of the artifact only another window onto a creation that had become in acquisition solely hers, though eventually that impression too had lost some of its heft, slowly diminishing until by the time of the robbery she hardly ever went down to spend time among them. They'd begun then, in a way, to exist as much in her mind as anywhere else, like years of music after so many hours on repeat, an impression that, post-disappearance, revealed itself no longer so true: as suddenly—in the absence of any continuous impression to refresh by—the gap in her understanding feels that much more flimsy, lacking true definition: instead she finds only semblances, misplaced impressions, none of which ring right in the fact of what they'd really been, no ongoing sense of intent as designed by their creator, instead her own revision of a vision now only held preserved among the dead.

The result is a massively diminished sense of presence in the space, one that seems still falling out from underneath her, in a cold way, as she returns to that blank, despite her persistent furtive expectation that some hidden dam in her might one day break, at last disrupting the suspended feeling she'd carried her whole long life, supplanting its memory with some reaction: at least a sense of loss, remorse, regret. Though, if anything, she finds the lingering feeling of her house's violation is like a revelation, a sense of something long unspoken now made known, as if the real crime had been ever deigning to own the artworks in the first place, a state made all that much more intoxicating and repentant now that they are gone.

That same feeling appears redoubled as she comes around the vault's partition into its second flank, a space designed to match the first completely as if it were an optical illusion, the absence of display points underscoring the match. Here before had hung Anselm Kiefer's *Winter Landscape (Winterlandschaft)* (1970), with its pink blood bursting from the neck of a disembodied head floating over a punctured landscape in silent pain, once seen in troubling juxtaposition alongside the face that spans the canvas in full of Jenny Saville's *Knead* (1995–96), its sickly subject half agog in coming to with breathing tube forced between her teeth, which on sight alone Alice had always felt she could feel deep in her own lungs, filling her innards with a queasy, leaking feeling, as if subjected to a virus passed by sight; and, last, Henry Ossawa Tanner's *Georgia Landscape* (1889–90), its cooler colors no less abstruse, a world unto itself, devoid of life, into which the longer she stared the more there seemed nothing else left in the world, its simple, sagging sky the only sky there'd ever been.

Capping the far end of the vault, where in the prior space had been the door, the mirror left behind in place of the Rauschenberg now awaits, its initial presence made more certain in still appearing, no longer just a figment in her mind. Its reflection of the room around her appears to slip against its own impression as she moves, the interplay of angles of the blank walls deflecting any obvious sense of what shape the space maintains beyond a vortex, without subject, white on white, further emboldening in its illusion until, as if from out of nowhere, there she is, *Alice*, held in its grasp. The crown of her head appears first, along the low end of the object as she appears with its plane; followed then by face and shoulders, rising up cut-off within the scape of monochromatic dimensions spanning behind her, more and more nowhere.

She can think of no reaction, faced with the unbidden object once again, now at an even greater remove. The mirror's surface seems different now, she realizes; she sees something odd there about her eyes, or at least a difference in how she would expect her eyes to look: a fuzzed-out phase to their pale green hue in reproduction, as if a mist has rolled up in her mirrored skull and come unfurled. Her pupils seem diseased, she thinks, struck with tangled lines as if from trauma, high without the pleasant reeling, only drift. The recognition makes her living body pang then, too, readjusting to incorporate the difference whose substance she can't quite apprehend, in either origin or intent. She stands and stands there, seeing herself watching herself redoubled, until time as it passes feels less alive and more on pause; a draw with beginning or an ending, awaiting some form of consummation yet to come.

Alice raises her arm then and indeed sees the other of her raise its with her as to match. She grimaces and sees her grimace equally returned, each gesture lacking actual emotion, a performance interested only in reception, without fact—and still there seems something lost in the translation, Alice can't help feeling, their shared expression somehow belonging to the glass's image more than hers.

Closer still, wanting to see clearer, Alice sees the difference held between them continue to refine, not just in position, but in substance: the lines of age progressing in her face, growing more pronounced, deeper conditioned; the bones beneath the flesh slowly protruding, pores becoming paler and more patchy, as from bad upkeep and too long away from sun. Each time she begins to see herself again in her complexion it immediately corrects itself just slightly further, leaving no time for any central take upon which to lay claim; it is as if her face is molting away, bit by bit, in rapid aging, its condition influenced by each measure of intent, as if—were she to hold still and remain—nothing thereafter could be changed; she could live forever as she might be now, or now, or now, if only she would forgo any and all else in existence.

And yet the very sense of wonder in seeing herself anew makes Alice want to understand what could come next: how she might look pushed to her limit, beyond change. Within a few paces the skin around her eyes tightens demonstrably, her chin becoming rounded, her knitting brow. Nearer still, the pixels of her face begin to bluster and coalesce, new ridges forcing their way out of the sharper features and obscuring each prior layer, filling in with grayer, rougher tones, taking on age. The feeling isn't so defeating as it might feel in other contexts, peeling years of looks off of her life; instead she is attracted to the mirror, feels its craving fill her flesh, scrawling through it without focus, as in a heat wave, manipulating its own perceived design in kind by how it's read. It's almost as if there's a whole other person enabled in her image, Alice imagines, coming free only in accrued observation, decades of rot. She finds she wants to touch the surface of the mirror as it shifts against her image, to hold it steady; to be near the other of her so she can understand her better, learn what it wants; to know her body from the outside as well as all those who've ever looked upon her without permission.

By the time she is halfway across the space, Alice finds, her reflection has taken on the image of someone well into late middle age. There's no music to the moment, no nothing beyond the time lapse as it gathers from her aggregating form, her hair extending down around her eyes, along her back, thinner and flatter, all color eradicating itself as if being vacuumed up from within her, slipping out. *Though all of this is only true in the reflection*, Alice thinks; and indeed she can see and feel along her present flesh that nothing actually is changing but in the glass; she feels no different at all except for where a rising heat behind her face fumbles with empathy, not for her own reflected image but for what has been obscured between them, throughout time: moments already lost as soon as she could ever want to try to understand them; each captured instant of her as if she were a different woman through every hour of her life; and each then overwritten in transition, made merely another forced iteration, the newest outer layer of her persona, subject and object, in control for just an instant then just as quickly smothered out, never to be recovered. She can already feel the skin hid in her mind, as she'd last been, just now, becoming replaced by another layer, and the next layer then at once again the same, over and over; quicker and closer. The only thing that had held all these lives together before now, she understands, was delusion, some false premonition as transmutable as any painting touched by flame or any elapsed memory made bereft, and nothing in her carried over louder than the questions she could only hope to never know an answer for, so that she might spend the whole rest of life in wonder, the only thing that, despite its pain, kept her living through the rubble.

Though when she feels her actual body try to speak—to slow itself in its transition in the mirror by objection, the sound exuding not through her mouth or even pores but through the gap between her living body and the other of her in the glass—it comes out so loud it hurts her hearing; as if there's something even louder locked within it, rounding out the corresponding feeling of having had something to say once covered over with mass dark. Then at once there's nothing left she can remember but years and years of heavy volume, inner-screaming; the countless versions of her fraught in anguish across their catalog of silent lives, amplified together within her to drown out her present understanding; thereafter splitting open, unscrolling innumerable other tormented voices carried on in every offshoot of her past persona, where at the center underneath it there's no true sound there, but endless blank, its flimsy, shrieking flesh becoming thin against her, stretching up through her brain and over her eyes. Then, on the far side of it, suspended, she can perceive a simple, terrifying calm: such blistered mass packed fat and crammed so full and filling that there's nowhere left to fit, nothing alive within this feeling but the sense of no longer being capable of feeling anything at all, no longing or outline or intent to fill her future life; only the feeling of the bending inward of her logic turned against her, pressed to burst. And then, briefly, as the rift glides: flashbulbs crashing in the overwhelming brightness; a sea of hands, as molding clay; a rush of wind so wide and far apart it rolls like water; silence.

She cannot remember how to live. All sense of what had always been required of a body to keep being suddenly seems warped, capped full of continuously elapsing turns at each of which one might become fixed forever to its intention, washed away. *Time is not a shapeless thing*, she hears her voice say, *but sets of cells on cells one could become sewn into, immobilized unending; a heat not fused from heat but glazed with film, edge-hard, undying*; the words each coming undone as they are uttered, so that even trying to think anything else burst worlds apart, all potential edges of desire beyond the present's nowhere pressing mud in her blood, each passing intention sprawled through her heart and born again into a lower, indescribable form of sense, beyond any emotion or expectation.

Her reflection's flesh is soft as anything, she finds, now that she is finally able to reach out and touch it, beyond its image, in the ensuing blind; so permeable it might as well be putty, and yet drawn up against some harder structure clasped within, against which she finds there is a force that wishes her to continue, to press her whole sense of central self into the fold, leave no space between the known and unknown therein remaining. Even as she tries alike to so comply she feels it lurch, and beneath that something grinding, metal on metal, each presence at once worn away on either side, like lines in a book that disappear as they are read.

The room was blue. Then it was white, as with day passing, and back to a blue of dimmer shade, whereby in being seen once and parsed it could no longer continue being what it had always been.

Alice is there. She can hear her thoughts as in dictation, somewhere above her. Between the thoughts, nothing exists.

I was watching myself as if from above, and at the same time as from inside me. I had to close my eyes and focus on the texture of my body to begin to see again out of the face I knew as mine, to go on managing my life, though when I saw out of my face, there was nothing but this sick, mislaid expanse of sun and dust, a deranging phase forced through the hue of blanking out, which then became the brightest, widest blank, in all directions, wrapped around me. I still felt everything I had to feel— the recognition of myself in the reflection, the understanding that I was already not who I'd just been, each second leaving my prior self behind me as an image, ever-off—though in a way more like having it described to me than actual experience.

Alice is not sure where the house is, beyond the mirror's edges. She knows that she has felt this way before, infinite times: such as the morning of the appearance of the unfather; such as this morning too, the day the cameras claimed her, unable for hours after waking to move or open up her eyes.

Wherein, behind my eyes, I saw bright snow, the kind from old-time rupture in our signal, when we still believed in local weather. How often something so much like hope would fill me up from the inside despite how

I could not remember anything else about where I'd been, what I'd been doing; as if regardless of all that, when at last I came around and found myself again, somewhere within me, it would be the same as it had been, in days when I felt love, when I knew who was waiting for me where and why, when I could remember my own name without trying.

Each time, though, when the snow touched to my flesh it immediately melted, as I was burning, full of bloat, and as the colors again widened, in between them I saw other people on their knees; saw them in the worst ways, fumbling, broken, each at once so much like me, grasping for faith; each only ever granted relief in at last turning over, giving in; at which point I realized I was no different from any of them; I was here trapped in me for a reason, beyond life; beyond anything even something like God could comprehend.

Every word dissolves into the ones subsequent, becoming absorbed in the running language of her thought's sentence as it sticks. She keeps waiting for the state to end, the way a dream would, returning the structure of the space to how it had last been, though the longer she waits the more it's like there could never be an out, that her life has ended not in fracture or in tragedy, but in simply coming to a wall.

——

The scene cuts out. The air around where the screen had been begins to shudder, a simulation of physical motion that doesn't seem to correspond to what she is. It's as if she's being turned over on her side, but for both sides at the same time, a mass of force without effect, framed by their speech.

I'd already lived through this before, her voice is praying. *I'd traced this faulty plot already, its living layer lying hidden and waiting to conform me to it like a flesh. Each instant that I lived now was only the conflation of all prior points of culmination competing in me to retake the helm, seize the controls, and all the pending world awaiting a lost relation to the present person I must be still standing strong enough to hold the claim.*

And when I looked in search of any world that might remain, I saw the sound of all time becoming broken open everywhere around, the glass of endless windows, mirrors, sight on sight, where through its rupture of my perspective I could then begin to hear another kind of speaking, the loudest, thickest voice I'd ever felt, compromised from all the people I'd ever known, each of them speaking at the same time, their choir brutal and unrehearsed, spreading through me with its sick yearning. It wasn't even sound as much as motion, spurred by an intent my own actual fiber could not trace. It numbed my arms and legs and face, then up and in through my intestines, working quick and hard around my heart, spreading out an instant, insistent warmth that made me want it never to stop coming, surging, living in me, like a passion; an act of understanding.

I had never felt so small, and at the same time so full and flooded with the sense that there was nothing left about me that was mine. I mean, I could not breathe. I could not see anything. I was sucking on the air no longer there, clutching at my body for ways to slip out, the words of urges flooding from my face. Everything I touched thereafter became a part of everything else I'd touched already, including light and air, including me, as did every other lifetime having touched the same space before or after, all the lengths and breadths of every face; and though I did not feel any pain in such erasure, neither mine nor someone else's carried on, when I closed my eyes next they would not open, nor would they want to ever.

Alice is holding the mirror in her arms. She has removed it from the wall, she finds, hefting it up against her chest, bracing it tight against her face. The mirror's flesh is overwarm now, as if from sunlight, its surface sticking to her skin where pulled away. She is surprised to find, too, how little it weighs, only hollow between sides.

The mirror's gleaming hurts her eyes, somehow shining in the room's absence of any fertile hue—like the meat of the sclera, the margins of the pages of a book. She feels an urge to look anywhere else but directly at it, searching for traction some long, lost time before she finds the will to look away, to lay the mirror face down on the floor where she'd been standing, the ground beneath it left to reflect the dark back at itself in hidden space.

The silence seems different then somehow, an active mute made negative, capped off. The backside of the mirror bears the same hue as the walls, unadorned but for the glinting outline of a small metallic placard installed into the upper right-hand corner of the otherwise bare field, engraved with a clear pattern cut into its substance, in relief. The edges of the etching glisten where the light behind her head still hits from certain angles, allowing its latent logo to resolve:

The pattern's shining weaves and stings, hard to look at quite directly. Alice rubs her thumb over the cut edges of the lines, feeling her flesh press into their divots, as if imprinting. The tines between the cuts are warm, like liquid; its gather clings against the pads of her prints, making the skin stick briefly before lifting away. In looking up again she sees the remaining expanse of what could only be her vault, standing long and flat at her periphery, recohering, coming down, the firming ground beneath her all that she can ascertain therein so clearly, left again with no way in and no way out.

In retrospect, Alice found in her later years that she could recall passed time only as played out under heavy glaze, as if it were all one long day; the withstanding larger world, too, impossibly obscure, bound by an illusion of immensity that connected nowhere else but back again upon itself. No matter how far she'd ever walked in one direction in her childhood home, the only place she'd ever lived, she always found her way arriving back to where she'd already been, despite how no location felt at all like her own, even given the countless points of passing recognition: the texture of the sheets of her own bed, cold no matter how long she lay within them; the closet full of clothes that fit her body as if sewn for her and her alone, no matter how much her body changed; the workbooks she'd been supplied for education full of logic problems none of which had any real answers, complex equations full of symbols and no instructions. Some days she'd grow so tired she could hardly see or think at all, stuffed full as if she'd eaten way too much; an object like a locket or a doll she'd loved would disappear completely, nowhere to be found no matter how many times she retraced her steps, then sometimes later turning up again wrapped in black plastic in the backyard, or for some reason stuffed inside her pillow, or on the roof.

Still nowhere, throughout all that time, following her unbrother's introduction in her life, had Alice ever been able to connect her supposed flesh and blood to a full person, no matter how much or little she tried to care. The door to his room remained locked from the inside even after she'd stopped hearing about his sickness and then eventually stopped hearing about him ever, the name made verboten between her and her mother once again, as had her real father been, still for no reason she could state, making Alice wonder if he'd died. Thereafter, the unfather refused to let her near him, as if the mere sight made him ill for dearer child; instead he began spending all his waking time locked in the den he'd converted from a sun room, blacking the windows with layers of fresh paint—so that he could read and think in solitude, her mother stated, caught up with a series of thick jacketless books he'd been subscribed to by a friend, and about which he would not speak, responding when prodded by her mother in a hoarse, high-pitched, clipped voice like some sick toy, in text that didn't even sound like English, his eyes unfocused, far away.

For the most part, though, Alice did not go seeking company, her prior efforts to hold a sense of home together quickly dissipating into a more focused isolation, bleeding from her teen years, straight through into early middle age. Her lone tie that kept her tuned in was a rising, constant worry for her mother's health: how she'd seemed at some point to go off a cliff, from out of nowhere, and thereafter, once acknowledged, to worsen by the day, suddenly gaining weight so fast it was as if it had never been another way. The woman then began spending all her time in bed, hidden away in one of the house's many guestrooms, which she and her supposed husband never appeared to share, her internal faculties going haywire one by one: first her desire to wash herself, to use the restroom, then to realize she needed to at all; then, not long after, forgoing any sense of when or where she was; then who she was, who Alice might be, why. It was as if whatever shred of personality or passion Alice could remember of the woman became as covered over in her as her bones under her accruing pounds of pasty flesh of no known feeding. Alice began then counting down to the time she'd soon be able to move away, an urge she couldn't help but hate herself for feeling, no matter how well earned, for how in turn she'd done no better for her mother than she for child, each stranding the other in a corrupt offshoot of their own ailing lifeline, related strangers.

In the end, the doctors said, it wasn't weight that killed her mother, or even immobility, not exactly—somehow underneath it all her heart was fine. Rather, she died of what they insisted be called *shock*: some sudden battery of hormones and adrenaline so strong it had changed the rhythm of her pulse—not a heart attack, but an immense stress. *Something that occurred upon her, or within her*, the doctor had written in the reports the police eventually provided, what seemed far too long after the fact, *like emotional spontaneous combustion*. Alice had never understood how they could decipher such definitions from a blood test or a graft; nor had she been expecting it when she was informed that her unfather had taken his own life, in the same hour as her mother, according to the coroner, via a gunshot to the head; the man had hardly even seemed able to remember her mother's name in those most recent months, much less to be so devastated by her loss as to kill himself in response, unless the two events were somehow only coincidentally timed, which, improbable as that seemed, who could prove otherwise?

This had all happened, apparently, as Alice slept, through another night of dreams aping her daily reality, frozen faceup in the bed, waking the next morning to find the house aflood with men with badges, bodies already removed from the scene, the necessary work of investigation under way. Any suspicion she might have harbored about wrongdoing in the matter, whether by her unfather, or by the authorities, or even by Richard, could be confirmed by no actual evidence in hand, nothing certain beyond lifetimes of ongoing psychic malfeasance that when described aloud in the presence of outside authority only ever seemed to raise eyebrows in *Alice's* direction—as if she were the one gone off the rails, informed by a worldview that to anyone who hadn't been there seemed unreliable, full of holes.

Such as: How long had she been out that night? Alice couldn't remember lying down or getting up, as the dark between held on all blotchy, endless, comprised in chunks cross-stitched together with the sour drag of a hangover in their wake. She couldn't piece together anything about the night in question, really, in her own mind, until later, when she read back the statements she'd apparently offered that same blurred morning they'd brought her in and shook her down, all of it transcribed and signed in her own name; describing a night that could have been any other she recalled: staring at the depth of night for hours, face at a window, reading the moon, before turning in just as the sun began to cut across the land. Which in the end had apparently been enough, as they found no evidence that anything about such claims was untrue; and in the end the case of the death of her parents, as they were, had been closed as quickly as it transpired, despite what seemed to Alice *some great wrong*, a sense of cleaving she might have welcomed were it not so ugly, out of whack. All the evidence was beyond her, supplanted by facts counted more real than anything she could offer, somehow adding up to what the law deemed a full picture, apparently; and so too, soon, it was easier to let it fade away than try to fight, her waking daily plague of familial terror at last finding a point from which it might recede, even as she was haunted newly not by what she'd done but what she hadn't, still unsure of how or why she could have changed their dismal course.

—

Most confounding of all, though, if in a completely different measure, was her inheritance—*their* inheritance, she should say, hers and Richard's—which included not only the house and all its present contents, but a sum of money so large it didn't seem correct, or at least not an amount their family had ever demonstrated access to. Alice had known they were well enough off, according to figures, though her parents hardly acted as if that were true, and certainly not to the extent the local coverage said they had been, detailing their fortune in abstract digits as enough to live out a thousand other lives, all of which was to be split down the middle with her unbrother—made legally now her actual brother by definition, his name right there on paper alongside hers. It was so much money, really, that what it came to mean to Alice eventually, more than all else, was that she might never fully rid herself of an association with her unwanted lineage; it would haunt her in its essence forever after, like a virus, despite how over time she'd try to spend it all or give it away, eventually going all in on the purportedly priceless works of strangers, each with a different life all their own, and unaffected as the world continued changing, until now, in their destruction.

Likewise, the ongoing state of sickness Richard had been said to live under, locked in his room through all Alice knew of his whole life, upon their parents' death itself had shifted gears. It was not days after their cremation—and the eventual scattering to local waters that Alice arranged to have performed by caretakers in her stead—that any remaining suggestion of Richard's presence inside the house was packed up and shipped out, as overnight. Though half the physical body of the house had been named his now, he'd left her to it, even taking his name off the deed, as if in trade for his unauthorized absconding with most all of what had outfitted their house's innards all that time—from the strange lace curtains in her mother's bedroom to the unfather's peculiar miniatures collection, a sticky group of countless tiny dolls strewn throughout the house; the candles and the maze games and the folded maps of foreign locations and the steak knives; even the carpet they'd installed just months before, a deep green color that blurred the eye, its removal leaving bare strange black paneled floors of interlacing diamond tile, which Alice could not remember being under there before—anything not bolted down, as the saying went, that had been a feature of their family; including every picture of them, from all their eras, leaving behind no photographic document of any of their lives—including shots held over from her mother's childhood, or those of Alice by herself, without which, Alice found, she found it increasingly difficult to remember how any of them had looked, including her, her memory mutating instead to whatever phantom relics she'd recorded in her mind. Sometimes she found it impossible to remember ever having any other face than the one she currently wore, as if she'd had the same features in every incarnation, no matter what age; sometimes she couldn't even imagine that present face without staring back at it directly, and even then it didn't match. And so, with her mother, passed any concrete semblance of attachment to all they'd shared, however wrong, the scaffolding around those years thereafter eroding, coming open.

Alice found, too, that she felt no real sense of mourning in the dissolution, as much as she might once have suspected she would miss even such ongoing pain when it was gone. She had been mourning the absence of a home, a love, a self for so long it felt her whole life, partitioning every prior feeling she and her mother had once shared, before the becoming of the unfamily, into its own state of disregard; as if any living bond between her and her mother as she'd once felt it had been itself the true mirage. If anything, it must be pure relief in the release, Alice encouraged herself to imagine, no longer forced to live on pressed between the possibilities of anything returning to how it had once been, that soft and false nostalgia battered so far down that all it had do was crumple up and crawl away. It would not be long, she felt sure, before she would be unable to remember her mother's voice at all, nor any moment shared between them, beyond sudden desperate flashes felt through night. Soon the very idea of ever having had a family or unfamily at all began to integrate itself into something long begotten and undone, a rotten joke no part at all of her real life, such that more and more throughout each waking hour her way of being became the only way it could be or ever had, held in the here and now, all her own, with any other sense of budding explanation only fodder for some fire in her heart, burning up along the very wire of *today*.

——

As for where Richard went or what became of him thereafter, that would remain a mystery to her for more than two decades, if one she found bizarrely easy to forgo. It all seemed so much more flimsy after the fact—his needs, his phantom motion, all the rest—much as each coming day did, all the time, the present point of focus slipping only further and further from its own foundation in retro-context, however marred as it remained. The whole disarming fact of having lived among the family had come and gone in what seemed months, leaving no trace beyond the chains of empty rooms she could not count, the insufferable moods that came over her as from out of nowhere amid the new shape of going on.

Even Richard's room itself, which had come to signify some sort of central emotional coordinate of that prior era—its door remained locked, without key that Alice could locate, the space itself remaining as inaccessible as it had always been, after the fact, though at the least she'd long since stopped hearing his mumbling echo in the nights; his phantomic lingering in her periphery waned away. She might have kicked the door down or removed its hinges, gone in and seen at last what else was there once and for all, but she couldn't summon the will; and soon she no longer wished to know. She would rather go on as if none of all that stretch of time, however long it had actually been, had ever happened; his prior space surrendered unto nothing. Alice could start to live now, as she saw it, with her and herself alone, somehow a pair, as if it had never been another way, keeping on only a last name that already felt like someone else's.

Alice's newfound isolation, however, did not mean that no trace of her old life would yet be left behind. Despite the summarily executed evacuation, the damage of what had gone on in or through the house continued to hold haunt, no matter how efficiently Alice designed her life to move along.

It showed itself in early days as only a distant sense about the air held over in such a trauma's wake: some sinking, overwritten feeling carried in the wood grain and the drywall; half adrenaline, half dread, intermixed with a continuous anxiety, among which the sleep that had always been hard enough grew harder as she aged. Alice found her nights extending one atop another like rungless ladders, allowing no firm place for resting as she climbed, no better with her eyes closed than eyes open. Occasionally, too, she'd come across some trinket passed over from before, a remnant of the way it'd so long been, appearing as if from out of nowhere to remind her who she was: a hairpin on the floor, caught with a single follicle of what could only be her sibling's slick, dark hair, as seen in pictures; a loose pill, brightly colored, possibly any other of her family members' regular dose, marked with cryptic engravings by some corporation; unnervingly often, crumpled notes in cramped, childish handwriting she could only imagine must be Richard's, so barely legible it hurt her head to read; and yet she couldn't overlook how each fragment seemed to correspond to her own life, as might an omniscient narrator describe it, in the third person. *Alice is walking down a long white hall*, one such note read, the ink all smearing where she touched, *in her old house, as it had been once; but is it even her? She hadn't looked so young in so long, though the girl clearly is wearing her same face, her deep-set eyes ringed with acne, deeper bruises all down her arms*—sourced presumably, as she imagines, from how often she had fainted as a child. *But where is she going now? What does she live for?* It gave her gooseflesh every time, reading and rereading someone writing of her like that, as if she were some chess piece to be paraded around, made a game of; as if the author could directly mold her past, her coming fate.

Alice is looking for her brother, another note read; today is his birthday, which also happens to be hers. *This year she has a gift to give him, one she'd found buried in the yard beneath the tree they sometimes joked about hanging themselves from together: a small black book. She had not opened the book without him, saving it hidden beneath her pillow for just the right time to give her gift; she wanted him to be the one to read it aloud, unto the both of them, in his small strange voice, so much her own, adding his own parts in as he went, between the lines.*

It really had been her birthday when she'd found the scrap, a fact she might have wholly passed over in her mind without reminder; and though he'd clearly made up the thing about them discovering the buried book—had he not?—she did at least know what he meant, referring to the series of novels the unfather had spent much of his last days with, so caught up in its entangled, epic plot that he couldn't bring himself to turn away. And though Alice had always wondered what the books said, wishing she could steal one for herself and read it locked in her own room, far from all eyes, she would never have wished to share it with Richard, much less to have him read it to her; and either way, she'd never found the courage to set foot in the unfather's study; instead she could only pretend to read them with her mind, envisioning the contents typed out against the darkness as she lay awake all night, beyond sleep. And so these fragments, Alice realized, must be their author's own attempt to do the same—to make something out of nothing; *another world*—although, unlike in her own imagination, this conception referred not to ecstatic fiction, but to their own *actual lives*, generating variations on the present hour as it passed, which in tone seemed to her something like incantations, like hexes that could change the way she saw herself, the world.

Alice would get the sense at times that these fragments were being left behind with intent, specifically for her to find, even if she could not begin to sketch a reason why. If not Richard, then who was it? And so she'd started burning each further scrap as soon as she'd found it, dozens of them, hundreds, stuffed in the kitchen sink, along a fan's blade, between slices of bread right out of the bag—*sometimes several copies of the same phrase, only a word or two varying between them, sometimes whole sets of other word erased.* So much smoke rose out of such a small amount of paper, she discovered, as if its fibers were thicker than they appeared, causing a stink she couldn't get out of her hair or clothing no matter how many times she washed.

▬

Other similar manifestations were much less indirect, seeming only to appear during her sleep: a new foyer, for instance, one cold morning, leading from the dining room where no one had ever together dined, into a hall so long she'd thought it never would end, until it did, upon a stage with velvet curtains thick as her chest, beyond which she found only a shallow alcove that bore no lighting and no proper seating for their guests. Or, then, another evening, elsewhere, a window that looked straight out onto another window just the same, each nearly opaque with blue-black glass, visually abutting into a section of the house that, try as Alice might, she could never seem to make connect; and always with the sense that someone else was performing the same on the far side, approaching and inspecting, just out of sight. These shifts felt different compared to how the house had changed when she was younger, now more and more blatantly defiant, no longer even trying to hide what they transformed.

Even more damaging than these physical alterations were other trace associations, new memories and meanings that cropped up in her experience of what space did seem to hold its shape around her, no matter how much time passed in between; such as what had been done to the living room beneath her bedroom, one of the few areas that had survived emotionally intact through the transition from one father to the other—a small, low-ceilinged space, harbor for their own flat jokes about its cramped dimensions, which never dissuaded either from insisting most every evening after dinner that they retire there all together, as a family, gathering around the glowing screen in total silence, to receive what it presented of the world. It was in this room, Alice remembered in post-transition years, that if she closed her eyes and tried to wish herself away, she could feel as if she were very young again, still there in what she'd come to think of as the prior version of her life, possible for some brief glimpse to carry on within a familiar form of her existence, happy, safe—a needed gash of hopefulness that for some time kept her going, no matter how quickly with her eyes again reopened the feeling faded, became like all else.

Even that sensation now, though, with the house in both her and Richard's name, had not held over. The room felt less itself each time she came around, if still strong enough inside her heart to seem a beacon as she wandered the house searching for places of comfort, common sense. It always managed to retain the same door, at least: dark wood with a polished gemstone doorknob, marred on the inside with claw marks along its bottom edge, from the year they'd tried to keep a feral cat—a memory she did not remember having until she ran her nails along the markings' deeper grooves and listened in— though the space behind it each time seemed even smaller, soon more like a closet than a room: the walls so near on every side, the ceiling low; the TV itself, one of the few things she understood Richard had intentionally left behind, no longer able to find any channel but marred globs of static, no matter what brand of service she installed, what signal was sent through the wires; as if this room, as it was now, could not be reached.

It was through this room's steadfast nostalgia—if nothing else, so long withstanding in her mind—that what would serve as her most vivid memories of Richard began cropping up, bearing timeworn associations he had never previously attained; on both sides of her understanding of their family, pre- and post-shift; as if in each phase he'd always been there, in both versions. Suddenly she could remember no other way it hadn't always been: the four of them together, crowded in for entertainment all those nights—Alice and her mother, yes, and either the father or unfather, depending on the time; and then, alike in both fraught eras, her living twin, his presence overriding whatever else the revision of her life had once entailed; as if, regardless of who the supposed progenitor was, Richard, the son, fully her brother, had always been there just as she had, one and the same.

Very quickly, in tracing this feeling in its appearance, Alice found she could no longer track the nature of the difference between the real father and the unfather; not because they looked alike, but because in the now-revised memory of their time alive together in the TV room, the body of the father had no face; instead there hung a smear of pallid outline where there should have been clear features, the skin around it caving in with waver, rods and pills. The same was true then for her mother in such memories too, as if the lack of recognition in the adults had copied itself onto her source of birth, leaving of all her family's faces only Richard's fully formed, and so at once her only living link to who she'd been, who she still was. Richard had simply *implanted* himself there, she felt, worming his way into the last remaining parts of her she could maintain, tearing down the wall between them that had survived their parents, either kind—and therein begetting adherent memories at last no longer part of an erasure, but bound within it, shared between; such that he too had been a victim, of whatever happened, a bond between them that no one else, even their blood, could understand, regardless of what kind of unword she used to differentiate between them. Then, yet further still, it began to seem as if in fact *he* had been there even before *her*; such that, from his perspective, Alice had been the one who just appeared from out of nowhere, living sick; she the fulcrum around which their *shared* world had been forever changed, beyond all compromise or correlation.

Even then, as she relived those memories newfangled, still nothing of Richard's actual physical presence would appear. His image in her memory remained merely a suggestion of a person, someone who *must have* been there but about whom she had already walled off all the facts; whose face and self remained from her perspective out of field, same as she'd sensed through all their hours, but now dipped in living glue, if still never actually *on camera* in any version, no matter how convincing her burgeoning memories began to seem. Once she had felt such association, even as barely there as ever, she could feel him from that flashpoint leaking further out, pressing at the edges of all the rest that she remembered no matter how much she tried not to, an itch she wouldn't scratch in fear of it inflaming, taking hold.

▬

Even more clearly than anything about the family in their shared time in the small glown dark, at least as she recalled it from that point forward in Richard's newly apparent wake, Alice remembered them watching the ongoing broadcast of a particular dramatic serial, one so popular or otherwise nationally backed that it had appeared on every channel at the same time, repeated back to back in syndication between the debut of each new episode, which seemed to have no set schedule or duration. The show was simply on all night every night during the timeline of its production, which seemed to Alice to have filled up several years, carrying on a sprawling plot, depicted from a point of time not in the past, but the near future, that centered on a retelling of the foundational history of the United States.

Alice could not recall the program's name. In retrospect, she remembered watching the episodes as if they weren't fiction—though she would later decide they must have been, despite no actual confirmation of the fact, given that she'd never heard anyone else discuss the show, had never read about it outside itself—but instead, according to her young attention, as actual news: captured footage of real living people, so she imagined; no famous actors, and often characters who would never recur, living or dead.

The series depicted crime and turmoil during the fallout of an epic plague that deconstructed all emotional logic, and then nostalgia, then all the rest, beginning with the supple heads of all our young, by means of a continuously mutating viral fire feeding off human experience, propagated by a furtive federal authority that once invoked could not be stopped. This power promised to eradicate all sense of self from those exposed, an inevitability that could be avoided only by those who refused or otherwise ceased to consume such form of media, ever, including the serial itself. The viewer, then, in viewing, was complicit, assisting the progress of the virus by providing mental bandwidth to its participation in the plotline of the show, the general thrust of which as stated never ever really came to light; all backstory assumed and passed by rumor, word of mouth, never onscreen. And yet somehow this did not stop the continuing broadcast and development of the series; nor did it dissuade a record-setting audience, due in no small part to how, as far as Alice could remember, there was nothing else to watch.

Each season of the show, as she had understood it then, by context of the commercials and store aisles crammed with themed merchandise, was based on a series of books penned by machine—the first major work of art created by an entity of artificial intelligence, she recalls, or at least so it was marketed, though there had never been much information presented about the generative apparatus itself, except that it was the culmination of a project funded publicly by taxpayers, and under way for decades. The show had become so popular, so well-regarded, that no one seemed to miss the programming the show must have replaced, both in ongoing production and in retrospective understanding, until there was nothing left beyond these generated worlds; its single work soon known to all, of any age or situation, as the only book or show that'd ever been.

Was that correct? That was how it happened? These were the same books her father or unfather—could it be both?—had grown obsessed with, to the point where he eventually never spoke of anything else, and eventually stopped speaking at all, his eyes glued to the lines inside whatever edition of whatever number in the series he'd taken up to read or read again even while driving, walking, bathing, starting over as soon as he had finished the series each time anew. Eventually he'd started writing his own extensions of the story, hadn't he, even seeking their publication, dictating them aloud to himself throughout the night, until eventually his own work took over for the obsession, as he spent all hours hidden away typing, typing. Or had he been writing all along, throughout his whole life, searching for purpose within his own imagination, until eventually he gave in and melded his ongoing work to this model universe? Either way, the books seemed always there throughout her life, in both versions, as they merged, their physical manufacture seeming long outdated, and by her father's compulsive usage, worn to pulp, riddled with loosened pages that would come out from the spine at any touch, held together by bands and pins that Alice would find scattered all throughout the house: stuck in a wall, for instance, or wrapped around a statue's face, hiding its eyes.

There were twenty-six volumes in all, as she remembered, each of various length, the largest too heavy to hold above the lap for very long, and each corresponding to a year's worth of viewing for the family in their translation to the screen, according to her father's extemporaneous explications of the context of the program at the dinner table every night, allowing no interruption or retort, which still poured forth even after the series was eventually outlawed in all formats, labeled by courts as heresy, pornography, a cult belief. The nightly broadcast went back to more varied programming thereafter, most of it reruns and lighter fare, the series no longer aired or even mentioned in larger media. All copies of the books, too, were supposed to have been confiscated and mass-burned, under the penalty of life imprisonment or worse for those who attempted to hold out—*the creators had already gotten what they'd wanted*, her father theorized; having witnessed their technology's effect, they now had bigger, better plans for it, perhaps, ones that required no cooperation from the audience but to return to a state of virtual unknowing, as if they'd never seen the show—a feat quite easy for millions of others, enveloped as the pap refilled their screens; and yet her unfather, or her father, whichever he had been at either time, had not complied.

He kept the books hidden, locked in his office, putting both himself and the family at risk, evoking a feeling of household vulnerability that had kept Alice awake through endless nights, expecting at any second the front door to be bashed in, sirens wailing as they dragged away her father and his contraband and locked him up and ate the key. She'd even thought about reporting him, as such, removing his presence from their family for good, though whenever she dialed the number for emergency assistance, tapping through submenus to find a living representative, all she ever reached was a recording, followed by the opportunity to record her own voice message for review, none of which, as far as she knew, ever received response.

Still, more than the books, none of which she'd ever been allowed to even hold, it was the show derived from them that occupied a vibrant quadrant of her mind, growing only that much more vivid the further from it time elapsed, as if the show kept growing inside her long after its pretend ending, feeding off her, framing her life, such that for some time, as a young one, she'd felt its duty to uphold within her carried on.

Season one, she still remembered, followed a war that lasted eighteen years, though the way the war was fought was not on land or sea or air, but inside our memories. In season two, all free speech and understanding were made uniform and monotonic—including the scripting of the show—such that for long periods all you could see passing the camera was miles and miles of open smoke. Season three then chronicled the obliteration of the Earth by way of its collision with a planet sharing identical features, and upon which existed exact copies of everyone on our planet who'd ever lived—our ideal versions, as we'd described them, if not in language, but in aspiration, all our lives—that is, "one of everyone *but you*," by which Alice knew the you meant precisely her, in such a way that no one else but her had understood, imagining every other person hearing either nothing or the phrase *"one of everyone but Alice Knott,"* leaving it up to them to wonder what it was about. To Alice this felt like a threat of sorts, a warning intoned so coldly throughout the program that she had to watch with her hands over her eyes; which ended up feeling even worse, she found then, than really seeing, as inside the blackness of her mind was where the program really came alive, its landscape no longer conscribed to the terrain behind the glass but also inside her, through and throughout her, by the night, unbound, the burgeoning link between the once false-feeling and now fully present lives of her own family made only stronger in the ever-sprawling body of the program, which as repercussion even the changing laws thereafter seemed unable to cover over or restrict, its fact mired in her mind as strong as any, impossible to ever actually expel; better, then, she thought, to watch and not stop watching, to at least try to control the shaping of its influence by attending to it directly, while she still could.

And still, throughout the countless hours they spent suspended like this, in the watching, nothing broke. The air held hard, sewn up on all sides by the show's intense, relentless score, a wall of white noise–like melodic feedback often so loud, regardless of personal settings, that you could hardly make out what any character said, its vast impression remaining frontloaded in her ears for days thereafter, a living whir. By the end, she couldn't even remember how they'd gotten through it, all those seasons interlocked in running breadth, all of it seeming to have required lifetimes to experience—though it never seemed to find a true end in its conclusion, the final episode spanning at least half her lifespan before it vanished from the air: a weeklong marathon episode, broken only by commercials that made it somehow even harder to shake, and featuring a dialogue-less chronicle of the massive cloud of earthly debris and dust left over after matching planets had collided, as every living being on our version of Earth slept—culminating with the shattered, golden impact, an instant that burned so brightly through the screen that Alice found it impossible to think or move, much less turn away, splitting the viewer's zoned-out throe into a fully palpable state of shock in every home, upending all previous intention in their lives. In this shock we'd learned, after several sweeping hours of gnashing blackout, that the collision somehow killed no one; instead, as Alice understood, it simply forced each person and their double to directly overlap—and so to *negate* each other as active forces, in compression, each pair becoming one, like the remaining land behind a full eclipse that never passed on, overridden with memories that held no water and pending fates that made no sense given the prior framework of their lives; neither to be the same again thereafter, all a jumble in their own minds, each that much more vulnerable to subsequent alteration, though by what or whom or in whose name remained unclear. By now all Alice could remember of the blurring glut of that last broadcast was how it passed through thousands of shots per second, all while Alice and her family still looked on, rendered inert, unable to assess the program's gist for hours upon hours with anything like plot or even image—and yet the thrust of which, over the course of its compilation, began to take hold inside them each, to claim true form: eventually assembling the crux of not only two versions of the same life held parallel, but innumerable emotional universes crushed in upon the haunted cognitive coordinates of every being, past and present in the same breath, the dead, alive, and yet to live alike, thereby unveiling a common landscape in our wake, one wherein time did not exist, nor did any person's prior perception of their own persona, no certain aspect of any fate.

In the last seconds before the show's end, Alice could hear the monotonic, slowed-down voiceover of what she thought at first must have been her father or unfather's voice over the noise, at last offering his own form of unwanted running commentary as he so often did with other shows, though which now looking back she could think of only as a living form of omniscient narration, spoken aloud by no human person, live or onscreen, but somehow emerging from somewhere deep inside the show itself, explaining how this moment was only the beginning, a seed from which *true liberty would eventually emerge*, wherein we would soon discover what had felt like freedom previously was only vile, a hoax between us and our worst versions, in the dissolution of which we would now be allowed to truly see—a promise heard by each alone in their own way, in their own context, as living scripture actualized at last after so much meaningless struggle for meaning, faith, passed along and on now through the impending waves of light and slow-dissolve filling their faces, blanking their features, until they could tell no inch from any other. In passing on through all of this, Alice could recall nothing else about the broadcast—only how in the morning after she could still feel it humming in her flesh, leaving large bruises in her sternum, down her throat, marks in her scalp like blank tattoos, a rising dizziness that would linger on forever after, all her life.

As for what the other members of her family had experienced during that last viewing, Alice had never understood. The posture of her peripheral parents' blurry-faced bodies never shuddered, no blink of eye or motor twitch beyond the passing sense she'd had of their inescapable virtual collaboration in the screen's thrall, wholly unremembered the next morning, any day after. Instead they went on watching calm as grass, the pixels flickering blue-black across their heads like living waves, not even smiling, blinking, arms loose in their laps. And there beside her, she could recall now, always Richard, plugged into the thriving body of the room, now in remembrance, staring not into the broadcast but at her, Alice, directly, grinning with his braces glinting on his teeth in the taut air, his mouth half open like a ventriloquist's, transfixed not by the program but her reaction to it; his eyes drawn in and only to her own, searching for something there come open, something attained; how he seemed to take pleasure in her terror, in how it bound her; how the ruthless feed around them carried on, as if to him her sense of understanding was the central pinion not only of the entertainment, but of all creation.

0002

The second viral video begins in close-up on a large, chrome oven.

At once, an arm enters the shot; it turns a handle, pulls the device's door down to reveal its cavernous innards, thickly coated with a black matte of caked-on smoke.

Into the maw, we see a short, flat painting carefully inserted, still in its frame—identified as *The Strength of the Curve* by Tullio Crali (1930), a late but major work of the Futurist movement depicting an abstract red, white, and blue assemblage of cold, athletic lines.

The oven is then closed. We hear the click of an ignition; then, through the slim viewing panel, the blue-white glow of active flames. The shot remains static on the immobile body of the machine as it does its work, altogether taking less than fifteen seconds; then again the viewing panel returns to dark, and the oven's mouth is again opened.

Little remains but cinder and soot, their blackened chunks at once swept free from the machine onto the floor to clear the space. Another painting is then inserted: *La Primavera* by Botticelli (1482), itself as well subjected to the same incineration.

This process is repeated without comment across the initial 2m 24s of the video, including the destruction of *I Don't Want No Retro Spective* by Ed Ruscha (1979), *The Trap* by Kara Walker (2008), and *Still-Life with Bouquet of Flowers and Plums* by Rachel Ruysch (1704). There appears to be no order to the sequence of these selections, as Alice sees it, the image of the mirror still looming front and center in her mind, having just come back up from the site of her own shared violation to find the latest evidence of incurred damage played in loop onscreen as live TV—no common era or outlook linking the artworks beyond their individual importance, no defining school of thought, as if to underline how any work ever could be the next annihilated. Likewise, the sound the device makes in processing each new subject remains indistinguishable from those before: a subtle humming almost imperceptible without the volume raised to abnormal level, interrupted only by the gestures of the operator, the raising and the lowering of the gate of the orifice.

Then, following the insertion of *IKB 191* by Yves Klein (1962), the video's perspective becomes freed. It recedes slowly, revealing the larger room surrounding: a massive warehouse, we see then, its gray interior crude and uniform as any mass manufacturing plant ever known, lighted from above with a stilted but steadfast incandescence filling the ceiling's false sky above with fabricated glow.

Stacked into abutting queues beneath, what looks like several hundred yards of other paintings wait in rows, spanning the room's horizon far as the eye can parse. Most remain unidentifiable, obscured by the next propped beside it, though among them, many might perceive countless well-known works, each numbered with a placard affixed to its frame, again without clear logic to the organization, though belying that there is organization here indeed: a plan set into faceless execution.

The camera lingers only briefly then before again shifting upward, to the right, leaving the archive behind and out of view. Its gaze continues moving then along the expanse of the lifeless metal warehouse wall, panning for some unnatural duration across the silver, spinning and spinning without frame of reference but the motion in itself, until suddenly, mathematically, coming to a hard stop, front and center, on a wide, reflective square; a mirror, we can see, it must be, shown reflecting at an angle that reveals the camera, and as well the remaining space beyond chrome plate. It seems to be the very shape and texture, Alice realizes, of the mirror left behind in her own home, the space of that memory somehow loosened, ages ago in her already, a memory rendered under significant duress, here again tightened in around her, its face somehow too close up in the screen, too real to remain just seen as light and glass; as if at any instant the very boundary between viewer and viewed might crack, shatter apart, allow the looming lens of the recording to come on through, to actually touch us, until the video cuts out.

The virtual reach of the second destruction video surpasses the previous in record time, shared and reshared in insane proliferation across all platforms left to sprawl; and in its renewed wake comes a further propagation of publicly destructive acts, however connected or unconnected in their adherent mania, as reported by the sets of talking heads behind the glass.

Within hours, for instance, a collection of eighteen paintings by the classical French Baroque master Nicolas Poussin (1594–1665) is noted missing from their temporary display in the Hall Napoléon under the Pyramid at the Louvre; where once again no alarms had been triggered in the process, nor is any evidence of tampering evident beyond the removal of the work itself, including the same blanked-out security footage of the area within the time of the occurrence, just as in Alice's home's robbery. The total take, it must be incessantly repeated, remains "literally invaluable," with various official estimates assessing the net worth lost around $2.2 billion. "And perhaps more, even as we speak," says one pundit, "as now the price is going up. Everybody wants their own piece of Poussin now; he's the absolute hottest."

The museum's security provider, an entity as highly reputable as the one hired by Alice, is placed under investigation, as are all current employees of the facilities, rendering all public access for the time being on hold; in other words, as the unpopular news anchor puts it: *The museum will be indefinitely closed.* Rumors about potential internal sabotage, given the entity's alleged dire financial status, as well as more outlandish conspiracies regarding the questionable authenticity of the museum's collection, begin to circulate, never so beyond possibility that even those most in the know find their dreams haunted, their sleep devoid of rest, the night alive.

Who else is out here among the world with us, we wonder, studying our behaviors, keeping their masks clean, biding time? Everyone at once so all on edge we sleep with automatic weapons, bark at our loved ones over parking, have another drink, another drink. It's business as usual, really, and business is booming; it's what we were born for: to partake, and to respond; *to find our voice among the rest.* Meanwhile, even nature's in on the prank now, up to its neck in human drift: as in masses, trees all over the world begin dropping, from out of nowhere, their roots discovered stunted, wrung with worms; flocks of disoriented birds disrupt a major air traffic control center, interrupting long enough to lose two jumbo flights en route to a major vacation destination, killing dozens; their blood will sink into the seas; it will wash up in swathes of gray foam with massive schools of fishes already rotting as they cover the white sands of a calm shore, a child not yet old enough to know a language awestruck by their fetid color as she hangs strapped to her mother's chest during their morning walk searching for shells, the first memory she will remember having all these years later. After all, it is our memories we want; more than expression, even, more than information; *please leave me be with what was mine.*

Meanwhile, overseas, the feed reports, at Centre Pompidou in Paris, a screen displaying an early print of Kenneth Anger's *Lucifer Rising* (1973) is head-butted by a fourteen-year-old, shattering the glass and causing profuse bleeding from his face. The family's legal representation will later sue the museum for emotional and physical damages, eventually resulting in an out-of-court settlement. Versions of the video remain available online. Now who is watching?

Hours later, at the Stage Hermitage Museum in St. Petersburg, a young man dressed all in blue takes a pocket lighter to the face of the angel in Albrecht Dürer's *The Dream of the Doctor* (c. 1498), scorching the skin of the face of the image, directly mimicking the original viral video, before being tackled by a local bystander, taken down. The culprit, during his arrest, will reveal tattoos marking the flesh over his left shoulder blade of what appears to be an illustration of the sun exploding. And underneath the point of impact, an inscription:

> *dream*
> *dreXm*
> *dreXX*
> *XreXX*
> *XXeXX*
> *XXXXX*

"I woke up one morning and I had this burned into me," the young man explains, speaking with his eyes forced closed on camera. "It has throbbed every single hour since. Finally, I couldn't stand it. I knew what it wanted, what I was meant to do." In coming weeks, he will be worshipped by fashion and fan-fic forums alike, pursuing a modeling career while simultaneously, unknown to most, establishing a new religion, XXXXX, in his name. By the end of the year, all members of the group will commit suicide by intentionally botched lobotomy.

And, at the Vatican Museum in Rome, Marc Chagall's *White Crucifixion* (1938) has a nail driven through it in the center of Christ's chest by a mute woman, who then uses the same hammer to attack all who try to touch her, shrieking at the top of her lungs the chorus to Michael Jackson's "Thriller" in a deformed register over and over: *"No one's going to save you from the beast about to strike."* All charges against her will later be dropped in recognition of her recent diagnosis of Creutzfeldt-Jakob Disease, one among many the world over, as in a wave.

And at the Tokyo National Museum, Suzuki Harunobu's *Woman Visiting the Shrine in the Night* (Edo period, 18th century) takes three gunshots to the center of the forehead of its subject before the high-school debate star wielding the gun turns the same weapon on herself, splattering her blood across the image, a gaudy mismatch for the composition.

And, at the National Gallery in London, still in the same day, *Sunflowers* by Vincent van Gogh (1888) is spray-painted over in neon pink with the words *THE SHIT OF LORD*, injecting the phrase into the public lexicon as it replicates uncensored through our screens, destined to become trivia.

And at the SFMOMA, Agnes Martin's *Falling Blue* (1963) is beaten with the long lens of a camera attached to a vintage device loaded with an exposed roll of black-and-white film, which when developed reveals a series of pictures of the attacker smiling and happy, with their family, waist-deep in the darkened water of a manmade lake as once again the world approaches dusk.

And at the Ludorff in Düsseldorf, Gerhard Richter's *Fuji* (1996) is taken off the wall and flung like a discus by a Japanese civil engineering major visiting from abroad, breaking the nose of a nearby bystander, herself in the midst of writing a personal email on her phone to her father concerning her future, about which she is quite afraid, having been waking up each morning finding herself in an unfamiliar location, far from home. She will go on to have a successful career as a spokesperson for a dementia medication corporation—which must remain nameless here, for your protection—during the coming era where it becomes the most prescribed drug in the world.

And again in Miami so as in Johannesburg, and in Mexico City, and Detroit, so as in Barcelona as in Sicily and Montreal and Tokyo and Dublin, so on, the names of cities cited as hosts of local crimes against creation brought about by persons whose names we won't remember after all, only their urges, passed by mouths from mind to mind like mental tiles lining some lost floor locked and gleaming in the dirt beneath our feet, the tally of our steps together passing without clear marking no matter where we imagine we might go, thereafter only remembered as emotions, so much weather, clogged in our secret longing for dreams of death of our ideas.

Even the concept of *the Idea* itself now feels like a plague of its own making, the loose ends of what could be done and has not yet been all flailing and flapping in the breeze of our communal desperation, as the shapes of faces of the arrested and the suspected through our TVs feed together back to back, as the list of affected works aggregates with increasing rapidity, the incurred damages tallied in moments of segue between acts of more ongoing social harm: the crashing of the planes into the ocean or the menace of global warning or the criminal acts of candidates for local office in the throes of their campaigns or the newly discovered sex tape of the surgeon general or the dark object newly rumored to be growing on the dark side of the moon or the reign of Alzheimer's or of Parkinson's or of whatever else we absorb between the colors of the commercials and the LCD glow of our laptops and on the airwaves flowing through us whether we tune in to hear them now or not.

Regardless, the surrounding context of other damage blends seamlessly within the voice of the news anchor, the local op-ed, as if there is already more to the story than we might know, which will be presented to the viewing audience as it is allowed, mandated by some civil architect behind the psychic curtain, veiled away, and yet whose pulse we can hear beating in our bodies, tuned just a hair off of our own. It is already hard to remember almost anything for even minutes, and it is only getting harder as such violent fauna fills our brains, seeking out the holes in us that most need fodder and taking hold.

"Our art has become completely penetrable," one rapidly emerging conceptual artist tells another, as an aside in conversation at the opening of her latest exhibition, dubbed by big names in the art world as *the future*: a series of one million blank and unlabeled videotapes onto which she's bootlegged her solo remake of the movie *Rambo*, to be burned all together in the parking lot of the Mall of America on a significant anniversary of September 11, a live video presentation of which is already available for streaming preorder, while the destroyed remake itself remains unseen. "And so why should it not be penetrated, over and over and again? The joke turns on itself at last, revealing no actual comedy; a mark forever on the face not only of the culprit, but all of man, its cost carried in the creases of our total legacy, binding us together in what is yet to ever be."

———

Alice sees the frenzy unfold as from a daze, afflicted in her own right with what seems a burgeoning condition of mortal confusion she has been victimized into feeling part of, as if the story onscreen is not some coincidental catastrophe but the next page in her life. It all feels at once too real and unreal in the same breath, apparently actually happening but not in a way that affects the strong, warm light that fills the house, the sense of something still needing to be done. She knows she should feel trepidation, maybe even panic, at how the ongoing vandalism might somehow be asserted back to her; all the faces flashing in the newscast feel like actors, employed in dramatic reenactments of some terrible event offered up to most would-be onlookers as theater, nothing that would ever rear its head in their real life—in much the same way a younger Alice had come to think of God, after years of finding nothing yet to count on, nothing that would not dissolve right out from underneath her given the chance. There was so little anyone could prove of anything, wasn't there, even in the context of their own living, much less the larger story of the world, so why believe in any one form of nightmare over another? Why expect anything but that which could never be expected?

Alice knows she is still awake now because the TV's gross glow insists so, the way it burns and burns on through her eyes, not in actual pain but more a reinforcing feeling that lines her waking hours with a sense of never quite being fully there, and that it could at any moment stick that way forever, confining her perpetual existence to endless sprawl. How else left to live but in between the lines, then? From where Alice sits, after all, nothing has changed: the walls are still walls; the reach of daylight stands moored in the same station as the day before and so probably tomorrow; no one and nothing but her inside herself again, alone, laced only with the snaking suspicion that time isn't actually passing, nor has it ever—there has only ever been this instant, now, and now—a seeming falsehood that could only ever be negated once it's too late, which is always, which is how we stay alive. Hell, if they did come to arrest her, brandishing some further culmination of the fragmentary evidence as yet supplied, would it even feel so bad? How much further could someone else's failing information take her? Alice can't remember even moving in what seems months, despite the still-warm remembrance of feeling burned up herself, feeling in midst of some slow continual inferno as she passed from room to room today or any other—all of which feels more like a recording than a live event, becoming simply another part of who she once was, an active grime that floats on her surface but won't stick.

"No, we still do not have any idea who made the films," someone is saying, as Alice tunes half back in from some time staring through the ceiling. The voice seems to wash over her, as if lapping at her brain. "Yes, we are still looking, and yes, of course, we want to stop them, whoever *they* are; because yes, we believe in the value and beauty of art in the lives of our people overall; and no, we don't have any leads; no, we do not understand what any one work of art itself was trying to say or even represent exactly before it was violated, nor do we have any idea why someone would want to violate it despite that lack of understanding; yes, I believe my child could probably do that too; both the art and the destruction of it; absolutely, we thought that was a pretty picture, though no we can't understand why anyone would pay so much to take it home when they could have owned a yacht instead, or a small island, really, or part of a sports team; yes, we do love to watch our sports, though we are aware of the many other ways time spent viewing could be spent; yes, we believe every citizen should respect the flag, regardless of personal experience or specious feel."

The man looks so much like one of the cops Alice remembers from that same morning, she imagines, peeking out through half-closed lashes, near adrift. His bloated body, even in blur, seems too large to fit onscreen so well, close as they've zoomed in. "Yes, I believe we prevail," he carries on, "regardless of the various statutes and procedural red tape keeping our mechanisms of public investigation from ever reaching full potential. No, we have not received any reports of threats on human lives, unless you count the hardworking children in our schools, who we are at this point no longer sure about and can't expect not to assault themselves; we truly hope the youth might take this rash of events as an opportunity to tend toward a career in something more practical than art; and yes we are standing by, at all times, locked and loaded, ready to react to anything that's thrown before us, without a moment's hesitation, as when forced to guess we must expect the worse, for our own safety, must we not? If only we could read criminals' minds finally, if we could be allowed to prosecute on the grounds of our suspicions, to cut the violent urges off at their own possible pass; think of how much trauma might be saved, for instance, if the kid wearing the hat with the marijuana leaf on it could be detained, preventing what worse fates for him might yet to come; yes, of course, ma'am, artists are people too, and so are addicts; yes, I believe I saw that recent major motion picture, based on real events, or so they claimed, though no I did not enjoy it as entertainment nor do I understand the fuss and the awards, nor did it improve my experience of life on planet Earth as a known human, in revelation, and as such I would prefer not to have to hear about it all the time, thanks; yes, I do fancy myself a sort of armchair critic, if you must ask; actually, I'm a writer, too, myself, though I'm waiting until I retire to get started; after nearly thirty years here on the force, I have so many stories you wouldn't believe, though for now my wife and kids will have to suffice as my best fans; yes, I think experience is more important than imagination, what do I look like? No, sir, I do not share the desire to destroy art, though I can't say the thought had never crossed my mind sometimes when people act like a pile of sand is the second coming; yes, I believe humans are inherently evil, if I may; yes, that includes me, if not my children, who are true angels, all seven of them, each bearing my same name; so at least we have the children, which is the only reason I show up and do my job. Yes, I am aware of the compromised state of mind of many of the offenders, as well as the general rise of cognitive impairment in our times, which some have suggested as a contributing factor to the events; my own mother and father both died of mental complications in their own right, and I saw firsthand the conditions they were forced to live in when I shipped them off to the same assisted living facilities where their own parents died, despite my suspicions of what goes on behind closed doors in places like that; me myself, I'd rather die; no, I did not mean that as a threat or even a possibility; no, I am not terrified for the future of our time and country, but yes, I am generally on edge now more than usual, you might say, both as a father and a husband and just basically an all-around happy-natured guy who wants to see his team do well and his best interests protected by the representatives who I've in no small way helped to elect."

No matter which channel Alice changes to, among hundreds, what they broadcast is the same, picking up the same thread where the last had just left off, like spinning plates; no choice but to listen, absorb.

"Yes, we have discussed the possibility of restricting public access to all nationally owned museums, at the very least, for a brief time, to limit access to those who might be inspired to contribute their own act of vandalism during this time of heightened visibility until we know more; no, we do not wish to have to resort to that, but yes, we carry active weapons and know how to use them, or have been trained to at some point in the past; yes, I am in favor of the bill to put guns in the hands of every human, because yes, I must admit, I don't always feel safe in my own home, much less my skin, despite my longstanding, nearly spotless record as a lawman; yes, I realize not everybody has it as good as everybody else, and I am thankful to the lord above who blessed me with my power and influence, not to mention my good looks, and yeah my kids; yes, I understand some people are very desperate, now more than ever; suckers; yes, we are seeking a speedy end to these events, despite our lack of clear direction as it stands; yes, we are diligently at work despite our necessary periods of rest, as even God took the day off, didn't he, so says the holy record, penned by his hand; yes, I believe in one true God, and yes I have a personal relationship with him and several of his family members, including his son, who we destroyed too, and so much else, though no I don't let it come between me and my work; yes, I still sort of see my job as holy, or else I wouldn't do it, though I would prefer not to use the term 'holy war'; yes, we want things to go back to the way they were before everything bad started happening day in and day out; no, we can't remember how that felt either, to live so much less encumbered by our conscience, allowing that those of families less fortunate than, for instance, mine must foot the bill, but yes I am thankful for their ongoing service as unskilled workers, even if sometimes seeing them coming, I'll admit it, I told my kids to cross the street; yes, I believe in right and wrong and feel equipped to tell the difference, even when others don't agree; yes, I believe sometimes people deserve to die, if only to provide better conditions for those remaining; yes, I am a student of our nation's history, including the bad parts, though I prefer to think of kinder times; yes, we hope we one day will feel better than we do now, or that our children will, at least, or their children or someone else's, any second now. Any more questions?"

At last the man has finished talking, so it seems, noting as she looks into the screen again how the speaker could only be one person, no one else, a head as recognizable as any, ever: it is the president, his squinted, arthritic profile definitive and sure despite how it's been digitally polished beyond flaw, unto a flesh so flat it's hard to remember how to look away. The broadcast, no longer local, comes live and direct from one of the leader's many vast vacation homes, somewhere undisclosed in the Caribbean, or so suggests the notating text onscreen alongside the garish ads for skin pills and memory cream, encasing his broad executive visage front and center against an empty beach at dusk, so obviously projected on a green screen that it might not be.

"I can remember when I was six," the ninety-nine-year-old figurehead intones, his voice digitally altered to sound younger, kinder, already digressing. "I saw a painting at a carnival downtown. I don't remember where it was, or even who the artist, though it probably wasn't someone you would know. I mean like it could have been a local dad, painting while the toddler squirms in his lap, or in the nighttime, while all the rest of us are dead asleep."

This man must be wasted, Alice notes; he can hardly keep his head up, or his hands from shaking; or at least so he would like to seem, she imagines, so as to feel closer to the common, inundated citizen; anybody's pawpaw. She can't remember anyone who didn't seem drunk as hell in at least years, perhaps her whole life; and yet no common world felt in between, nothing left to pin her down to who she had been but her own exhaustion, loss of resolution.

"Anyway, it was a picture of a giraffe. But you only knew that due to the label, *Giraffe in Paradise*, like a little brass caption below, because the content itself was totally I don't know: the most disarming image I'd ever seen or still have since, all this time later, to the point words fail any attempt to correspond. It wasn't getting any much attention at the show, I noticed, as there were free cotton candy machines and a clown that knew some tricks to fool the rubes. The whole rest of my brothers and sisters were in the goat tent, doing free goat rides, which of course I loved. But you know what? That goddamn picture, I mean that painting, it changed the whole shape of my life, right there on the spot, like being drowned. I'd never seen anything like it, understand me? Nowhere in creation. I was at once transfixed and overrun, filled up with power; I didn't want to ever have to leave it, and realized I'd do almost anything to spend the rest of my life in its regard; like I would have got down on one knee if I had had a ring, and if it had fingers, maybe a mouth to say aloud, *I do*. Anyway, I begged and begged my mom to buy it for me, to bring it home with us, like I have never begged for anything since in my whole life, or at least not up to that point; and believe me, I can be one convincing S.O.B., not to be denied what I desire."

Alice can hardly even tell by now who's really speaking. The man's voice sounds like every other man she's ever met—the cop, her father and unfather, the unbrother, whoever else—somehow all of it nearer and louder than it should be, all throughout her, parsed in darkness. *Like when my imagination's saying all the things I never wished to have to hear, the world's darkest wishes made manifest against not who I am, but who I will be.*

"Between me and my mother," the head continues, "my everlasting mother, may she rest in peace, we worked out a little plan, where for one full year all of my allowances would go to pay off the picture, see? Instead of all the junk food I could have had, trips to the movies, toys, I sacrificed it all just for this picture, passing loaned-up cash to its creator, whoever they are now, tendered definitively from hand to hand, and I took it home with me and into my bedroom and locked the door, and boy I thanked my lucky stars for the fact I'd been allowed to make it mine, for only me to ever see thereafter, no one else. So did I hang it on the wall? I did not hang it on the wall. I had much bigger plans for it than that. Grand plans, to change my world. And so I hid the painting in my closet, see, as something private, impenetrable but by me, the same way other boys around my age were hiding materials of a more, let's say, unmentionable nature; I had always been slightly ahead, slightly my own god. So I would only take my giraffe out when I could lock myself inside my room, hidden from all else, and, friends, I must admit, I would take all my clothes off. And what would I do then? I would stare. I might spend a whole weekend in there like that, staring, scheming, meditating, just me and the picture, titled *Giraffe in Paradise*, did I say? It was scribbled right there on the back of the canvas in pen, without a signature from any artist, as if formed from out of time. But in my mind, I called it *son*; that is, it felt like my own child, before I even had good, working sperm. I would lie with my son flat on my chest and think about who he might be and yet become in growing into himself more fully over time, how I might better come to know the colors as they'd been rendered, how the colors were as much a part of me as any other part of who I was. How through growing closer to its grace, get it, I could now understand my own coming future—you know, my destiny."

Until I can't tell where his voice ends and mine begins. The speech's words are all bunching up in Alice's cerebrum, blurring together, fomenting sicker, darker language in between, all else unspeakable, without a surface, through which Alice feels in unseen blaze against her face, firming in around her, walling her in.

"And you know what? To this day, without that painting, and my years with it, the experience I felt it granted me, like a drug, meaning the good, prescribed kind, I know in my heart I never would have embodied what it takes to run this country, about which furthermore, between you and me, my fine constituents of faith, I will say I never meant to become a politician in the first place before I found that I'd become one. There was so much I had to overcome to be able to maintain my ability to oversee, to direct. I don't believe I could have survived my birth mother's suicide, as they graciously named it, or found the desire to continue to carry on from such immediately meaningful death and become what I am now, or rather, who, which I can assure you I am no less sure than you are exactly what that is, despite how I am I up here standing still trying to be it, every second, just like you are doing with your own self, in whatever little slice of your own life you feel you've taken charge of."

If she could close her eyes, Alice feels certain, she could identify the source behind the sculpting, the subconscious lurch within the utterance and its rendition making her feel crowded on the insides, wracked with unscratchable itch. She's been staring so hard at the screen for some time now, she realizes, that she can't remember ever having not, a premonition corresponding sharply with the deeper-seated feeling of how the receptors behind her eyes might at any moment crack and come apart, disrupting her ability to grasp anything thereafter if she refuses to oblige.

"None of us have any clue what we are doing, is what I'm saying, people; including the people like myself who act for the most part like they do, who dictate orders all the rest must observe and obey, because we can, no matter how little or from how far away they ever seem to see us, how much they must know what will work out to the common good better than any of us know it by ourselves. This is the fundamental law of governing, as I have come to understand it: there was always someone else to blame; the guy behind the guy behind the guy and so on, where eventually, certain of my fine colleagues would have you believe, there eventually, appears the ultimate authority, which most of us, like I did even as such a young boy, would learn to see as God. Not God like the *drink wine and live forever* God, but God like you are mine and mine alone, and you will do exactly as I say, forever and ever, not only in your waking life, but into death and yet beyond."

▬

The president reaches into his pocket, then, removes a square of folded paper; he unfolds the paper to reveal a scrawl of messy scratching, faded hues, in some way resembling, according to the text scrolling beneath, the body of the precious image he's just described, held up for all the cameras, hiding his face. Though the paper might as well be blank, as far as Alice can tell; there's nothing to it, its hues and hashmarks worn away to zilch with age and friction, nothing left, strange given the leader's testimony.

Likewise, Alice can feel nothing of her body, only its surroundings; the same whorl carries on inside her as she feels her lids click closed in thoughtless capture, like a camera, and so much longer than a blink; and just underneath, constrained in darkness, the pull of something shifting in her immediate terrain; altered, as with the touch of wind or silent terror trapped in suddenly remembering something previously thought forgotten, some day so far gone now it could be any, which Alice finds the longer she allows herself to dote on, the gravity surrounding the silence in the absence of the president's ongoing voice billows with weight, accessing something like atonal music carried in her, a mutant choir made of blood, her cells all pinching. It is unclear how long this goes on; it takes another lifetime to remember how to pull away, to make the flimsy scenery inside her lifelines dissolve back into nowhere, and then to even less. As Alice opens her eyes again she does so at the same time as the president appears to tear his precious artwork into two; and into two again, again, again, allowing the shredded fragments to fall beneath him like unmelting snow against the black deck of the set.

"I am very much like you, perhaps you see now," the president utters, clearer and stronger now with every rip, until there's nothing left but empty hands, "and yes, as you have long known, I am in all ways on your side. There's nothing you can feel that I have not already felt before you, in your stead, so that you might never have to, despite how so often you insist on feeling pain. Reality is very jacked up for us right now, isn't it? Indeed, I feel it is my duty now, in being frank, to admit that we, as a people, find ourselves at the cusp of a great emergency, one absolutely more dark and ominous than any other ever known. Some of the very best of us are being seized by terrible sickness, one that's wound its way into the heart of every mind, a plague programmed out of the understanding of the first law of the market, taught to me by my great mentor, whose name I cannot share: *They will take what they are given*, which includes me myself no less than it includes each and every one of you."

Alice can no longer tell if what she's seeing is being projected in the blackness of her mind or on the screen against the wall; there seems to be no difference, as all there might be ever again seems made only of language, a projection, forced feed.

"And listen, I know I have come to you before to warn of great danger many times before, and many times among those times it was not true, or it was no more true than that it is always; every second, every day. But I must tell you now that we've been looking in all the wrong places all this time: it is our own people we need to be afraid of, more so than those beyond our walls; and we must consider now, as well, that perhaps those people aren't simply evil, but they are animated by a force they don't even realize they've let in, despite how it's been hanging for forever right in plain sight, on the walls that line their lives, that fill our houses, define our space. Friends, I believe it is our imagination that's turned against us. It has filled our insides, changed our brains while we slept, which many of us experience thereafter diagnosable as medical conditions, many more common than ever, which we believe might yet be stopped. But it is our very surroundings, too, the nature of our creations, that has changed; something has zapped aware within what for so long we saw only as passive, beyond mind. This was once a great country, a hopeful country. Preservation of who we'd always been was a source of endless pride, a way to remind us both of what we'd been and what we could be. And yet, this is not an open system, not ours to alter. By allowing outside influence in over our spirits, over and again, we have forgotten how to wish, or what to wish for, and what it means to want to wish alongside billions of others also wishing, in their own lives, all at once. The volume is as high now as it has ever been, I'm saying, so high there almost is no longer any sound we can shout louder than, to get it out. Instead, we must learn to hear again, within this deafness— not to *listen*, but to *hear*—a process which begins by accepting exactly what you have been given by those who know better than we might, myself included, without the luxury of understanding, at least not yet. We must respond to the ineffability of rampant peril by providing it no station, no reflection. Our living blood must be the only channel."

The president peers into the screen, across the land. His unblinking corneas are blue now, where at the beginning they'd been gray, she recalls now—the same blue as her own eyes, her mother's and brother's, both her fathers, each all alike now as she remembers, and so her own. The whole screen seems to tingle in recognition of her recognition of their shared traits, the relentless light a celebration in its own right, leaving only temporary, passing places in the blind.

"About all this, though, I want you to relax. The game is already covered, end to end. I come to you with all this information so that you understand that you can trust me; that I am with you, through the illusion, soon coming out the other side. We'll take care of the details, me and my great people. We always have been, all this time. All you should want to do now is lie down on the floor and feel the ground, bask in its hardness. The ground has never once yet let us down, after all, has it? Ever beneath us throughout each step on our march to brighter light, as together we find a common will within to overcome what we've done to us, what we'll keep doing, and desiring to do, forever, sight unseen. The world is ours."

The face so near the camera now it is actually touching, Alice sees, skin to screen, into all homes. It holds and waits there like a world, eclipsing even its own features, pores big as holes one might slip into, makeup caked so thick it could be almost any body underneath; where as he blinks his eyes then and they close, so her eyes do too, meeting at once with massive, unlimited darkness.

▬

Alice inhales slowly, in rhythm with the pulse of the TV, her exhale matching too, in mirror, beyond control. Something like time continues passing; the edges of her understanding ridged as if with something brittle rubbing past it on either side. She can still feel the room around her stuck so still it refuses to let the moment shift, waiting for the landscape to awaken, to allow Alice back into the access of herself, the same way she might have waited through the night as a child for the sun to rise again, whole lifetimes passing in between.

Meanwhile, in between heartbeats, she hears the news broadcast's signal carried on, another voice left over from the last scene, its dictation drawing her attention back up into its ongoing story.

Renowned performance and installation artist Alice Novak, the speaker intones, *age sixty-eight, was found dead this afternoon in her studio workspace complex in downtown X., following reports of "strange animal sounds" and "terrible music."*

Alice's eyes unlock then, as if on command. There, where the president had just been, she sees only the image of a woman's face, front and center and impossibly large—for at some point Alice had moved unknowing, she finds, to touch her own face against the screen, on both knees. The woman's face seems at once familiar, if in a completely different way than the last face; there's something both soft and yet constrained about it, surely, in the woman's obvious old age, long white hair and round jaw, pierced ears without earrings, something worn down about the aged flesh thinned by years. Behind her the outline of an ocean appears, gray and flat, reflecting the sky above the waters without stars; nor any sense of time or space extending from it, as if how it's captured is all it is.

Police entered the premises to discover the artist's body naked and faceup on the floor, surrounded by a series of seven separate live webcams broadcasting to seven different independent URLs. Several dozen other artworks, recently recalled from their display at various international museums and estimated to have been valued at more than $380 million, were found burned on site, allegedly by Novak herself.

There's something wrong about the woman's eyes inside the picture, Alice senses. They don't seem human, somehow: cloudier, deeper, glazed over from the inside. They make the whole rest of the face feel not as recognizable as it had been at first, the longer she looks; something missing, a black cat stuffed in a bag. And yet Alice finds she can't stop staring back into the woman's gaze, how it sees *through* her, as if there's something yet to be transmitted, some desperate phrase; though the feeling breaks up as the broadcast transitions to a montage of the artist in life and work: first at a flat black charcoal-colored desk in midst of typing; then in a room surrounded by camera heads all installed into white walls, her face enwrapped with silver fabric; then wading through a sea of prosthetic bodies dressed like cops in a gold warehouse, pressed in so full there's hardly room to even see; and in a cathedral filling up from one end with a cloud of flooding smoke burst from a vial of hair placed on the altar.

Best known for her reality-bending performances and interactive landscapes, including the landmark Telecommunication *series, Novak had not shown or discussed work in more than twenty years, though it is believed this period had been an effort toward what she referred to as her "most crucial human work as yet."*

Each image beyond the first few passes too fast for Alice to acknowledge its variation, the montage blurring, cell to cell, packed fat with faces and locations spanning a supposed lifetime; and yet she can't shake a feeling of private attraction to such a display, the way one might feel a painting by a stranger touched them in a way no one else could understand, a song written just for them, despite how the whole world can still hear it, if never the same way.

Novak's death has been ruled a suicide, and is believed to represent the first of a series of conceptual works—previously assumed to be theoretical—collectively titled Devoid, *alluded to in a lengthy, leather-bound suicide note she'd left behind; the note has since gone missing; any info as to its present whereabouts should be immediately reported.*

Alice waits for them to show the woman's final face again, as it was last captured before she died, some curtain in her heart pulled back to show only another curtain there behind it. Instead the broadcast returns only to an anchorwoman at her desk, apparently the owner of the narrating voice, though the texture doesn't seem to match, her mouth barely moving as she continues the dictation.

Devoid: A Memorial Exhibition, introducing the artist's final work, in adherence to her will, alongside a selected retrospective of her career, will be held in her hometown of A. tonight at six o'clock, and is free and open to the public.

Alice repeats the event's subsequently displayed address and phone number aloud over and over, rushing to transcribe it, its characters rolling over one another in the unfurling landscape of her mind, such that by the time she gets it down on paper she's no longer certain the information is correct. Still, she finds herself dialing the digits at once into her handheld either way. The line at once starts ringing as it should, loud enough against her face to fill her whole head with the sound, followed by a quick click and the dull hum of an open line thereafter, not a word.

"Hello?" Alice whispers into the receiver, cupping her mouth to shield it from the room. "Anyone there?" Her voice sounds funny on the line, like she's talking through a filter that makes her sound older, lower pitched; more like her mother, she imagines, whose voice had all but turned to gravel through her last months, eventually so low it was unintelligible from groaning. Either way, no one responds; there's only hanging air, and perhaps somewhere far on in there, Alice imagines, the sound of her own breathing there reflected, as if the line itself only connects to a recording of itself.

Alice spends a minute studying the silence, waiting for reception, and is on the verge of hanging up when suddenly she hears a scrambled sound, like language played back at high speed, followed by a sudden, earsplitting bleep, its shrillness spreading cold and hard between her teeth, jarring her fillings. The beep repeats immediately, this time less jarringly so, delivering her into a much different sort of stillness. She doesn't want to be the one to speak up first, for some reason, diminishing her power. Instead she sits holding her breath, waiting them out, eventually moving the receiver to rest against her jaw, her neck, her chest, until she gradually nods off altogether. It's been so long since she's had good rest, hasn't it? Longer than she can remember, maybe never. Something about the drift between her and the phone feels so complete, as if she should always do it like this, every evening, all her life.

Later, when she stands again, lightheaded from some cold draft sent through the space like a lost breeze, she lays the receiver on the ground still connected, already forgotten, its open channel holding steady as she moves amid the TV's fluctuating glow across the room, toward the only window, parting the heavy gray curtains by slipping among them, winding its cloth around her flesh, same as she had spent so many hours in childhood hiding from everybody, the cloth soon rough and tight around her bones, a second skin. Peeking out beyond the flat, cool pane, she finds a heavy, intense sunlight spanning all as far as she can see, with no visible motion even so small as a breeze or cloud there within it, a day so much like every other she remembers how could it not be.

It was only in the years following her mother and unfather's deaths that Alice felt Richard's influence come alive inside the house, in a far more affecting way than she had felt him when he was said to live right there in the room beside her own. Now that both his belongings and their supposed mutual parents had been removed, she began to sense not only that was he still in there with her, sight unseen, but that he had *just been* in any room she entered, as if he'd been adjusting a would-be set for her appearance, lining her path, yet always remaining just out of eyeshot, as if he were watching her through holes in the walls or from behind two-way mirrors, more there than ever now that, at least theoretically, he had moved on.

Alice would spend whole days, then, repeating the same small serial behaviors over and over in little loops, waiting for Richard to slip and appear there where he had not intended to, at last revealed; and yet no matter what methods she employed, how many permutations, she could not catch him in the act, make him appear; and so she had little choice but to continue trying, as she saw it, always on the cusp but never clear—to the point where she began to move without actual belief that the present condition would ever end; that soon enough, if she couldn't break through, she would become so ingrained in her own patterns of behavior, like a phantom, that she would soon no longer recognize an exit, become locked in amid the haunt, the same way her mother had lost her mind—and still nothing, not a knock of Richard, beyond some ineluctable trace of pressing presence, the nights all growing over into one another, drowned in time, each act finding her only that much older, slower, further gone.

All of this corresponded with the initiation of Alice's drinking so heavily she would be hospitalized half a dozen times in half as many years—a fact that suggested itself as sufficient explanation of her mind-state at the time, the ongoing substance abuse a front they never failed to hang upon her as the only answer, shooing all sense of other disturbance aside, though Alice insisted that the drinking was the only thing that had kept her sane throughout; without it, as she saw it, she would have suffered even more; would not have had the will to get out of bed or want to eat, much less quest after answers.

And while she did not fully associate the cause of her self-harm with all that had happened to her, nor with Richard as a person—she felt essentially no emotion for him beyond a sense of inarticulable wonder, as in religion, her only source of trepidation being her inability to connect the dots between what could be felt and what was seen—there was no mistaking that the coincidence of such events marked her persona with a flattened, folded feeling, as if there were a second flesh beneath her flesh, and there within it a second set of attributes and memories in constant friction with her central person, never to settle. She felt herself totally exposed to misinterpretation, given her wont for passing out in public, the sudden seizures from not eating, the constant pain that pushed her to walk around glowering, grumbling, beyond clear mind; yet this was simply how it felt to be a human, Alice believed, in her most sober moments, the same trepidations pressing down on each decision she had to make to leave the house, much less to ever get help to move along and find a different way of life; though, then again, she knew for sure that the drinking made her nightmares worse than ever, filling her mind with visions of endless fire each night as soon as she closed her eyes; with endless depictions of her own beheading, of drowning at the hands of unseen forces holding her under black water, of being beaten to a pulp by screaming children in the streets; every inch of any rest packed full of brutal sounds and aching color that made the waking world feel small and wrong and far away. *One way or another*, she'd learned to tell herself, hardly in jest though it never failed to make her snort, *you had to become obliterated enough in daily going that in the end you could no longer tell the difference between life and death, between seeing and feeling, where and nowhere.* And still, no matter how identical the days between seemed, no matter how each time she lay down she imagined it would be the last, still she woke again into another day still unforgiven, seamed in with enough corresponding personal memory to assure her that she was still who she believed she had last been, regardless of what might have gone on outside her attention, while she was under, in the hands of anybody else, and what they now knew about her and her world that she would never.

And even now the room seems to be turning over underneath her, Alice imagines, a feeling of vertigo she'd long carried on with, only intensified by living in a space simultaneously so stolid and so pregnable to change; a place where, if she thought too long about it, the floor might at any minute collapse by sheer weight of premonition, underlined by a shameless anxiety that even recognizing its implausibility only strengthens. The screen of the TV still glows long across the room, as if to mirror back the shade of open sunlight all around her, its brightest pixels overwritten with the residue of time spent absorbing past and future entertainments, each slowly sculpting the nature of her life in their design, forcing information into us day in, day out, until we are starved for escape into the pending night.

Stronger than even that, though, is the slurred sound like winding gears Alice can now hear bearing down around the edges of her vision, replacing the space where the voice of the media had spread its hold with a new feeling: an ongoing sense that her every act was being not only recorded but witnessed by a live audience looking back at her through the screen of her conception, however motionless her life remained. Her ears seem stuffed beyond capacity, overloaded by the void of every hidden signal that might be parsed by other animals with sharper sense, or so she feels; placing every action under the impression that it's missing nothing but also never solely hers, just out of range.

Suddenly the room seems slightly smaller too, and again smaller upon such confirmation, followed by the feeling that she can't remember a time when it had not been shrinking ever toward its present size and on from there. It is the present and the past at once, she thinks, somehow coexisting in the same mount, forced by the different kinds of light straining her eyes, from the TV and the windows and the light within. Stronger still is the feeling that the larger world beyond her house is shrinking too, its landscape unseen behind the unending curtains, only the sheen of her imagination placed between them to defer the shifting logic: every waking second another line etched in the ongoing creation of the *yet to come*, like keys somewhere being pushed, changing her intention without warning, all of it part of the shapeless history of all that has gone on just out of sight.

Alice no longer wants to move or even see, much less to think; she doesn't want her hands to be connected to her body, to her brain; even the flow of thought feels like a structure placed upon her, printed out like subtitles, framing where she stands for all but her to see. How many people had experienced this same thought before, for instance, whether in assessing hers or having felt it as their own? How many versions of a person would be allowed to abuse the same array of evidence, emotion, language? How many hours left to watch?

The walls are banging then, Alice imagines, somewhere beyond her, so hard it seems to shake the house. Between each point of impact the surrounding silence mutates in anticipation, a space awaiting interpolation, further graft. It takes another several bouts of banging before her brain clicks loose and she remembers where she is and what could be: someone is at her door, it seems, though which door and who? She can't remember why someone would want to be here, when she herself would give so much not to; she can't imagine what more of her could anybody want. Eventually, she imagines, whoever knocks will go away, will grow old and die, will turn again to dust and blow away, whatever motive had once spurred them now grown inconsequential, numb.

And yet with each knock she blinks, then finally stands to cross the room, her body moving as if without approval. She presses her face against a peephole, seeing through the tiny eye in the face of the door she can tell by feel is the only one left in the house that allowed a person in or out, the others having been revised out of her memory amid the ever-changing proliferation of doors that led to other doors and hallways, void of firm direction. Through the narrow haze of the eyeglass, she can see another body standing on the far side: a human, for certain, oblong and boxy, its finer form compromised as if in mist, preventing further identity beyond the idea that someone is there, having shown up on her front step for some reason they must know and she does not.

Perhaps it is her own future self at the door, she thinks. She wouldn't rule herself out from acting better on someone else's behalf than her own. And even if it's just the cops, she feels, she'd love to give them another piece of her mind, demand to know why they haven't found the felon yet, recovered her belongings. Or had they? Had something else come down she can't recall, an answer she's already been granted but allowed to wear away? She hears her voice speak into the glass to seek an answer, but whoever's there either can't hear her or she can't hear them or otherwise there's no response; no shift even in posture or position, judging by the person's outline through the glass. Which should mean she shouldn't open the door, correct? It could be another burglar out there wanting in, come to claim all that remains; or perhaps something more—a murderer, for instance, having selected her at random to die today, depending only on the willingness of their next victim to assume *I am not the one to whom this could ever happen*, though if so, with her, they've got it all wrong: she feels she knows very well what yet awaits. And yet she undoes the latch—in fact, she's glad to—her hands and arms moving as if they've already performed the necessary action, the muscled meat lining her body already performing its own work, afraid of nothing; *come what may;* or rather, more correctly, *come what does.*

———

Behind the door, now open, stands a body. Long brownish hair, spectacles, old sun damage in its face; an older man, it seems, or at least as old as she feels. Wearing some kind of military garb, or at least a uniform espousing order—though he is clearly not a cop, his glinting insignia of a different code. He's speaking something, or at least his mouth is moving, though no language is coming out, so she can hear, or nothing substantive enough to register beyond the long low hum of the outdoors, its heat exploitive, crammed with damp.

Alice regards the man for several moments, waiting for traction, though the longer it continues, the more the thinner air there feels suspended inside of her head: *like spinning gyres inside an overheating hard drive*, she thinks, *a web address that won't connect.* The wide world's colors well up around the edges of her vision, burning at her eyes to try to see the world beyond, burning her brain to try to want to understand; instead she waits and looks and strains as the man whose voice she cannot hear explains himself unheeded, as if unaware of her distention, the cognitive gap held on between.

The man reaches into his pocket, then, fumbling for something; *a knife*, she thinks, *a gun, brass knuckles*, though even such idea can't shake her free; if anything she goes even stiller, expecting something worse than simple drift.

Instead of any weapon, though, the man's hand presents a business card, handed over with a wry wink. Printed shrill against the dull-blown field of cardstock, in silver letters, Alice reads his identifying language, word by word, aloud:

A. B. Smith—*Senior Adjuster*
AVOID CORP., INC.
Your first and last line of defense since 1901

Of course: *Smith*. The name had always struck her strange, no matter how often she met someone who used it; it shook free again the lacing feeling of both her unfather and unbrother's would-be lineage, none of which she had any context for beyond the pair delivered to her life, two from out of millions named the same way. So what sort of Smith was *this* Smith then? How could she ever know which Smith was one of *theirs*, of her unfamily's, comprised from some supposing fork off her own blood, and which was not, all someone else's? Biblical logic— far as she remembered being lambasted with it as a child, before the serial show filled in all such inlet of her life—suggested we were all descended from one person, tying our lives together by its lore; every pending person a possible Smith, then, all driven onward through the temporary lunge of birth and death, each living id moored to their own version of center stage.

Beyond that, Alice feels she already should know why this one *A. B. Smith* is here, what his directive must be in showing up on behalf of her security after the recent losses, though she can't make the words stutter out. The air flooding in from outside at her through the door is as warm as infant's milk, no feeling logged within her brain beyond its flailing blankness, like how an astronaut might feel after being cut free into outer space.

Smith starts speaking again, still incoherent to her, a wall of unknown sound. Once he has paused, she hears her own voice come out oddly loudly in reply, yet also muffled, as if rebounding after passing through several layers, deep within. She's already unsure what she is saying as she says it, the actual words obscured both in intent and receipt, her hands splayed out before her as in prayer.

She watches him produce a document from the side pocket on his briefcase, holding it up toward her without first opening it to look inside. The printed words list out her account's most recent details, likely supplied by some analyst in some huge building, far away, including the date and time of her home's trespass, a brief neutral description of the incident as interpreted by someone who wasn't really there, and who can only report on the representation of the action, according to record. Further down, she sees details derived from their last contact—dated from today, it seems, earlier that afternoon, though the only call she'd made, as she recalls it, had not connected—somehow here transcribed and dispatched with her comments about need for further service, passed on so fast that here he is, standing at her door. And before she can finish inspecting the fine print as it remains, perhaps to suss some sense out of the interaction, the man withdraws the paper and returns it to his briefcase, his intent in making this appearance now fully certified and stamped, leaving no way from here on to turn back from what must be their business, as if every step they'd taken, she and he both, their whole lives, had been designed to bring them to nowhere else but where they are, right now, today.

Alice feels her mouth moving again, saying something she isn't sure of; she feels the vibration of his communicative energy as he echoes in response, using his hands to gesticulate some series of abstract gestures Alice finds her eyes tracking more than anything so far—as if it is part of a magic trick, a small performance meant to impress as well as satisfy. The man laughs then, as at a joke he's slipped into the routine, and then Alice herself is laughing too, though more at the apparent incongruence in their interaction, still unclear in its objective or intent.

Nevertheless, the man appears to take her chortle as progress, and so bends to take his briefcase, as if they'll continue forward unto some task. He brings his eyes up to hers directly for the first time, and Alice realizes they're still standing in the doorway, despite the feeling in her mind of already having brought him in, told him to make himself at home. She presses back against the doorframe, suddenly embarrassed, creating a slim aisle of open space through which the man may enter, though for some reason she is unable to step back into the house herself to clear the way, extend an arm of welcome; the man in turn accepts the outlet, their shoulders gently brushing as he sidles by. Alice imagines closing the door between them, then, leaving herself outside, locking herself out, walking off into the light alone just like that, with only the clothes she has on her, leaving him—that is, still, Smith—to have her house all to himself, while she starts over elsewhere. This could be the start of something new in her life, she thinks, and perhaps his too, each defying what already seemed to have been planned for them some time long ago, following a theoretical inevitability once based on some set of persona-defining trivialities each selected so far back neither of them could remember how or why or even by whom; no day ever not interrupted by what had once been selected as the engine of their desire.

Then there they are alone together inside the house; the door already locked behind her, out of habit. Up close the man's clothes smell so much like two-packs-a-day-for-thirty-years she can hardly keep from choking. The air is twice as thick with him so near no open windows, all still air. He has his own heartbeat and intentions, she understands, staring back up into his *disarming sky-blue eyes*, which seem different out of reach of sunlight, fake like colored lenses, looking back into her face but not quite right at her as he goes on speaking in the mute, still no more audible even up close. Still, Alice finds herself continuing to respond to his apparent points of question. She smiles and nods between the cues, mimicking listening, receiving, still centrally unsure what it is about him that makes her want to go along, beyond the fact that he is here apparently in service of a claim initiated at her request, regardless of her more immediate desire that the whole world just disappear.

Fully inside now, away from the world's noise, Alice can better hear her own voice, in her head, speaking too fast already, hardly leaving time to breathe. She finds herself describing the night the robbery occurred, a span of memory throughout which she has no direct account of beyond its results, elapsed in sleep; as for the actual time of break-in, all she remembers is another strange recurrence of a nightmare she's had on and off since she was born—nude and hanging from a tree, accused of witchcraft, a fact she understands as innate to the fabric of the dream—*Why is she telling him this*, she wonders, in third person, unable to restrain herself from pressing forward, *why right now*. The only thing visible from her perspective in the dream, strung by the neck above the ground in throes of pending death, had been the presence of endless flashbulbs, their buzzing fibers knitting together all around her a spastic, intermittent light, through which, as she understood it on the inside, everyone else could *see straight into her thoughts*, into parts of her mind she'd pressed away, so to avoid; a psychic spectacle put on display not only for the large, hazy crowd chanting in tongues beneath her, but fed as well out through circuits, wires, to endless screens, unto all eyes, such that millions, the world over, were there to witness her demise.

The dream had gone on forever, strung out along a drastically slowed timeline—exactly seven years, in fact, a span she understood as dictated by a digital timecode burned into the filmscape of the dream, filling the fray of her thoughts with every passing second's exact, excruciating drag. Each moment then felt unique in agony and trauma as it passed, her system held there on the verge of strangulation and also bleeding out, stabbed and battered by caretakers assigned to make sure she stayed awake and half alive through every instant of the suffering. She could feel every cell inside her body wailing, boiling over, lapsing only long enough for her to form a passing thought of some eventual relief, though nothing changed. That night, the same as all the others, she'd hung on through the nightmare by a thread, and when she woke in searing sunlight through the window above her bed, she'd sweated out so much she could not move. She'd found herself seven years older again in mind if not her body, even more exhausted than when she'd gone to bed. It had then taken her the same duration to relearn how to operate her limbs, to find the ability to stand, such that by the time she was up again it was nighttime, the world again encased in endless dark; only then had she gone down to find the front door left wide open, the door of the vault disarmed, its contents long gone.

To hear her side of the story now, Alice realizes, is to experience it as for the first time; she feels ready to move on from it all, to let it go. Yet there is something about this man, his face, his posture, that sets her subconscious neuroses, raised to hackles in the telling, at an ease; he seems to be looking back into her as if not only really paying attention—the rarest feeling—but as well seeing her for who she is; not the question mark she'd been made to feel like from the TV, made up of only surface measures, premonitions, gut reactions, but someone struck up in an ongoing march of pain, across not only the trouble of the robbing, but the further miles of rubble in her heart. *He understands*, Alice imagines, *he can really hear me.*

Now they are standing together in the vault, Alice finds, punching her self-awareness back out of the autopilot effect of telling and into the present, already unable to remember having led them together down the stairs and past the requirement of entering the system's entry code without even thinking beyond language, the way one might drive for hours without realizing all the tiny motor actions spent between. But if the man is annoyed or taxed by her, by her physical vigor or emotional confusion, he doesn't show it; he simply looks at her, calm, nodding his head, writing nothing down—perhaps he's recording it, she imagines, or perhaps his memory is that good, or he's heard it all before. Either way, they're in here, live; the time is clicking.

———

Alice shows Smith where the walls of the first of the two legs of the vault once had displayed the artworks, now purged of sight, the absence still louder in her mind than any other element in the space; she wonders if he can sense the same. She can feel him study her instruction closely as she outlines where light-altered impressions on the surface demonstrate the relief of what had once appeared, the tiny eyeholes in the plaster where nails had been inserted. She assumes the company, his overseers, already have a list of what she'd owned and for how long and at what value purchased and at what amount valued in the event of its loss, as is the case now, the very reason he is here—and yet he wants to hear her say it, her own version of the whole plot, perhaps in search of cracks in its foundation, in her persona.

She follows suit, the language coming out of her more easily than she would have expected, despite her not quite knowing what to say. She explains how what looked when it had been here; she demonstrates the level at which each image had hung, shaping her limbs and posture as if still able to see it. His eyes remain on hers at all times, even when directed by her elsewhere; Alice gets the sense there is more suspicion in him than she'd first read, a kind of judging stance for which now she must perform, though she finds herself wanting to play into the doubt, if only to spite it, flip it over. It's all a game, this day, this living, or it could be, one worth pushing over where you can, to watch the upturned wheels spin in futility. Yet she also wants to understand: what his experience might draw out from the flesh of evidence as it stands, and why she feels like there is something unsaid even in his perceived misgiving, his presence a checkpoint to be passed.

It's not until they work their way around into the vault's second chamber, coming around the end of the only wall between them, that the adjuster's eyes leave Alice's. He stops mid-step, stuck staring head on into the mirror still hanging at the corridor's far end, just as before. Alice is surprised he notices it so quickly, when to her it had seemed to blend in so well, to disappear. She hesitates to face it directly yet herself, a sudden internal roil filling her blood in its presence, somehow even more so now with another witness—as if she herself had made the mirror, and finds herself standing now in the presence of a critic, being judged. She wrings her hands together, trying to turn him, standing awkward, looking for words to fill the space between. She feels his attention on her, by their reflection in the object's open face, the features surely hazy from such distance, each of them almost like other people.

The impending silence swells. Time seems to slow again, though only all around her; as if she might act outside the present on her own, undo its mettle by provoking what she wants; a feeling she hasn't had in long enough to not know how she wants to use it. She waits and listens as she lets the adjuster do his job; she sees him raise his arm toward the wall, pointing at their image in the reflective glass, and thereby too the image pointing back out at them in return. The man's arm is trembling, she sees, in both versions, his posture stock-still, held in file. He appears visibly thrown by the mirror's presence, his expression in the reflection pinched and tense, almost sickly in the cramped discolor of the room's bright. He looks *betrayed*, she thinks might be the word, or else exposed, as if he might not have come down here at all had he known what waited.

"It was my brother's," Alice hears herself say, her voice suddenly loud and clear outside her head. She's thrown to hear the term *brother*, not *unbrother*, though it doesn't slow her. "He kept it hung above his bed, gifted to him on his last birthday in the house, before our parents died. It was supposed to be a family heirloom, but I'd never seen it before in my whole life, and wouldn't for years after everybody else inside the house was gone. But my brother loved that mirror. I know because I would listen at the wall all night, almost every night for several years. I could hear him in there talking to it, singing, praying, if always in a language that made no sense; like some long spell he had to practice a whole lifetime to eventually get right, that he was performing not only for himself, but for all of us; everyone ever. I'm sure he knew that I was listening; that more than anything, I wanted to live like him, hidden away; or even to become part of him completely; to switch places, so I might feel some of the concern and the affection that his ongoing sickness garnered, all I wasn't getting. It became like a secret kept between us he didn't even know I knew about, that neither of us could quite control in application. This went on for what seemed years and years till he got worse; till he grew so sick they had to move him away somewhere no one would ever see him, though by then it was too late."

Alice can't place the source of this account in her memory, can't remember how much of it is even accurate once stated, though it feels no less true than whatever else; as if at last she's establishing a version of the story she might believe in ever after. *Where are the facts within the facts?* Regardless, the adjuster's posture relaxes at her telling, either bored or awed or both; his arms fall limp at his sides, his pupils dilate, his face—still in the reflection—looks tuned-in and open like a child's. The widened silence that fills in around her voice thereafter, where she pauses, seems only to feed the rising fire as it stands, each transition in their interaction giving way to more speech lurched from the first, a suffocating kind of freedom as from behind a mask.

"The next time I came across him—I mean my brother, Richard—he was all over the TV. It had been almost exactly seven years. They said he'd killed at least a dozen people since then, maybe more. Hunted them, kidnapped them, kept them, did not feed them, filmed them, called it *art*. He was going by a different name by then, and he'd put on a ton of weight, up to like four hundred and fifty pounds, but it was clearly him. I could still see the same child in there he'd always been: his eyes so unmistakable, even given how much he'd grown, what had come over him, more than flesh; something he had been designed from birth to perform, he felt, and so he had performed it, without what seemed any other choice. I really do believe that: how there was no other way he could have turned out, no matter what else he might have wanted, what better life might have soon arrived. It was written in him, and all around him. He'd been selected, and at the same time he volunteered, by remaining in his person, taking his own orders, from the condition of himself. They did him a favor, I believe, by finally cutting off the option of his life, or so was claimed: The verdict was that he would be executed by lethal injection four days before my thirty-seventh birthday, drawn up as headlines in all the papers, though I never saw any subsequent report confirming completion of the event. Instead he just kind of disappeared from public eye, left unmentioned far as I saw ever thereafter, which seemed like a relief at the time, absolving us at last of hearing about him, even his demise; and yet as years passed I found its lack of confirmed resolution even worse than an ongoing stay, as each night when I closed my eyes to sleep I saw his face behind my face, as if he had always been right there inside me; his thoughts squirming in the silences between my own, holding me over in my own flesh, feeding off me; his prints all over everything I touch."

Sweat is pouring profusely down the adjuster's skin now, Alice notices, his pallid flesh clearly visible through his white work shirt. There is a developing uneasiness in him, she senses, some kind of *breaking off* from past intent, where out of a bearing once rigid with influence, he has curled up and wound down inside himself, in shock. Alice raises her hand to touch him on the shoulder, gently, as a friend, so as to verify he's actually still there. And though she can indeed feel his flesh's texture against hers, actual as any, the lines beneath the surface seem to waver, thinning in real time. He still will not look at her directly, only at her face in the mirror; he is grinning, for no reason she can place. When he speaks she hears him clearly, as if her touch alone is the sole conduit through which his presence may be parsed.

"My own father had this exact same brand of mirror," she hears him saying, "or one just like it, in his den when I was young. I wasn't supposed to ever go in there, as an unwritten rule, though the door was always open. He'd sit in there reading for whole days at a time, not even standing up to eat or use the bathroom. He always read from the same series of books: bound in black leather, no titles or name of author on the outside. It was impossible to tell the difference between editions without opening them, which I wasn't allowed to do; he insisted that no one must touch them besides him, as the price he'd paid to make them his was worth more than *all our lives combined*. Anything we wanted to know about their content could be transmitted through him, he said; all you had to do was ask. And so he would come into my room at night to ask me, to give his answers, though no one other than him cared."

Why is he telling me my own story? Alice wonders. *As if it were his own story to tell*, as if he had lived it in her place, taken it over. Does he really believe this anecdote was his? Or is he trying to use her life against her, to scare her off or wear her down, to in some way get down to what really happened? He even seems to have absorbed her tone, implanting himself into her disposition, in narration, tapping into all she remembers of her life. And yet his version isn't quite the same as she would say it, slightly shifted in ways hardly noticeable to anyone but her, and even those impossible to prove beyond her mind.

He refuses still to look at her directly, speaking aloud toward the mirror as if speaking to himself more than her. Along the edge of their reflection, within the captured room, the glass begins to fill with something like a mist; the mirror is sweating, it appears, the air suddenly tacky, humid, traced with heated moisture that seems to well from pores in the mirror's surface, bloating out; the very dimensions of the room in the reflection become muddled over in the mix, more and more vague around their flesh. And still the voice of the adjuster seems unfazed, resisting any impending panic, regardless of what seems to be burgeoning between them; as if *the story is the story, all there is now*, the only remaining common ground.

"For years it went on like this," the man continues, seeming calm and only calmer the longer she allows him to carry on, "all as if the same day forced repeated, just slightly off enough to be ignored. My mom was gone around the clock each day, earning a living while my father stayed in with his own work; that is, the reading; until he eventually took ill. I never felt certain what sort of sickness he had, or where it came from, how it took hold of his whole life, though it was said to be rooted in our family's bloodlines, an inevitability in time. And still his fading and our lack of traction didn't stop him from going on and on about the books, if almost never about their actual substance, only the surrounding mythology of it, the lore. There were supposed to be twenty-six of them in all, each bearing the same title, no variation, though he'd managed to collect only the final twenty-five, missing only the first volume, of which, so he claimed, there was only ever one: *a single copy somewhere no one knew*, which could be accessed only by *a true believer*, in his words. It became my father's total life obsession, to get his hands on that edition, so he said, though he never actually did anything to find it; he just kept reading the other volumes, trying to decipher from them a kind of context by which he could infer its origin; to intuit what kind of information the missing book might need to contain, as if it could only be written by omission, in his infested imagination, never needing to actually exist in human hands. Therein lay its ultimate power, so he claimed, even as what that power meant or might be used for remained impossible to parse. And no matter what ongoing inconsistencies appeared in his own logic, no matter how much sicker he grew by giving himself over to it, even certain death wouldn't dissuade him. By the end, he'd even begun to believe he'd already read the missing volume without having had to; he decided that the origin must be hidden throughout all its subsequent components, the answer right beneath his eyes all this time, revealing itself to him more clearly as he grew ever weaker in its transference, eradicating all other aspects of his life. Eventually he even tried to give it our own lives also—his *quote unquote family*, he called us—though he became only more terrifyingly unwavering the longer we refused to participate. So many nights I'd hear him wandering the house from room to room, often carrying a weapon, going on and on to no one about how close he was to discovering his fate, what everlasting glory awaited him on the far side of himself, within which all prior questions about life and death and what came after would be given answers; and even more so: given flesh."

Alice's whole body is trembling, she can see then; for how much about her he seems to know, things she hadn't even thought of in forever, so much so she can't be sure they're really hers, or otherwise some coincidental simulacrum, unintended in how exactly they overlap, about which the man doesn't seem to realize, given his placid, piecemeal gait. She finds she doesn't want his speech to stop now, as if by allowing it to play out long enough she might understand what really happened to her; and in the same breath, finally so might someone else; that is, for once she might no longer have to solely be herself, stranded alone in her own life, but to share time with someone else, as after years of marriage, or as in the way she'd always thought of death: not as an end but a beginning.

Still, already, she feels the idea collapsing, losing its conditioning;

she knows that, as far as her strong sense of recognition had felt true, it was only in a plagued way: uninvited, involuntary, strained. The walls of the room have grown so hazy that it's unclear where the vault ends and the house begins, much less the larger, looming world beyond. Somewhere above, in the house outside the vault, Alice can hear the sound of banging, dragging; distant voices, as if people had come in behind them and started moving things around: other employees of the company, perhaps, or burglars returned to claim what they'd left behind. Yet she does not try to move, to crack the present and call attention to their presence; instead she stares at the man before her, as if he might explain it all away, or otherwise amend the situation.

By now, though, the adjuster's grin has grown so wide it bends his face. Each time he blinks the room is flatter, and at the same time, she imagines, somehow more real; or, rather, more like it had always been, just out of range. She can no longer hear the sounds from upstairs over their shared silence. In the mirror, their bodies appear to have rapidly aged, stretched so thin and feeble that Alice thinks they might collapse on contact, even as the world around them continues on its fat blank, scaling toward nothing, flatness in all directions, for forever, only waiting some day to be filled in; or, rather, to continue expanding until there's nothing else left.

"Somewhere within the years there, as life continued, my mother got sick and died," the man is saying, "from complications of the birthing of my sister, which took place behind locked doors, while I slept, and who still looked exactly like me, even all those years apart; I would despise her for that forever, both our mother's passing and the shared likeness, until almost exactly eighteen years later, when my sister also died, in the same way, birthing her own daughter, though that child by all accounts had come out as hardly human, just a blob, whose parts became recycled, donated to science, for who knows what. Her name would have been Alice, just like you," he says, now suddenly looking up, if not directly at her, but so as to appear to, just slightly off, "though in the end she never had a name. They were too embarrassed, too desperate to move forward, to erase the most painful subset of their whole short lives." He watches her, then, waiting that she might interrupt or add something, ask a question; and still all Alice can manage is not to blink. "Regardless, no matter what waking hell our life became, my father refused to shift his course. He hardly even seemed to notice that my mother was no longer there, allowing me to run the house and raise his newborn daughter by myself. At some point he stopped leaving his den at all, and speaking only by quoting directly from the books, in an unrecognizable language."

The last remaining light between them is filing in, becoming covered over; and yet Alice can still see him speaking, the rest of the remaining world no longer required. The story is no longer even hers at all, as she would tell it, its course now clearly veering from her own; as if the programming might now be altered, rearranged; what might have once been her own speech editing itself, becoming something else entirely; and yet, to her, it feels no less familiar than the rest, maybe even more familiar as there's even less left to rely on; as if, even in her own mind, acknowledging the revision of her own story out from underneath her, it must continue shifting further still—but for whose purpose? Hers? Her brother's? Someone else's?

"Finally, one night I decided I was going to burn the books," the man continues, suddenly leering, "to end their existence once and for all. It seemed the only way to undo what was becoming of our family, much less the whole world."

Alice feels the breath inside her bristle, lock—for, though she hadn't lived this version of the account, she already knows what's coming, and now can't make it stop.

"I told my father there was another kid I knew at school whose father read the same books as him, and who supposedly had a hard copy of the missing first volume. *I had seen it with my own eyes*, I swore, and *a book so large it could not be held with human hands*. My father's reaction was not at all what I expected, at least at first; he became overcome with rage, started screaming at me, demanding to know where my friend lived, what the other father looked like, how old he was and how many kids."

Was this how it actually happened? Alice wonders. *More true than how she otherwise might have remembered?* Suddenly she can't seem to tell the difference either way, as if no matter how the story's told, it leads to *now*.

"I provided him with a false address, even directions, at which point he gathered some things into a bag—including a knife, I noticed, and a large bundle of cash, with which we could have been eating all this time. I was afraid he would take the rest of the books with him as well, but suddenly he seemed to have forgotten them completely, as if the rest were no longer necessary in the light of the missing version."

Had there even really been more than one book? Could it have really been the key to all those other volumes, their whole world?

"He left the house at once, then, locking me in it, telling me not to answer the phone or even raise my head or think until he got back, which should be soon, he said, if not tomorrow, or by next week at the latest."

Every day thereafter, every hour, under the expectation of some arrival, if not of her father, then of someone, or something; all these years.

"My father never returned. I would never see him again in this world, waking or dreaming, except for when I closed my eyes and said his name; then I would see only my own face there reflected, right inside me, so old I don't know how I could still be left alive."

The story seems to take further and further liberty in the absence of any friction, Alice imagines, absconding with the events as they must have been. She finds she can already place the next word the man will say before he says it, right alongside him, as if in the end she is the only one who can cut the thread.

"As soon as he was gone, I gathered all the volumes of the series into a pile in the floor right there in his den," they say together now, aloud in tandem, suddenly the only way to speak. "It almost didn't even occur to me to look inside, to read; I didn't want to know what the books were about; I just wanted them gone from us, forever."

Yes, Alice can feel her body thinking. Yes; though in her mind: *miles of black smoke; the inseam of her own face hot and melting in long rivulets that puddle in her stomach; endless loops.*

"But the spines were such thick leather that they refused to catch from any spark, so finally I opened a random volume to light it by its pages. There was nothing printed on the paper, at least far as I could tell. I remember flipping through one volume, then another, feeling this strange elastic feeling moving through me that deepened further the more there was nothing there to read. Though it was not a simple blankness, as on new paper; instead, it felt like being drawn down into the page, the trace of the lines accessing their way inward, all around me, as I moved my eyes across the absent lines, the world left undescribed there in its languagelessness more like the world I knew than any prior recitation; a feeling both electric and made of drowning; starved for attention, out of reach."

His and her voice by now are bound together in her brain, indistinguishable from any other she recalls; so slick and black it's more like silence.

"Immediately I closed my eyes and struck the match and lit the book there in my hands. This time, because I could not see, I could feel its flame catch on the paper with ease, begin to spread; the same true, too, when I laid the burning object on the ground there with the others and opened my eyes to see the fire open up between. Within minutes they were ash; the smoke amassing in upon itself and dissipating smoothly, as if devoured by the hole made in the books as they consumed themselves."

Smith turns toward her then, at once and fully for the first time since he appeared, his attention at last breaking from where his eyes had held transfixed; the whites all bloodshot at the edges as if having been awake for far too long, pupils large and starving, the only fixed points left in his blurred face.

"And yet by then," they say together absolutely, without emotion, as if cold reading from a script, each syllable a placeholder for another, sicker syllable behind, "as you must know, it was too late," her hands in his hands, squeezing and throbbing, impossible at last to pull apart, "as once I'd felt that feeling, of having read the page, seen it come alive before me, move into me, I would not stop feeling it thereafter, from then on; and I had never felt it elsewhere, in no person, place, or object—until now."

The man is gone, then: his voice, his presence, even the feeling of where he'd been, all of it now covered with ambient warbling, a wake to fill. All Alice can see is where, in both the reflection and her flesh, nothing exists beyond the empty space enclosed between the house's walls surrounding, clear as day; nowhere else to be but within what remains visible before her or within her; no other land.

But the larger world is certainly still out there somewhere, she remembers, feeling the light above from which she'd let the man into her house still brushed upon her skin, how it had burned her even on the inside, all her life; all she has to do is find a place where she can interact with it again, return to its context, and then remember how to move; though even as she tries to make her head turn, in collaboration, to shift her leg to start to walk, she finds her equilibrium thrown sideways, legs rubbering beneath her as she fumbles to her knees in pitching forward, to be embraced by winding colors wide as a horizon, all across her.

The ground beneath her descent is off, then, she finds, only eventually coming to a full stop after what seems far too long spent as in fall— the floor beneath her now no longer hardwood, as her vault's had been, but something soft, rough on her flesh. There's patchy soil there, some brittle grass across it, a suspended feeling. As she stretches forward all lightheaded on her hands, reaching for any sign of home, she finds only earth and dander, no wind, and no construction.

The longer she lies there, the more the daylight holds together held above her, as in a field, adjusting to the long, stunned open glow. Somewhere amid the white above, firming from nothing, the sky is massive, monochrome, almost large enough to imagine how and why a creator could have placed it there: to distract; or more directly: to pose a mirage through which a larger, strong presence always pended, awaiting just the right time to puncture through. Alice feels her blood churn with viscous pressure, crowding her innards' edges as if for outlet, to become spilled across the land; at last, to be seen.

Otherwise, the soil beneath her feet is pale and dead, in some way unnatural in texture, like turf. The open air stinks like expired cream, wafts of meatsmoke. Ahead, in all directions, her view is broken up every few yards with a waist-high white wood cross crammed into the earth; for miles and miles there, hundreds or thousands of them, without clear layout, any center.

None of the crosses bears any name; when they are marked, she finds it's only with odd sets of years burned into the wood, no months or days:

1920–1964
1922–1975
1939–1979
1971–1996
1957–1998
1906–2002
1929–2005
1945–2006

And on the cross marking the plot where she'd been lying:

1979–2020

Far against the distance just beyond, slipped into the airspace, Alice can see the looming outline of what could only be her home, its position held in place by all the land her family had owned longer than she's been alive, left unattended following her inheritance, unto rot.

I spent so much time here as a young one, in this same field, our family graveyard, Alice thinks, rubbing her thumb across the nearest dates, relieved to find her thinking now returned to her alone, if still somehow like being read to. *How in the year before my mother died, to give my father some space inside the house alone to write, she brought me out to witness what was said to be the last solar eclipse. This was just before my real father became replaced, as I remember, before I began puberty; he was working at that time almost sixteen hours a day, locked in his study, writing and writing, which at the time I did not understand: that my father made words that other people read, and so allowed into their bodies, like a plague.*

Alice finds her instinct to interrupt her own remembrance locked out now, left over as a spectator unto herself, recalling each line soon as it's uttered as the way it all had been; and still the thread of it keeps running, slithering through her: *Nor could I understand why my mother brought a mirror to watch the sun with, and kept insisting I not look up into the light, but instead at the copy of it on which she'd caught the light and held it between us. Each time I turned my head up to look directly, she would scream and pull me to her, as if the brightness overhead were a hole into which I might be sucked.*

The present light itself is also strong, she realizes, almost matching her memory in its intensity, if subject to the whim of such wide clouds. *Finally she forced her hand over my eyes to hide the damage, releasing only when the sun was completely snuffed, which seemed to last a lifetime, then another. I remember feeling then that we were the only two alive, the only people ever in the world, and, there within that, the understanding that I would never need to move or breathe or eat again, that I could stay like this forever, without a motive, not even fear, though such a flash of full contentment passed so fast I hardly felt it, beyond how thereafter, as the years passed, it only served to hold me down, to make me wonder how long before I could find a way back to that feeling, to live inside it.*

The crosses spread across the land from there: miles and miles of plots for bodies, multiplying as she scans them with her eyes, beyond history.

Only now do I realize that all the time that's passed between that instant and the present was not mine, her mind suggests; *that the only place I've ever been is here, forlorn but not alone, without a grave, waiting for my body to find a way in to what the light had promised.*

The light is wide, all burning at her.

Then, again, my mother covered up my eyes.

For eons I could not think. Nor could I describe or feel my perception. Even where before I'd felt numbness, now there was not even that; no sensation, even including the absence of the feeling of absence; no past inferred but in the echo of carnage, made in our image, in reinvention of all the mush that rose and fell. My senses were all silver, fuzzed out from focus where I'd tried to learn again to see the coming day as it remained. In whatever way I'd felt before that I could contain any remembrance, there was only every prior hour crushed so completely into the present that it had no remainder, no skin left to be felt; and so once again it was as it was and always had been forever; sheer hemispheres of landscape ground down into nowhere, same as what would come out of burning up a picture or a table, indistinguishable now from flesh or floors, each tick of time so conflicted it's already over as soon as it begins, beyond even the shape of information, story. And so no story left to say; nowhere but what exists outside itself forever, now coming open; integrating.

Inside this expanse, I closed my eyes and clasped my hands. I heard the pages of my past life turning in my person, no longer flesh but only flow, made of expired language claimed out of all the open time we'd never witnessed pressed together, then welling out from its compression, so that whenever I tried to look or be front and center, I could feel many potential forms of future, each written over by another as they struggled to remain a dream: miles of vibrant fire populated by massive machines, gunmetal black; flame unfurling like dumb lava through some deformed architecture without map, churning putty and smoke in clouds that weep; hordes of masses packed together around a high, wide, silver wall, waiting to be let in, perhaps, or for something to emerge; the only open sound the sound of their whining, gnawing, starving; dirt becoming overturned; masses of birds with deformed wings flooding out in fever at the light; children bawling in open fields; windows smashed out of buildings as looters take whatever they can find, not to have but to destroy; globs of gold dust sticking to all the glass there, among roving clouds of open blood; the tide of the sea no longer moving, still as the land is; piles of money in the street not even good enough to burn; reams of celluloid and tapes weird with emulsion, dumped into bodies of stagnant water overflowing, filling gorges where plots had been; books and canvases and audio tapes being ripped to bits by machines with human faces as packs of cops stand calm and smoking in the sun, no features to their faces, no fingers to their fists, smoke all over everything in layers; each person not completely crippled carrying a copy of the same book, like an appendage; shots of countless planets, ours and others alike, seen from roving monitors above each square mile; construction crews set up in action in wide deserts, erecting a translucent screen installed as a ceiling just beneath the sky above; silent troops in white gear moving across locations as barren as lost film sets; piles of blood, slathered across landscapes, floors, unknown locations; each, even in repeating, bearing down upon the grain behind it, wearing through it, thin. And where the image occurs, the blight behind grows stronger, burning through the very shape of its idea; no repetition and no subject; the miles of fire spreading over all below, ash raining down as from some high eye; people shrieking in the streets with arms raised and mouths forced open, inhaling the cinder written all among them and above them and beyond.

Within all this, when I could feel myself again, the world was not the world as it had been, nor was it any of the days I'd ever passed through in my life; it was not a world at all, really, but an apparition, more real than all the rest, full of air from fields of buried dead, their flesh disintegrated into soil and heat, even their brains and names only a loam. I couldn't tell the difference between one inch and another, nor *could I remember how to want to care; every hour had fallen into the same hour, each passing pixel contained in each new frame; I kept finding my eyes were closed when I had believed them open, and as I opened my eyes again the eyes would burn, as looking on through countless frames of light and sound all at the same time, like every film I'd ever seen or book I'd ever read or paintings I'd passed by in rooms at once all laid on top of one another into a field of conflicting signals so loud they defied certain shape or hue; so where in every inch lived every life, splitting out through what must once have been my point of view, one of many billions of our skins draped all throughout eternal night, each corresponding lifetime in its own mind larger than all else as yet combined, its gravity so dense it could not stop spreading through itself, eating itself, and at once echoed so intensely by every other it split each color from its name, until soon, so on thereafter, there would be nothing left between us, no edge to anything.*

By now, Alice finds, the dusk is coming down; the night all leaky, having slicked her clothes and skin with dew. She's wandered far out among the plots, she realizes, without direction, no longer able to see any definitive landmark or location like her home or the idea of one no matter how she turns, no other living shape under the sky. She might imagine she is lost, too far to find a way back, were she not standing front and center in the pathway of a car; a white stretch limo, rather, its engine running and high beams left on, cutting toward her on the air.

She recognizes the car at once, despite having never been allowed to ride inside it either with her father or unfather—she can't remember which—who'd purchased the machine, or so he'd claimed, to be used for free delivery to their own funerals, each of the family, a morbid punchline that always made her mother cackle with crazed glee. And yet, even if it were indeed a punchline, he hadn't strayed from its sole law: to keep it clean and shining for when the day came, never driving it otherwise, or letting anybody else. She can't remember the last time she'd seen it, after it was stored so long in a sealed air bubble in some garage Alice always avoided for its stench of mildew; nor has she driven herself anywhere in so long she's not sure she still remembers how.

The body of the machine is hot to the touch, she finds, sticky with sundrench. She puts her head to the glass, expecting to see a driver there inside, perhaps even someone she should know, or who has more information for her, though there does not appear to be anyone in the front seat, nor any passenger in the long, slick back space, large enough for a dozen or more.

The limo's doors aren't locked. The keys are still in the ignition, too, attached to a keychain bearing the initials a.b.k., same as she'd shared with both her parents, as she remembers, though in the moment she finds she can't recall their full names, each possible moniker sounding wrong, not a real person.

Still, it feels good to sit in the driver's seat, she finds, pulling the driver's-side door closed against herself in the freezing rush of hard A/C; to feel her hands around the wheel, peering out through where to see anything beyond the glass she has to wipe an eyehole, the cool air inside causing thick white condensation on the glass, same as the mirror had, covering the world up and over again each time as it fills back in. The seat leather sticks to her skin, its deep cupped bucket wanting to surround her, draw her down, until she's soon hardly high enough to see out or over into anywhere.

———

Alice puts the car in drive and hears it speak. The machine's voice is like a woman's, mottled with digitization that betrays it as unnatural, though this does not dissuade it from commanding her to *proceed to the route*, its program already somewhere well into a set of ongoing directions once abandoned, now revived. At least for once there is an unquestioned destination, Alice imagines, an authority to point the way, and though she has never used a GPS before—never trusted it, never wished to—somehow now it seems exactly what she needs, hardly a choice.

Driving seems easier than she remembers, a motion still harbored somewhere in her habit's memory, awkward mostly in how the world beyond still defies her direct recognition, even miles out: no familiar landmarks or significant visual stretches looming up from the landscape in her mind. Spaces move past her, continuous patches of blurred terrain, never standing out long enough to inform her present position, her blinking cursor in the open document of space and time. There's so much world out here, she finds, and so much empty, so much alike and just the same, not even any other passing cars. The night is wholly silent besides the rushing wind and the ongoing, canny voice of GPS, which she relies on blindly, finding pleasure in following its instructions toward a future destination apparently already entered, bearing out the continuing surprise of each new turn; each step in the dictated directions arriving just as quickly as they feed into the last, only to disappear again as *somewhere she'd once been.* She's hardly even really driving, she realizes, as each time she notices where she is, she can't remember having acted, for which she feels thankful, already unsure which lever to turn or nub to press to make the car do anything.

Then, like that, just as she's enjoying the procession, she's arrived; or so the device announces, ceasing its dictation, returning to its default state to await the next command. Through the windshield, the façade of the site where she's arrived is lit so sharply it's hard to see in full expanse, the high lines of the massive structure rising up as if in direct competition with the half moon, all polished metal and massive, opaque plate glass panes that do little more than deflect the eye, giving the whole grounds a floating feeling, open wide. There's no indication that the place is even actually in business, or ever has been, far as Alice can tell: construction all so new, no defining signage, no cars at all beyond her own in the massive lot flanking the wide grounds, each space numbered with absurdly long strings of ID digits. She hears nothing but the hollow fall of her own feet on the fresh pavement, breath and heartbeat loud in her head, all other senses suddenly stuffed.

The structure's exterior appears to have no entrance, in fact, she finds, no matter how far around it she continues: all only further matching walls and glass. She passes benches for sitting without clear reason; a fountain of a pyramid spurting white-glowing water, full of coins to make a wish; the whole back half of the property blocked off with a seamless forest overrun with stunted trees, their lower limbs all cut off within reach. Why isn't there anyone else out here, Alice wonders? Though perhaps the better question remains: Why is she? She can't remember what urge had brought her to leave her house at any point, ever; much less her bed itself, the heavy fiber of her ongoing exhaustion already filling out her moving muscles, full of gunk. *It would be so nice to lie down*, she can't stop thinking, *now and forever; if only I could remember where was home.*

She's already begun tracing her way back to the limo, uncertain which outbound direction leads to where, until around another hard curve in the narrow structure's surface she runs head on into a face: a flat, massive woman's head, floating before her, part of the building, overridden upon with rising daze, from out of which she sees cheeks and teeth, first, then a set of nostrils, each as big as her own skull, like open portals punctuating the flesh between the face's pursed lips and the lids of its closed eyes. Only as she steps back to take it in can Alice gather context: the same face of the same deceased artist from earlier that same day on the TV, here captured in the midst of speaking or breathing out, or so it seems; the same static ocean still spanning the background, without waves; the same wide silver sky looming above it parallel and overseeing all.

Alice is terrified, seeing the woman again now so larger than life. The face seems able to see her even through her eyelids' skin, leering and alien, likely at any second to open her mouth and start to speak; or perhaps to swallow her whole there, into her body, and the bowels of the world beneath. Alice herself can't quite seem to clear the image from her mind then, or catch her breath; she starts backing away on tiptoe from the intolerable image, its impression seeming to follow as she moves, looming out around her in vibrant animation the more she tries to resist or turn away, to undo herself from its influence, its expression.

She can't remember exactly how to move then, each gesture somehow resulting in something more like falling backward in slow-motion, the space behind her rushing out around her to fill in where she is not. No matter how she contorts or blinks, the face's gape continues in and down upon her, leaving no outlet but to go on edging further and further back as best she can, soon finding herself pressed back against another surface behind her in relief, its wide white premise even more formidable from so close up. As she tracks her eyes across the divide searching for sky, the flat beneath her splits in half, yawning apart wide unto a sudden silent gasp of too-warm air, flooding out around her like a hard wind at all sides, a rift rendered as in inhaling, luring her along into its gait with both her arms out, spinning for bearing, before the would-be automatic doors slide back into place just past her eyes, their wide white backside sealing her within it, part of t he building.

■■■■

The lobby of the gallery, as it resolves like déjà vu, is brightly lit and claustrophobic; white like the walls in her home's vault. All further sound is absorbed by the wide tiles beneath her feet, which form a strangely interlocking pattern that for no clear reason brings her instant calm, an infectious flattening projected by the space's tempered, steady light. Otherwise the entry space is empty—no one on duty behind what appears to be a welcome kiosk spanning the far side of the space in her approach, its countertop bare besides a leather-bound guest book left propped open, full of names, into which Alice adds her own mark without hesitation: just her initials, the thin black pen buzzing at her fingers as she writes, leaking its sharp blue ink over everything it touches, leaving nothing legible among the blob.

There's only one way forward then, from there, besides just leaving, about which Alice senses an inclination to do just that, yet instead finds herself following the pattern of the floor into the adjacent space, its corresponding layout much like the first but longer, thinner, as if a copy of the lobby had been clicked and dragged to open up.

Printed onto a wide part of the wall, visible only as she draws near, in shimmering texture changing color with the angle, she reads:

ALICE NOVAK: A Memorial Exhibition

And beneath that, in smaller, darker font:

I Retrospective
II *Devoid*

The wall beyond the marking for some distance remains bare. Alice has to proceed for longer than it should take to span the room before she finds some form of exhibit, installed onto the wall aligned in matching silver frames: a series of photographs, each unlabeled and identical in size.

The first photo shows the same woman from the display outside—Alice Novak, context predicts—but as a young girl, perhaps age six. She appears wearing a gray smock, standing on black sand far as the eye can see—the same beach as in the prior image, Alice imagines, judging by its consistency, but decades earlier—which in this depiction looks so much like the land surrounding the manmade lake behind her mother's parents' house; the place where they'd both died when it burned down, long before Alice was even born; the lake itself had been eventually filled in, according to local ordinance— something about a contagion in its waters, one that could not be diluted or broken down, which had then spread, as Alice recalls, across innumerable locations, far and wide.

The next few photos show the same girl amid the sprawl of growing up. The child looks more and more familiar to Alice as her face refines with age. She is always depicted, for some reason, amid nature: on dirt or near water, surrounded by trees or grass, not at all the kind of youth Alice herself had experienced, behind closed doors. And yet, as each image moves the child nearer and nearer to adulthood, Alice can't help but see the rising lines inside the captured face conforming, making sense, not quite a match for who she is now, but for who she'd once been, as if wearing younger Alice's own features, down to tics of facial behavior and innate expression so much her own. But why then do the places, the situations, seem so outdated, someone else's? Something in the timeline isn't adding up, despite the low-pitched grinding Alice feels already gathering, in gut reaction; something remains off between what possible actuality the images insist on and what remains in her own mind. She feels a shaking, then, just slightly, down her arms and through her hands, spreading upward and inward, made only worse as she tries to suppress it.

In the next framed image, she sees the other woman there again, now in what must be her early thirties, shown in joyful embrace with a familiar man: Alice's father, as she remembers—her actual father, without a doubt—alongside whom the woman seems aglow, a joy between them that was absent from the prior pictures. Together they are standing at the front stoop of a house, exactly like the version she remembers of their home before so much remodeling or mutating, as it were, and smaller from the outside than it had ever really felt, suggesting a much more modest air to the estate, a fact also reflected in their shabby, outdated clothing. There is no question, though, that this version of the woman looks exactly how Alice herself had at that age, however long ago it is now; it could be almost no one else but her—Alice Knott, not Novak—here depicted in what must have been her own mother's timeline's life, somehow the same age as her father during an era when Alice as she is now could not have yet been born.

Had her mother really resembled her so clearly back then? Alice can't remember ever being told that or seeing pictures that suggested such, much less ever recognizing such similarities herself in her mother's later, living face; although it had been so long since she'd seen even any memorabilia from those times, all of it swept away with Richard's supposed parting from the house. What was all this meant to be, then? Where did this Novak person get these pictures, and what could she think gave her the right? Or was there something else about all this: some kind of hoax photography, a trace of green screen, causing any passing viewer to format their own lives between the lines, their most precious memories revised and mangled into a display designed to simulate disorder, to confound one's own past and person right before their eyes?

Either way, the next picture, Alice discovers, moving along in heaving silence, unsure quite yet what to do, depicts the same woman but now as very pregnant. Here she's photographed herself nude in a mirror hung in what Alice recognizes as her childhood bedroom, the walls all gray and lined with silver etchings of no clear pattern. The woman's face seems unhappy, full of doubt, much as had Alice been through the same years of her life, a spitting image, though this could most definitely not be her here, she is certain; she had been declared infertile from a very early age, and had never concerned herself with sexual partners, as she remembers, much less even really ever friends. There was nothing in her mind of any person but her core family, as it stands, in both regards; if in a way no one but she would still remember, all others from that era by now long dead or moved along, her own resemblance even to herself subtle enough now with so much time passed, and so much damage, that someone else beside her looking on might not identify the link at all, or even note the similarities after having them pointed out; as such it remains a secret, between her and herself, she thinks, at once the only witness and the only victim.

The following image appears to be a more professionally styled portrait, like the one that had once hung in the front room of their house: mother, father, daughter, son, shown all together, whereas before Richard would have been omitted, replaced by backdrop. Here, though, the person she recognizes as a decade-younger version of who she is today has assumed the position of her mother, wearing the same black blouse and long gold earrings she still had on when she died, matching the gold band of the wedding ring still on her finger; and there beside her, Alice's real father, not the un-version, his face seeming sunken but still there, behind thick glasses that glinted sharply in the flash. The children, clearly, as she sees them, are Richard and her younger self—that is, herself the way she remembers appearing at that age, a clear match in her mind at once with whatever fractured memories she retains, and also a seeming match for her twin brother, at last presented side by side. It's hard to tell them apart, even to Alice, beyond the small aspects of their gender's shaping, each wearing the same coy smile, staring ahead at something looming above them, out of frame. Overall, all four of them together seem healthy, hopeful, held together, in a way Alice can't connect at all with how it felt to be alive during that time; the shock so sharp, rampant within her, that for once she has nothing else to say; her hands trembling so hard now it's like they're still.

A corresponding portrait, taken in the same studio it seems, depicts the same family some years later, maybe five, but by now so much has changed. The older Alice is still there, in her mother's place, wearing a white blouse now, sweated clear through in massive ovals along the pits, her earrings removed; the man standing at her side is clearly not the same as in the prior image, this one wearing shaggy black hair and a week's stubble, a ruddy complexion, like a drunk—the face of her unfather, exactly as Alice remembers him throughout, never aging regardless of how long his presence carried on and despite how hard she tried to forget anything palpable about his make, most of all his smoke-laden speaking voice, which she hears at once again on sight throughout her as at a distance, singing inside her head that stupid song he'd always sing, with the lyrics that kept changing each time it repeated, rolling its language, all now inside her turned to mush. Now, too, there are no longer the two kids, Alice and Richard, but only the latter, his aging face now glossy and disrupted with his acne, which would scar his features through adulthood; a flat blank in his eyes mirrored by braces newly affixed in his mouth, a dull, hard chrome hiding his teeth. Among the three, the unfather is the only one still smiling, his skin drained and pasty from not sleeping, his pupils dilated as if on drugs, wearing such a knowing look staring straight out into the viewer that it makes Alice's stomach turn, as if she's been punched—the same feeling that spanned all those early hours of his appearance, from which nothing ever would rebound.

The other two still in the picture—that is, her mother (clearly Alice as she is now, nearly identical to her present form) alongside Richard (bridging status as both her brother and her son)—look quite unwell, almost afraid, as if they wished they didn't have to be photographed, to even be still in their own body. Alice notices, too, and remembers as accurate, how her mother's wedding ring has changed—both in its placement, appearing now on her right hand instead of the left, and in design: a thick dark band absent of gemstone, costume jewelry—though her mother had sworn it had been the same through her whole life. The woman seems to bite her lips inside to hold them closed; her nostrils, shaped with heavy breathing, tunnel in. As well, for some reason, Richard is wearing a ring just like his mother's, gleaming dully from a fist balled so tight in his lap it had to hurt, given his long nails; the nature of his rage seemed so much like what she had felt amid the sprawl of it, the desperation, yet now instead appearing crammed inside *him*, as *his trauma, no longer hers*, otherwise unreadable beyond the sense of itching the whole scene holds, some tension yet to be revealed, as if something would be ripped out from underneath them just after the camera's shutters clicked.

Alice can only seem to think to want to laugh now, seeing her place invaded, turned on its head, shaken in place. She looks around the room as if verifying she is still in here, that she is seeing what she's seeing, waiting for someone else to come running out of the wings, letting her in on the trick that's being played here with her life: as if someone had come in behind her and switched skins around among her most known people, reprogrammed even the most basic facts of what she's known. But the gallery is still all empty, so it appears, no other guests, coming or going; she is an audience of one, allowed within an otherwise completely passive landscape, the quietest of nights. She's trembling so badly now it's like her flesh is made of blur; the strained texture of her aged skin brittle, veiny, in some way now less her own, a question mark ending a sentence she can't tell who's asking.

The last image in the series, hung alone on the far end of the wall, appears to have been taken decades after all the others. In it, the older woman from the blown-up face she saw outside—which she can see now is what she herself might look like in another twenty years—stands at the center of a group of about a dozen people, some casually holding cameras, wires, booms, all dressed in identical stark white clothes, in dense sunlight on a wide field of blackened tarmac, standing inside the shadow of a large, monolithic structure looming behind them on the horizon, hazy and oblong: the largest building she's ever seen.

Beside the woman, an aging, more obese version of who could only be Richard, his face still all cratered, hardened with sores, at an age unclear to Alice, before or after his arrest, stands with his arm around their mother. They both still have the matching metal rings on their right fingers, as do all the others. Among the range of faces, Alice sees, are ones she recognizes from *today*: some of them the reporters she had given her statements about the break-in, a few who might have showed up at her home as cops; even A. B. Smith himself, as she recalls him, though here pictured somehow older, wearing glasses that obscure the definition. Everyone in the image seems excited, triumphant even, except for the older Alice, whose eyes are closed as in mid-blink, arms limp at her sides, while all the rest of them are captured in the midst of waving to the camera.

———

There are no more pictures after that.

Beside the last, printed in gold ink directly on the wall, there is a signature, presumably the artist's: *Alice Novak*, shown in a scrawl of jumbled lines and loops, not at all like the mark Alice herself had just made in the lobby's open book, nor even how she remembers her mother making as her handwriting turned childish in those last months. The spastic marking hurts Alice's eyes even to look at, bearing a kind of sting that seals her prior feelings of helplessness, disconnection, into something more fully overwhelming and complete; the christening demarcation of a narrative confirmed, on its own authority, as decisive as any other fact.

There's so little certain left to understand then, she finds, turning back to face the space of the room she'd just moved through, its expanse remaining vacant beyond the hanging icons on the walls. It's as if whole dimensions of her person, passed through decades, even withered and undependable as they had been, stand now at risk by mere suggestion, under defeat. It isn't right, Alice feels sure; this narrative is not at all like what had happened; in fact, it's a willful degradation of her truth, so it appears, designed to pull the world out from beneath her, all explanation held behind some curtain she can't see. Who had set this up, and from whom did they gain access? How to explain all these fragmented memories of her life? What has happened off the record, between what she felt she knew and what appears apparent to the public, to every other passing eye? The questions throttle through her one after another, all unanswerable, their absent logic clogging her ability to even think straight, to assume anything.

Without further commentary, Alice calmly turns and stalks back past the display, coming to stand again before the image of the four of them, all happy, hopeful for some version of the future. She immediately slams her fist into the image, punching it square and center at no specific face but the whole sham. The pulpy surface of the print buckles and puckers against her knuckles as she repeats the blow again, again, each hit in equal measure, furious but focused, all a scrawl. The harder she hits, the less she feels the impact, each bud of stunning pain suffusing up along her arm, lost to the cold numb of the rest of her body, disconnected; until the blood covers her whole hand then; until it sprays on the museum floor in shining spots as on a map. Only then does she notice how the picture's pigment is coming off, too, more with each impact, the substance beneath its surface giving way unto the pulpy whiteness of its foundation's layers as the image comes apart.

It's not even a photo, she realizes. *It's a painting*, if one so meticulously composed they would be impossible to tell apart, until now. The paint is fresh, too, she finds, still moist beneath its outer layer as it smears across her runny wounds; the canvas punctured in small places that reveal the wide white wall behind its frame where she's bashed through. She finds that she can scratch the details away under her nails, digging in at once in curiosity against the depiction of Richard's face, leaving behind only a muddy smear there, blending together under duress. She finds the same is true of the subsequent image of their family in obvious emotional disarray, hung just beside, also a painting; and therein all of the photos now rendered suspect, of the same make—*must they not be?*—if still demanding a slew of different looming questions just the same.

And still she's not sure she feels any better, surveying the damage in her wake, photos or not. There's still something there in what the series of images intend to represent, it seems, something filched from her memory, conjured into some aesthetic projection left unclear, flooding her psyche in waves of mixed emotion, till she feels suddenly more alive than she has in quite some time, there in the room's resounding stillness. Somehow in all her furor she has triggered no alarms, she realizes, or at least none audible above her heavy breathing through her teeth; no one comes running out to calm her down or make her stop; no grand reveal of the nature of the game, as it might be, nor the face of the creator.

She can think of nothing else then but to lift the damaged painting off the wall, a task she finds even simpler than imagined; it weighs almost nothing, bears no firmer fixture, and reveals nothing there behind. She holds it against her chest there for a moment, feeling the loose weight of its smearing body pressed against her sweaty flesh, pore upon grain. She grips and squeezes the thing so hard that it bends, till she is hardly able to hold the remnants still; in the end she heaves it away, but it merely claps and skitters, landing facedown on the floor, its damaged image hidden against the looming darkness caught between where any two surfaces might touch.

It doesn't take her long to repeat the act for each other image, winging them aside as one might cards from a deck, until there's nothing left to see about the display but the withstanding wall itself, its blank white the same no matter where something had once hung or something hadn't.

The gallery's next room, beyond the first two, appears even emptier than those before: no featured objects, no specs for reception, not even windows, ventwork; only walls. The space appears to hold itself in place around the absence of what it could include at any moment, on display; beyond the nature of the light, the vertices and ongoing flat expanse, there is nothing there to see. The air feels stagnant, even dusty; warmer and warmer by the length, as if the air of the outside world could never touch it. She's already sweating so much she might come apart, she thinks, turn into goo, a pile of blood and muscle on the floor to be swept up and done away with, or otherwise absorbed into the space.

But there always seems to be another chamber just ahead, further empty space linked by lone archways wide enough to let a horde through, space that from outside the structure hadn't appeared large enough to house. Perhaps this is the intent of the installation, she imagines. The artist's final statement being no statement at all, a massive blank, though this seems less than inventive. Even the patterned floor has lost its color now, she finds, all pure mute, each tile by now the width of her chest. Her hand is soft and brittle against the texture of the guiding wall when brushed against it, as if to confirm it's really there, absent of any evidence of whatever else might once have hung there.

It's almost strange how well the space is made to keep you moving, she thinks. Around each corner she keeps expecting to come upon some display, some marker of tribute, for instance, or other obvious artwork, symbols or signs—and yet around each corner there's only more of the same: intersecting vertices that form small dead ends, blank displays, each at once alike and not the same. Soon she can't even tell for certain which would be the way back whence she came and which the way forward, she realizes, as she stands in a room bound by identical spaces on either side, as if it might only go on like this forever.

Then, like that, as if to correct her, the space's radiance divides. Where the edge of the present display room opens into the next, Alice sees no light filling the space, but only solid black, its interior imperceptible half a dozen feet beyond, full as all night. The darkness ahead, she feels in pressing on along it, is markedly cooler than prior space. The further she allows herself to edge into the dark, the easier it is to breathe again, to format her thinking within the linking calmness of the dark, away from all past suffering. She realizes she can no longer tell how it had ever been another way than it is now; no edge of light even where she'd last been, she finds, nothing left but more and more of the seamless and shapeless fund of dark, eclipsing her ability to assess or render anything at all. Every inch ahead could be the end of where she is, or the beginning of where she had last been, looped around again, no definition; and she already can't remember how far she's moved from any point. She should feel panic, she understands, even dread, but the acknowledged sensation won't take hold; no verve there where she might call for help, no means to sense who or what might already be there just beside her or behind her. She's not sure she wants to move further, as such, in expectation of what will emerge from out of nowhere; though when she does, the resolution is right there: another wall, so close it's almost touching, side by side. This surface's face feels slicker than had prior surfaces behind her—at the same time thicker, deeper, like heavy stone. The long line of its expanse's breadth continues, allowing her further forward, pressed against it, each space connecting on to further walls. Their height seems to tend down, now, leading further into depth, into space that narrows as she presses on, until she finds herself quickly shoulder to shoulder with what spaces remain, and no option to go back behind her, where the passage seems to have sealed itself, only down through deeper dark.

The floor itself has begun to slope, she notices, her skin so slick with sweat now it's like she's slipping, only barely under her own guide, as if the ground might split apart and open up unless she keeps moving, still taking care to keep her center of gravity underneath her as the plane of space extends onward, further down, growing steeper with her unintended cooperation, until suddenly she's struggling to stand. The walls on either side are at once no longer there, dissolved into a feeling much like falling, if without wind or friction, through the ongoing resolution of the opaque. It's as if the surrounding world is moving for her, drawing her forward into exactly what it wants. *Like all the hours between seeing and believing*, someone in her is saying, *the gap in who I am and what I was*—her thoughts so clear, at last, so all her own—until, when she tries again to move her head, to see another form of way, she finds she no longer still can; the ceiling by now is right above her, walls on each side, none below. It is as if suddenly the air were made to enclose her size and shape precisely, her and her alone, like someone's God in their own mind, with nowhere to move, no opening or passage to appear, only more and more nothing filled in around her, calm, as if it'd never been another way—the kind of place she'd always wished for, really, made for her and her alone.

———

Alice finds the ground beneath her now is soft again, more so than ever, made of loose muck. Its texture gently vibrates against her palms, a monotonic hum at once sedating and stimulating, like the feeling of being near one's mother from very young, knowing for once there was someone there to hold her safe. She hasn't had that feeling in so long, and now she finds herself craving it, even so uncertain in its source; to feel it closer, to find its heart.

The muck is easy to dislodge. Its quality feels ashen as she digs at it with her fingers, its packed-in surface coming up in clots and plumes, sticking to the wetness of her skin. It's in her mouth, then, the more she digs, and in her throat and eyes, making her choke; so too her mind, as if there's nowhere left for it to go but on into her, worming deeper. *She had lived for this so long*, she understands; *had been waiting through it all for now, to feel it come upon her.* But no, she hadn't, she responds; she hadn't wished for any of this, not a second; instead she'd been dying her whole life, wanting nothing of whatever else came, no matter how clear, or how destroyed.

Several inches down, Alice feels her fingers click on something cold and hard; some kind of hidden surface beneath the softer cover that glints wherever she scrapes the dust away, its exposed edges somehow faintly gleaming in the dim maw of what the world is. Finally, she peers and sees her own self's shape reflected there, in the flat, through its vast muddle: her own apparent double staring up from what remains below, held on in the lining of what seems another mirror, its surface damaged, wet with mildew, buried so long in its place.

And yet this mirror is unlike others she's seen before, Alice observes, spreading the acrid wet away as best she can to clear its face. She is surprised by its shape: how it has edges, its own body, against the larger darkness. In this reflection, she sees, her flesh is marred and naked, its fiber an aggravated patchy red in parts and charred to pus or scab in others, like skin once burned and now deep into firming over, becoming healed. As well, the hair has been melted off her head, leaving gross patches, her finer facial features bruised and ruined; only her eyes are recognizable among the mess of her complexion, and even these are ruptured, uniformly blackened throughout, as if each pupil has occluded the entire organ; her lipless mouth still beaming through its damage, as if inexplicably elated in looking back up at her other through their boundary between, now interlocked.

The room this other now appears in, Alice discerns amid its mass disfigured lines, is the same shape and configuration of the vault beneath her house, as she remembers, the missing artworks now still there hanging in the doubled image, if each also damaged by what must be the same fire that hurt her, each painting indistinguishable from any other plate of ugly char.

In the mirror she is kneeling, same as she is above the object; she can even sense the other's heartbeat in the flat plane of the mirror's silver, their rhythm only slightly out of sync, enough to suggest each has her own life, independent from the other.

We had passed through this same day as so many different versions, Alice imagines, relieved at least to hear her own voice still there inside her, if still not quite fully her own. *I had stood in this very instant and observed myself from years apart, without clear recognition on either side; had wanted into somewhere I distinctly could not go, somewhere sacred, indestructible; less inherent to my flesh and more to the curvature of a state of living beyond life, within which everything about the world as I'd believed I'd known and depended on it would fall away, making room at last for only one source code containing all my possible futures, a fate to define myself against as in relief; so at last to become anyone other than I had ever meant to.*

The mirror's face, in the meantime, has grown inflamed against her skin, warmer in a different way than sunlight, cutting through her, beyond pain, and upon extended contact releasing from her a thousand further questions she might ask of any of her prior versions, or those who saw her in the midst of those lost lives: people she had passed over in potential, avoiding any points of recognition with the many other ways she could have intersected with them, found common ground, or what she could have found a longer hope in or felt any truth through, all against the wide wake of her many other open wounds, carried in behest against the deeper aspirations she'd not allowed herself to see, covered up in rash expressions of bitter blame and shapeless longing, so well concealed from even herself it gave no pause. She can't begin to think of what her age is, then, nor her name, how she had begun this day or any other. There's so much space here that isn't hers; so much she could feel and never see but held so close; as if the mirror is a conduit of sorts, connecting phases without regard for time or light, any instant in all existence laced together in the same shot. If only she could find the language in her brain beyond the throbbing of its cells, or could locate some clear connection within all her past and future impressions of her pain, flowing over and within her not as a strobe or pulse but one long mute, without horizon, beyond the blank between herself and any other unremembered, unto now.

I had pressed myself into so many lives, realities, she hears herself thinking, through the mirror, *that to know that none of them was as much mine as I had once believed was to accept my own annihilation, within which what I was when I was where I was when I was who to whoever else I wasn't was as much me as the rest of the shape of everywhere I'd never seen; so much the same as any in their own life—including you, whoever you are, the same you who in no time yourself will no longer be: not even zilch, a void, but what exists only once it's all at once been made undone.*

▬

The ground seems not only just beneath her, then, but the same on all sides, as if there are not many directions filling out the darkness, but only one spread encrypted all throughout. She can't remember then quite which way to reach to brace her shape and maintain hold on where she is. The space within the dark falls in around her, its runny silt up to her ankles, then her knees, forcing her back down each time as she tries again to rise, and more so in every motion as she struggles to pry and hold the object of her reflection up above the muck, the shit, the wailing, to go on seeing who she was, what she could want, at once already unable to tell herself apart from her reflection, even in flashes, going under. Soon she can hear nothing but the sound inside her mind, awash in the black churning gush of every possible erasure of our world, the friction between land and object, flesh and spirit, all hours fused together as one long take, never to be split again or carried over, unto at last the only way it ever could have really been.

All time thereafter is a gnarl; no phase left to shape a recognition of itself outside its own best understanding, within which she can see and feel the present instant only spread apart and held in thrall, at once overridden with a further sprawl of possible oncoming coordinates and timelines so prodigious it blinds all further direct vision but in bolts. And now Alice can see as if *around* each passing second, not the present but the fragmented gaps between: spirals of smashed-in wishing brought on slow as windows never opened; everything not quite done and never since; all buildings ever, burning; the books all burning; the smoke together coiling all throughout it all: the breath of God. All passing seconds felt thereafter only as copies, wherein all copies aren't a copy but our only true and living fate; what we had once called our ideas, now only made more ours in their discharge, filling the air up without a signal.

0003

"The Persistence of Memory" disappears. "The Last Supper" disappears. "The Tower of Babel" disappears. "Self-Portrait with Two Pupils" disappears. "Self-Portrait as the Allegory of Painting" disappears. "Painting" disappears. "Apollo the Lute Player" disappears. "Bridgewater Madonna" disappears. "Mask" disappears. "The Autobiography of an Embryo" disappears. "The Son of Man" disappears. "Massacre of the Innocents" disappears. "Good News, Bad News" disappears. "Bare Willows and Distant Mountains" disappears. "Master of the Symbolic Execution" disappears. "The Broken Column" disappears. "The Ninth Wave" disappears. "Friendship" disappears. "Portia Wounding Her Thigh" disappears. "Self-Portrait with Bandaged Ear" disappears. "Composition V" disappears. "The Black Painting" disappears. "Black Heart" disappears. "Las Meninas" disappears. "Dance at Le Moulin de la Gallette" disappears. "Along the River During the Qingming Festival" disappears. "Femme assise dans un jardin" disappears. "A Mother I Remember" disappears. "Saturn Devouring One of His Children" disappears. "Dustheads" disappears. "The Dream" disappears. "Flag" disappears. "Masterpiece" disappears. "Pictorial Quilt 1898" disappears. "Silver Car Crash (Double Disaster)" disappears. "Triptych, 1976" disappears. "Infinity (Infinity Seascape)" disappears. "Bull" disappears. "Bird in Space" disappears. "White Cockatoo: Number 24A" disappears. "Target with Plaster Casts" disappears. "The Liver Is the Cock's Comb" disappears. "Portrait of Adele Bloch-Bauer I" disappears. "Woman with Crossed Arms" disappears. "Young Lady on a Red Sofa" disappears. "Diana and Actaeon" disappears. "Mahishasura" disappears. "Liberty Leading the People" disappears. "Oedipus and the Sphinx" disappears. "The Raft of the Medusa" disappears. "Krishna and Radha" disappears. "Death of the Virgin" disappears. "The Third of May 1808" disappears. "Louis XVI" disappears. "Girl at a Window" disappears. "The Snail" disappears. "The Fighting Temeraire" disappears. "Adam and Eve" disappears. "The Ambassadors" disappears. "The Lady of Shalott" disappears. "Veil" disappears. "Slicer" disappears. "Electric Prisms" disappears. "Bird Cloud" disappears. "The Encounter" disappears. "The Great Wave off Kanagawa" disappears. "The Migration Series" disappears. "Metamorphosis of Narcissus" disappears. "Crucifixion" disappears. "The First Part of the Return from Parnassus" disappears. "Still Life with Checked Tablecloth" disappears. "The Teacher" disappears. "Untitled" disappears. "Untitled [No. 25]" disappears. "Untitled (America)" disappears. "Stretch" disappears. "The Reader" disappears. "Cindy" disappears. "Aberration #8" disappears. "Sappho" disappears. "Buddha Footprint" disappears. "The Flower Carrier" disappears. "Pine Forest" disappears. "Ashes to Ashes" disappears. "Cultural Gothic" disappears. "Pink Panther" disappears. "Purple Octagonal" disappears. "Sweetie" disappears. "The Small Morning" disappears. "Everyone I Have Ever Slept With 1963—1995" disappears. "Nature Unveiling Herself to Science" disappears. "Tête" disappears. "Head of Apollo" disappears. "Head" disappears. "The Sower" disappears. "Sorrow" disappears. "Future" disappears. "Crowd" disappears. "Entrada" disappears. "Christ" disappears. "Human Machine" disappears. "Prop" disappears. "For the Love of God" disappears. "Spirit of the Night" disappears. "Sunflowers" disappears.

And so on and on like that then.

■

The world is calm. Its light is see-through.

Alice feels her body rushing up then from out of where she had last been and into now, full of something like panic on the cusp of blacking out, wanting no part of what could have ever come before.

She finds she is sitting in a very small white room; the dimensions are the same as the last space, with the mirror, which she does not actively remember beyond an impression, displaced in time; nor can she recognize where she is or where she's been. And yet she feels no panic in not knowing, as on the edges of waking: to imagine the past seems the same as imagining the future, or the present, any difference all a whorl; as if the edges of the room are also the edges of her experience; as if the world has just begun with her beginning.

There is a bed, a sink, a toilet, a door. A TV stands installed into the wall across from the bed, turned to no channel; only a white glow, matching the walls. Her hair is long, unwashed, mangy with age. She is wearing a white jumpsuit, marked with a number: 98,100,001,844. And, on her right wrist, a tattoo:

She doesn't feel surprised to see the marks, though she can't remember when or how she had received them. Nothing feels so different from how it always had, an aggregate of alike days repeating in the absence of so much of her memory beyond certain hot spots, flashes of an existence so far away it seems like someone else's. No way to know how long has passed in this condition except by the nauseous soreness in her gut, her heavy limbs unsure of what to do in any second; no other day forever but through this one.

Alice stands. Her legs feel strange beneath her; not weak, but slightly off, a moment's delay between her impulse and its corresponding motion; the joints run stiff, not quite all there. She half expects to collapse, and to see herself in freefall before it happens, her vision somehow several seconds just ahead inside her head, comprised in thoughts that do not completely feel like hers, words that come on like lines of script more than live action.

She experiences her body calmly moving across the room to touch the door. Its frame is as wide as her shoulders' span and high as her head, as if custom-made for her to fit. The door, of course, she already knows, is locked; has been for some time, maybe forever. Through a small panel she can see out into the hall beyond. There's nothing there from her perspective but another wall, of the same white as those on her side, seeming almost near enough to touch if she could only reach out through the partition, break the plane.

Instead, she touches her own face. The flesh feels fake, frigid beneath its semi-malleable outer lining, numbed to the impression of her own contact on the outside. Where she should see her own reflection in the glass of the door's viewing panel she does not appear there; the grain's all glare, obscuring any central aspect.

She can still understand how it had felt before to feel—though something's missing between her understanding of what she'd been and what she'd come from, who and how she still must be, despite the lack of active definition; the only difference this time being how she doesn't miss at all what she has lost. Instead its absence provides strange relief, a covering over of a covering over, as if there had never really been another place to be.

The cell door opens from the outside. Once it does, all prior supposition of what might be or had been in her dissolves, becomes another dislocated feeling.

Alice is sitting on her mattress. She can't remember having returned to the position. Nor can she remember having ever stood. The kind of air that seems to curl in through the open door is the only mind the room has.

A man in a pressed blue uniform appears. He ducks his skull beneath the transom so as not to bump it, though he has already been injured, apparently, as he's moving with a limp, his poor posture making him seem shorter, smaller than he actually must be. He's carrying a tray that bears a glass of thick gray liquid, which he comes to place at Alice's feet, keeping his eyes down from her, not a word.

The man waits while she studies the glass's contents, poking at its surface, sniffing its edge to find no smell. She is unsure at first what she is meant to do with it: Eat it? Clean her body? Rinse her eyes? Queries seethe against the lining of her skull like wire mesh, pulsing through the flesh around her eyes, but no words emerge to break her silence, more so the longer that she can't. *Where to begin even?* she wonders, not for the first time. *What does it even matter when and where am I, or why and who?* Everywhere within her where she might once have felt the urge to resist her bonds, her captivity, she feels instead a lurching feeling, like hunger laced with nausea, in the same stew. Already her body seems to know what it wants from her: She takes down the whole glass of gray liquid in one go. The stuff has no taste at all, she finds, despite its oily texture; it seems to spread out inside her like wallpaper melting, coating her linings with warm slur. When she is finished, the man takes the empty glass and tray again and gives her a cloth to wipe her face. He then turns back, eyes still averted, and approaches the screen set in the wall, upon which he summons a command screen and enters a passcode, bringing the interface alive. Alice can't stay with him long enough to read his maneuvers in the software, selecting options from stacked menus scrolling open into more, until eventually the blank screen shifts into a peal of calibrating static, then a printed title card on a white screen: ALICE KNOTT, Exhibit A.

The man turns to leave then, saying nothing. As the cell door closes again between them, Alice hears the tumblers scraping in the locks, like lobes of gravel ground together.

The recording, following its title, shows Alice seen from above and behind, standing in a room with bright blank walls, much like her cell but wider, full of daylight. It is clearly her, she sees; she recognizes the clothes she's wearing as the same she'd worn so many days, like a personal uniform, the arch of her own posture distinct to her from out of hundreds despite having seen herself outside herself only on film. Those are the shapes of the veins that run along her arms, she sees; there is the mole on her neck that sometimes grew so sore she couldn't sleep; those are the earrings she took off her mother just days before her death, to wear herself thereafter. The only difference she can tell between herself and her depiction is her age, equally indeterminate on both ends, as if her life had spanned so long a time it no longer sticks in any given state.

It takes another moment, though, before she identifies the space on the screen as that of the memorial exhibition for the dead artist, whose name she can no longer recall—however long ago it had been—except for how in the film here, unlike the empty breadth of her remembrance, there are many other people packed in, both in the current chamber and in those beyond, on either side. As she recalls there had been nothing hanging there but on the one wall of framed pictures of her family, but here there are works of varying size and disposition all throughout, many bearing images of wholly different persons and locations, abstract smears, none of whom seem familiar to Alice now at all. Many of the exhibits in the very next room even appear to be A/V presentations, like this one Alice is watching, shown through large screens that fill each spectator's face with diffuse glow.

Alice herself is standing before a particular display, in the same location as the one she recalls she had attacked, though she can no longer remember why. Instead of the portrait of her family there is a large dark object, the size and shape of the mirror left behind in her own home, or at least close; this one, though, is wholly blackened, caked with soot so thick no reflection might appear, nor any sign it's really a mirror there at all—beneath the resin could be anything. A tiny placard underneath it appears to bear its title, its creator, though Alice can't read the fine print so far away, the printed words there remaining any words at all.

On the video, Alice is shown standing immobile and unblinking, as if mesmerized by what she sees there in the black. No matter what comes on either side, she doesn't move, staying stock still as hundreds of other bodies pass along, crowding in around her, most hardly even glancing at the object as much as taking notice of her awkward gape. Her arms lie flat at her sides, her expression almost unchanging with the time, marked by the code at the bottom right of the screen, sped up to cram many seconds into each, playing out now for the present Alice to suffer through anew, watching herself stuck in a scene she can't recall, wondering what might be yet to come despite her lack of recognition.

The film goes on like that for quite some time. It seems more and more as if nothing else is going to happen, slowly loosing Alice's expectation into not boredom but increasing anxiety, until just after the film's code marks the passing of its seventh hour, when—without a sound above the muted aspect of its playback—the blackened object bursts; that is, its surface shatters, unprompted by obvious contact, showering debris and shards all over the museum floor. It's unclear what could have caused the event, as nothing seems abnormal within the space outside Alice's prolonged attention, which she has never shifted, although the subtext of the film itself suggests some form of connection; at the very least, it seems, she had known the incident was coming, if not also that her prolonged focus itself had caused or helped it to occur. This culpability is reinforced when, immediately after the demolition, the long-lingering Alice in the recording turns her back and moves away—not to exit the space, we find, but to go on casually observing other work, as if she hasn't even realized what has happened.

But the destruction of the object, as it remains thereafter in its fragments, suddenly an attraction for the nearby patrons as they begin to gather around it like maggots onto meat, reveals the innate structure of its manufacture. Underneath the char had really been a mirror, we can see, its face now fractured into a finite set of glassy shards, none of them alike, spilled from the compromised object's body as if they've been bashed out from behind it, revealing a previously unobservable cavity of colored gel, black as oil but tinged with fuchsia rust, a mass apparently still wet and gleaming in the gallery's contained light, appearing something like alive. One might even wonder if the event has been set up by the creator, as strangely compelling an image as it is—some immersive performance meant to comment and undo the very decorum of being viewed. But the reaction of those surrounding quickly makes it clear that this is not the case.

It soon becomes clear that the focus of the recording thereafter is not the ruptured object, despite its spectacle; rather, the camera follows Alice, who has yet to even appear to realize what's going on. She continues on calmly moving through the exhibit work to work, passive in posture, arms limp, by herself, while various bystanders now begin to fill out the edges of the video from rooms beyond, several of them already pointing and jawing at her unseen, holding their kids back. Others are already taking their own videos and pictures with their devices, as if in parallel to the central recording from overhead, immediately disseminating replications of the moment into the world beyond, on to loved ones and strangers alike online.

Even when two security officers appear and approach her at the room's far end, Alice remains composed, passive and still. She does not appear to respond to their inquiries by so much as nodding, even when her forward progress becomes blocked, until at last the cops take her by the arms, produce their handcuffs, bind her wrists, and pat her down. She watches blankly, both onscreen and in real time, as they remove from pockets on her person several prescription bottles, a flask, a fillet knife, and a handgun. No matter what they do or say, her recorded image won't respond, a helpless blankness in her eyes as if what is meant to happen is all that could ever happen, as if she's already lived through this countless times. She makes no recognizable attempt to cover her face or speak or struggle, even as they begin to lead her out of the screen and into custody; and it is only just before she clears the frame and the scene cuts that she looks suddenly straight up into the recording's POV, staring head on into the lens of the security camera, as if she'd known exactly who was watching all along.

Within thirty-six hours, the surveillance video—described by many in media as depicting *Alice shattering the mirror with her mind*—goes viral as well, shared at a rate not quite as rapid and widespread as the prior acts of destruction, but now accompanied by a host of further allegations over the supposed culprit, already a cult figure in many eyes, and thus subsequently generating renewed attention to the related prior videos in its wake—even more so then as what at first seems circumstantial soon appears more certain, as a thumb drive in Alice's bag is discovered to hold a bank of dozens of other previously unseen videos, saved with sequentially numbered filenames in an untitled folder on a disk otherwise blank.

Among the videos are recordings documenting the destruction of the eight major artworks she'd been known previously to own, including new footage from the originally leaked videos of the sandblasted de Kooning, and firsthand footage of the undoing of the other seven, including five by similar acts of fire, two by razor scraping, one by repeated immersion in an acid bath, and one compressed in a compactor down to the size of a remote control, which is then deposited in a public receptacle designated for common trash. Various other videos include evidence of destruction of a number of other missing works, many of them already reported stolen, others newly marked. There are as well several videos in which the works being destroyed cannot be identified by hired experts as noteworthy— that is, *famous*—which raises some question over the intent of the sum total of the acts: Who is deciding which should be demolished, and which not? Is a work left previously unknown, ruined in the same way as those of so many major artists, suddenly more valuable, more real?

Though Alice herself does not appear in any portion of the films—the faces of those involved in the destruction remaining either in costume, off screen, or otherwise scrambled—possession of the evidence is deemed sufficient to detain Alice as the primary suspect in more than one hundred counts of larceny, fraud, destruction of private property, and, in the mass wake of mimicked acts, incitement to riot. Her location in custody remains unpublished, another form of privileged knowledge.

———

By the end of the first week after the initial broadcast of Alice's arrest, the blackened mirror-object she had allegedly attacked on the most recent recording, titled *The High Cost of Existing (Under a Silver Sky)*, is sold in its current, damaged condition, shards and all, at private auction to a buyer who ceases to be named, for a higher price than any artwork in the contemporary era.

The following morning, depictions of the blackened screen—the newly infamous work—appear on the front cover of more than three dozen major magazines, spanning worldwide. It is now essentially nothing more than a large black square, far as most can see, dressed around its edges with slivered reflecting fragments, trails of dust: an entity impossible to recombine, but equally impossible to re-create, given the hysterical event causing its becoming. But its import, from there, is taken no less seriously; if anything, it acquires status it otherwise likely never would have. "Its fragments are a solar system of itself," one media critic writes of the work, "a mini-model of our confounded universe as yet to come."

Fifteen hours later, the purported buyer, an "antisocial," bad boy billionaire also known for his eye as a collector, is discovered to have killed himself not long after receipt of the transaction, by throwing himself off the roof of one of his many tropical properties. His blood is found toxicologically confounded with substances whose nature remains excluded from reports.

That blood has barely begun to dry when the now-notorious artwork again changes hands at public auction on behalf of the new executor of the dead's estate, this time fetching nearly twice the previous record upon its sale to a young hedge fund manager whose purchase is deemed to occur for no reason other than that its value in creating new fame, as this last sale resets the record not only for the highest valued artwork in our era, but of all time.

The name of the agency representing both the buyer and the seller in each of these transactions, it is reported, is Void Corporation.

Public repercussion of such exposure in coming days proceeds apace. Soon each act is just another icon in a conflagration without border.

At New York's MoMA, Henri Rousseau's *The Dream* (1910) is attacked with a straight razor by a local college professor of physics, who after screaming "I am the fuck of your reality" stabs the image of a full moon in the painting's upper right-hand corner eleven times before restraint. A video, less viral than prior efforts, circulates briefly, showing police beating the man into submission as he attempts to struggle free, screaming over and over for his mother by her first name.

And on the same floor, in the same afternoon, Umberto Boccioni's *Dynamism of a Soccer Player* (1913) survives attack in the form of a recently laid-off nanny's attempts to pry the painting from its frame, resorting then to punching the face of the image with her fists so hard the pigment would be forever dented, if in a way almost not visible to the passing eye. In her purse, they find nearly a week's worth of leaking frozen meatloaf dinners crammed into an otherwise empty vessel, with a handwritten note that says, *You may not eat me.*

Later that afternoon, downtown at the New Museum, a set of twins left briefly unsupervised by their young parents climb over the dividing rail around Chris Burden's *A Tale of Two Cities* (1981), where they are then able to run and roll in gleeful hysteria across a significant stretch of the installation's meticulously arranged landscape before their detention. It is, of course, the parents who will be charged, resulting in a month-long exposé in which the mother attempts to out the father, an accountant, as a secret correspondent for the CIA, claiming he had triggered the children to act out by placing his finger in their ears and administering a serum concocted and administered by the government for centuries in the manufacturing of the exact timeline of our history as it had already been conceived. In the end, only the mother will serve time.

And the next morning, across the country at the Hammer Museum in Los Angeles, Katie Grinnan's *Mirage* (2011) is assaulted by a security attendant who had been assigned that day to watch the very room in which the work had been displayed, a violent outburst that then continues onto nearby bystanders, leaving four wounded and one dead. "I could no longer stand to let it go on like this," the guard is quoted as saying upon arrest. "It isn't right. It isn't the way I am, we are, we have been. This disease. This eye within the eye. I am become overcome, my bones. No new future."

And across the ocean, at almost the same time, a recently married architect is arrested for trying to masturbate onto the face of Edvard Munch's *The Scream* (1893), succeeding only in exposing himself to dozens from a visiting middle school, amid their actual audible replications of the target's representative act. While imprisoned, the culprit will attempt to sever his genitalia with the bent edge of the leg of a metal bedframe and die from blood loss.

And a substitute teacher removes the section of mirror from Joan Miró's sculpture *Object* (1932), allowing it to fall free on the ground, as if the mirror had been scalding to the touch once broken free, shrieking in high-pitched furor as they come to stop her, unable thereafter to make any kind of human speech, only more shrieking.

And a Boy Scout with a pocket knife manages to stab Rembrandt van Rijn's *Judas Repentant, Returning the Thirty Pieces of Silver* (1629) twenty-two times without triggering attention of the guards before he stops and lies face down by his own will on the floor and goes at once into a coma; only later will it be discovered that he had been blind from birth, with no clear explanation for how he'd delivered himself from the home of his also blind legal guardian, his grandmother, her home more than one hundred miles away.

And somewhere else an elderly woman throws her body into Damien Hirst's *The Physical Impossibility of Death in the Mind of Someone Living* (1991), so hard that it shatters the glass and spills formaldehyde into the gallery, pooling out into the nearby rooms like a sick tide; the woman later tells the press she "wanted to take the place of the shark and let the shark live in sunlight forever instead of what I am because soon there will be nothing."

What is wrong with all these people's minds? people keep asking. Why did it have to come this far, and what will be enough to make it stop? Many have their own opinions on the outcome, the exposure, though in the end none will be true, never exactly as it happened; and neither, then, will be the story of whoever's left in years thereafter to pass it on.

Regardless, two different kinds of neon blue paint are sprayed simultaneously onto Salvador Dalí's *Girl at a Window* (1925) by the left and right hand of a young mother, who has left her sixteen-month-old child at home alone to fend for herself so that she might go and make the pattern of an upside-down cross over the famous image. In her absence, the child will be found having ripped all the pages out of a copy of the Bible passed down through their family for more generations than anyone might like to recall, her first work as a living artist.

And that same day Antoine Bourdelle's *Head of Apollo* (1900) is lifted up by a young violin prodigy and carried across the exhibition chamber at a run before being dunked like a basketball into the back of the head of an unwitting patron, inflicting physical damage that will eventually prove critical.

And a young housewife produces a steel baton from underneath her dress and attacks Glenn Ligon's neon-bulb sculpture, *Untitled (America)* (2018), then fends off security by cutting her arms with fragments from the wreckage, spraying blood she screams is "hell blood" at them until she is eventually restrained using plastic sheeting and a Taser.

And another and again and so on, all like this; the hour in the hour rendered full, as if to splitting, each act made done in separate rooms touched by the same air, hemispheres and days apart.

Each occurrence, once it is committed, has been committed. It cannot thereafter be unwritten from the replicating pages of organs of the media that continue to carry it forward by mouth and eye, regardless of how quickly we must continue to move on, accumulating more and more preposterous occasions into mass memory until eventually it's no longer possible to properly attend to any one.

And meanwhile, in the news of local politics and weather, birds keep falling from the sky in flocks, their pupils overrun with scads of parasite; six different elementary schools in the same district all burn down on the same day, a serial accident cited in connection to faulty work done by a major contractor, now running for mayor; a bag boy kills eighteen by slipping arsenic into each box of doughnuts that he is forced to touch by way of work; sales of Aricept reach an all-time high; Stonehenge collapses; a long wing of the Mall of America collapses; the president's twin brother appears on the nightly news to ask that we bow our heads with him and pray. It is unclear what any of these events have to do with what's being done elsewhere, how it connects; how it might have gone differently or could never have gone differently. Soon, one might imagine, there will be more instances of damage than can be accounted for, so much so we won't even be able to recognize the real from the unreal; a mass of incorporated acts eventually surpassing our mental bandwidth, lost in the gape.

It is, after all, just another day held over in our remaining hours, as some of us struggle just to stand; the light in the room of the ongoing reportage, tuned into by millions, maintains the same conductive quality as ever, at once neurotic and antiseptic, biding its lines, beneath the whites of the eyes of the news anchors in every local hemisphere as soft as something bled to death, too primed; against all of which the ongoing ambient buzzing of the production, the heavy lights, the operators, their flawless makeup, obscures the soundtrack just enough to make any one word seem off from what it meant.

The strangest thing, to Alice, in the midst of the world as it unfolds, both by word of mouth and in her heart, is how none of it seems actually strange at all, despite its lack of precedent. Not that it had already happened before, in another life even, but that she'd felt it coming her whole life. From her incarcerated state, each aspect of the present seems in its reception like something that could have been in one of her father's books or a plotline in the show they'd watched together as a family, neither of which she remembered as her own memory beforehand; at least, an echo of those, embodied by their air. The present's occurrence effectively affects her as any newly unveiled episode would have, even knowing that, even days later, often only one small scene or minor aspect of the production is all that will still stick—*the way* a character said something more than *what* was said, even; the stunning color of a walk-on's leggings or lips, perhaps, as seen moving through the background of a shot, elements not meant to have specific purpose, it seems, but somehow therein occluding the more formal aspects of the entertainment, larger than life. Though the walls of her cell are real, clearly—she can bang her head against them and feel no bend—the words within her don't feel like hers, seem to have no defining explanation beyond her own mind, their meanings fitting in her like a floodplain, one upon which the rushing waters have long already come and worn down the land to its barest. There could be nothing more there underneath, beyond a burning, the molten core around which churns the mutating crust of Earth.

Sometimes, in the flat of night there, running open, Alice can even hear the texture of her father's voice—not her unfather, for once, but the one who had been lost—reading to her aloud among the black space crammed into the air behind her eyes. And though she can't really seem to make out any of the single words themselves, their clusters, or what they mean, she can sense where the sounds of the spoken sentences pushed up against her flesh, the blood beneath. If she can fix herself just so, on the edge of hours passing half-asleep inside her cell as the world without her carries on, it might begin to seem almost as if she is still in her old room in her family's house instead of here; the mouth of his voice might still appear there reading the words out of the book between her and him, some kind of passage through which she cannot wriggle but can breathe; his whiskers brushing at her ear, his thick tongue clucking, the sound of the language stronger the longer she can go without asking where it came from or what it means. It is the clearest feeling she can count not still today, held so tightly down against her she might soon not remember having ever moved an inch or felt a way.

———

Whenever Alice opens her eyes again, coming to into the feeling of being watched from the outside, it's just the cell there, same as last time; her old body back in place within the waiting world and what it wants, which is nearly nothing now, second to second, in her confinement, as somewhere beyond the walls the rest goes on. She watches what she can of what appears broadcast behind the glass of the screen inside her cell, its trim eye coming on and glowing through a channel as if at irregularly programmed quadrants from out of nowhere, if always armed with information.

Her name, in the mouths of the pundits, does not sound to her like her own name; nor does it fit the facts of who she'd been throughout the hours leading up to now. So many seem to think they know more about who she is and what she's done, crimes alone notwithstanding, than Alice herself: as every other mention of her in the media in their continuing coverage of her case and its implication—always still the topic of the hour for some reason, at least as shown to her—provides further detail of the apparent facts that bind her life, all of it made new to her, live and then again in syndication: stills of her, several years younger, smiling wild-eyed, from her only previous arrest, a DUI; of her even younger, in high school, dressed in all black, baring her teeth (a photo she herself had never seen, though she could nearly remember its having been taken: a flash of light erupting in the hands of some human person she'd once felt raw for, full of love); and alongside that, most recently, the footage of the aftermath of her arrest, herself being led out of the museum by a small band of men, bolstered with reports provided by the courts and now made public, detailing how in addition to her extremely high blood alcohol content at the time of arrest (.402)—a shock considered she hasn't had a drink in seven years and seven months—she'd had significant amounts of various foreign substances in her system, including a nearly lethal level of crack cocaine, as well as smaller but not diminutive amounts of psilocybin, methamphetamine, and LSD, none of which, beyond the booze, Alice had knowingly ingested in her life.

Nor does she remember having agreed to allow blood testing, despite her clear initials scribbled into the margins of the paperwork as supplied on demand by the guards who come to maintain her upkeep—not that she'd ever developed any definitive process for that scrawl, even when sober, always simply putting pen down to paper and letting it rip. It could have been anyone who had signed for any of her, as such; any of millions, taking over in the guise of her own person, hacking her history with the simplest of commands. Now the whole world knew who she was, what she had done, perhaps more concretely than even she did, processed through facts she wasn't sure whether to dispute or to try to understand.

Could she actually have done what they were saying, she can't help but start to wonder, given the gaps in what she felt about who she was? Didn't they have anything better to report on, given the innumerable order of other worldwide horrors going on inflicted by the hour? Even the future, as it happens, feels more like a revision of what was meant to be than original events, pasted in and crossed out over and over so many times beforehand that when it actually arrives, it bears the same wear as all the rest, long rolled over and disremembered, left to suffer—the same way that the longer she remains locked in the long shape of such present, the less she finds she can remember of all else. Increasingly it's as if, in the same way her father had disappeared, whole parts of the world and the life she'd lived inside it are disappearing, are only there enough within her that she might recognize them missing, being thought of as for the last time: *The flower she had picked and pressed into the book her mother had read to her every night before the transition, whose petals had bled their color onto the paper, ruining the words. The blanket she had slept with through those same years, nuzzled through so many hours of sleep that by the end it was only threads and dust, indistinguishable from any rag to anyone but her. The soft spot in the forest where she had buried a box of undeveloped film, full of images of all those days then, whose location she could no longer remember but could still sense the color of the film's flat blackness stretching soft and far inside her face. The field of white dirt where she had always imagined she'd be buried, if there was anybody left by then to carry out her will, and that in the meantime she dreamed of not as a place of death, but almost worship, a small eye in the world where it had actually seemed there portended the aspect of the presence of a god.*

As she exhumes each above the piles of other psychic refuse, held between white walls, Alice feels their past locations folding over like a map, each fact of her existence lost within the contours of the day, in and over on themselves, erasing without even the echo of a report. If she herself could not remember them forever, who would? Who else could sense the dissolution of the very ground she had walked on anywhere, its surface turning over a new face that matched the old, despite how she had fallen on it, ripped her skin there? There was no such awareness of its significance in her own life beyond her mental borders, no tag with any hint of how these moments made her who she was now even still—and how, without them, what remained? What held firm about the future as it became the present and then the past, over and over, never dissipating, turned to mush? Any expectation could just as easily become the absence to which one's persona forfeited its identity, unto fate worse than mere death, and therefore any past fact might just as quickly have no floor. The world might open underneath her, yes, or worse, it might stop holding traction, its fiber no longer connecting to the space on either side. Like a person captured in a painting, or a model; or in their own life, placed here side by side with every other in every moment, every hour, and no one counting.

That evening, after supper in the form of another serving of the gray liquid, Alice is escorted from her cell, along a long thin hall of the same color, only to end up in another cell shaped just the same but bare of bed or toilet, and in the place of the display screen a huge bay window, wide as seven of her standing side by side. The whole breadth of the view is encased in hefty plastic, into which gouges like claw marks appear to have been rendered, perhaps by animal or by machine, though whether from the inside or the outside is not clear. The world outside the window is difficult to parse. Far out as she can look, the ground goes on flat and slight, paved over, or made of dirt so cleanly blasted by the sun it no longer bears a color. Only in the very far reaches of her vision can she make out a mass of smoke on the horizon, somehow insanely far away—a rising host of ongoing conflagration; or is it rainfall? She can hardly see, the thick glass in the face of the window for some reason easily clouding over from her breathing and her heat, against where on the far side, she can clearly feel, the air is freezing; so much so it hurts to touch. And yet she puts her head against the pane again, trying to see, better, anywhere she's ever been; though the scene now resembles nothing of the world in which she'd tried to learn to live, all possible paths she can imagine ending up only in the same place: where she is now, nowhere else.

At last, for once, though, at this wider window, which she still is not quite sure why they have brought her out to see—a reward for good behavior, allowing her a peek behind the scenes?—she finds she no longer feels it necessary to believe anything enough to not expect to one day ask again and receive a different answer. When she is most honest with herself, she knows that what has been abandoned would likely have been no better; that all she recalls as prior life was nothing more than further smoke; that the holes and interruptions that plagued her now would still have wound their way in, wrought their damage. She is only exactly who she is. Wherever any expectation might appear to differentiate from her past timeline meant nothing more than any other form of interruption, some commercial crammed into the narrative fiber of a lifetime, wrought by the same dark nail through every fate, if always obscured behind the veils of expectation and intention, all the flashbulbs and the gore.

As Alice looks across in the longer reaches of the distance across the flatness, beyond the edges of the farthest scope of light, she can make out other soft features encrypted even further in its immense landscape, just there enough to be mistaken, overlooked: white sets of scaffolding fit with wired lighting fixtures, like half-finished film sets, abandoned or in disuse; and then, beyond them, hanging cranes and stadium seating where countless cameras dot the necks of apparati installed along the sky, no audience where bleachers for millions stand as if free-floating on all sides, all of it lost among other patterns and minutiae just as quickly as she can parse it, sensed thereafter only as a refraction of cracks in perception in the horizon, small fits of sickly weather, the land rebuffing where it touched parts of the world too far gone to read from here.

Alice's bail is set at seventeen million dollars.

It doesn't feel like a real number—at least no more than the prices set and paid for the works she had allegedly destroyed, each more than most people make through their whole life. It's what some might call *an obscene sum of money*, though to Alice, in certain shock now, it only feels like another punchline to the joke.

Though there had been a time when such an obviously intentionally excessive penalty would not have been outside Alice's command— the impending sprawl of mismanagement of which had played no small role in precisely how she ended up here, so it seems—it has been some time since even that abstract financial reality could be confirmed as actual liquidity; all squandered away or blown through on purpose, or otherwise relinquished by her in her detesting of the obligation, whence it came, by now seemed as virtual as the manner by which such funds might have accrued, somewhere so buried in her bloodline now she can't remember having benefited from a stitch of it, despite the ledgers and receipts that must still exist, demonstrating her participation in said transactions despite whatever else about it she'd like to feel.

Alice no longer has the money, is the conclusion, and nowhere near it, if she ever even really did; whoever that had been seems like someone else, a story she had read somewhere, so long ago its source had long divorced its particulars, misappropriated its intent into her way, including the apparent demolition of the very assets she might have cashed in now to buy her freedom—though by now she can't recall the feeling of ever having owned those paintings, even been near them, nor can she remember ever having lived as if she had; no phase at all where her kin were allowed to live in any way but by the skin of someone's teeth, stretching to make ends meet, to make dinner. All she knows for certain now is that each time she wakes she is more tired than she had been and always has been, and nothing others claim as true really does seem true.

Maybe she's even actually guilty, she imagines? Maybe she did do everything they claimed, and thereafter just forgot or revised its memory beyond her, as she feels she had of so much of her life. The longer she allows herself to go on not remembering how she ended up here, what had actually happened, the more it begins to seem as if not only must her reported actions be true, but as if she can actually remember having been where they say she has, done what she's been accused of. She can even then remember, if she wishes: the nearness of the flame, the white-hot eye wielded in her fists primed for the destruction of the artworks, ready and willing to bring an end to anything that would allow itself to be; the incinerating cluster of the pigmented canvas melting away, turning to smoke and ash, can feel the leather of its absence stretching out along her limbs and through her lungs, her sternum, into her heart, igniting fast across each coming thought as it arose. Likewise, for once more clearly now than ever, she can understand the pleasure of such destructive power, what might bring a person to want to be not one who created, but who destroyed; someone who, for once, at last could be said to have even so briefly taken control of their nature, their direction, and, for better or for worse, altered the world. Who is to say the state might not know her better than she could herself, parsing what's available on paper into her blackest wishes, what she would not have even known she could be capable of doing? In what ways is it *not* her?

Alice begins to hear herself confess into the small cell, then, listing aloud everything she might remember wrong, or might have done different had she known better, or had not done but should have, on and on, welling up from there within her unstoppably once allowed initiation. For once the speaking seems to come out in what is really her own voice, even if she can't connect all of the utterances to facts, each possible thought sliding out between her lips as if no urge's requirement remains, and thereafter committed to her living record as soon as it has shape—as if all it takes to have performed an act is to say so, requiring not even one's own personal belief. And yet throughout it all there's something different about the language, the grain she feels against it. There is something in the logic of the sound that makes all the old words feel like shelves, places where things had been placed more than things themselves; as if what is on the far side of the wall of her small cell now is not another cell at all, but yet another room appearing in her childhood household, one possessed of endless ways to be.

When Alice wakes, the room is blurry and half formed. There is a face. The man in blue is there above her, leering with eyes that tremble in their sockets, all other features melding into their surroundings at the edges, half abstracted. He has no mouth at first, no eyelids; then, though, there is a mouth, fitted with gold, no sound about it but of a low hiss, speaking in a language hardly human till it begins to coalesce.

The mouth has to tell her several times, in several manners, that she must rise; and though she feels lightheaded sitting up and seeing the scape of the bed beneath her, logged with sweat, it doesn't stop her body from bending upright, lurching forward on the mattress, weak but operable, still there. She can sense at once that she's lost mass; less of her left there than there should be, it seems, in a bad way, as if the muscle between the meat has been sucked out, replaced with putty or rubber, the skin all raw and far too thick. Her mouth tastes strange, sour and dry around a throat that doesn't want to swallow without grind; and at her center, the dull roar of open aching, like hunger but wider, more overriding.

The man is watching her, Alice notices, unlike before, though his eyes seem to have no feeling behind them, dilated down to thin gray rims around their center's holes. He moves as if blind, only able to source her presence there by heat and motion, *such that if I could stay still forever*, Alice imagines, *he'd go away and not come back.* She feels closer to him then, suddenly, relieved for no clear reason she can separate from other sensations. Congruently, the guard cracks half a smile, his aged face fumbling with wrinkles that emerge only in expression, attached to longer modules beneath his flesh that pump and rotate, searching for ground. He closes his eyes as such, frozen in posture, waiting for some confirmation of intent to which he might react. He clasps his hands together and rubs one in the other with the milky hiss of skin on skin, an ugly rhythm. Meanwhile, behind him, on the screen, live, the feed shows a shot of the room with them inside it from overhead, offering a view of the back of the man's body while she stares past him into the camera from the bed. She is so pale, she thinks, studying her own representation, *so hardly there*. She sits watching the screen then for some time, expecting to see herself take action without the necessity of activation, as if the version of them held onscreen could carry on without correspondence with her person.

It is on the screen first, then, that Alice sees the guard, still with his eyes closed, turn and trundle stiffly back toward the cell's lone door; he stops and looks back to face her only briefly—an action matched in real time as she transfers her attention from the screen to where he really stands—before he then continues on out into the hallway linked beyond, this time leaving the door open for her behind him without instruction. She finds that every next motion on her own requires enormous concentration, each joint and bone having come loose now in her muscle memory of even standing, walking, seeing, each somehow disattached from how she is. It remains unclear if she's supposed to follow the guard or just wait here, much less what consequences await either choice if correct or incorrect; still, she lurches to her feet and forward, and likes the way the sudden motion makes her feel, like being drunk again, sensing doors where there aren't doors, walls where there aren't walls, despite how the world always seems to come around.

What walls there actually are, far as she can tell as she shuffles out into the hall beyond her cell, are flat and blank, absent of doors that might have entered in to other cells alongside hers, a fact that corresponds with the fact that she's seen no one else in here through all her time, far as she remembers. Which how long had that been now? How might she measure? A couple days at most, she thinks, though it's still strange not to have encountered other inmates, heard their voices; instead, the withstanding span of silence of the prison's space and her fading remembrance of years passed all runs together, disrupting her equilibrium in fact as she struggles to keep up with her ward already quite far ahead along the long drab hallway's line of sight. It is enough, then, just to focus on one step and then the next, and so on forward through the extending space, more like an office building than a prison, both in texture and in spirit, manufactured to maintain calm.

No matter how well she maintains pace, regardless, the guard is always out of range, just disappearing around another corner as she passes the last one, never bothering to so much as look back. The hallway never seems able to go straight for very long before it comes to roundabouts or doorless junctures that bifurcate the path, always limiting her visibility to almost precisely where she is, each length alike in hue and texture, without markings. Either way, she stays the course, following suit without comment even under the great effort now required for such simple work, never mind the looping wills within her own head, her heavy limbs, somehow starving and flooded full at the same time. She doesn't want to lose the guard's lead, for some reason, more afraid of what might befall her were she to end up lost here than whatever other fate might await her otherwise, the threat of deeper confinement or even capital punishment at all times pressing in against her mind, even unable as she is for certain to say why or how it'd come to that, or what else might still be wanted of her.

Occasionally, too, at certain sudden checkpoints, Alice's passage is interrupted by otherwise impassable security mechanisms, requiring her to present handprints, fingerprints, mouthprint, or nails and eyes as ID, which she performs without instruction from the guard— having passed their clearance some time before, perhaps, or otherwise finding their interface obvious, intrinsic. Certain devices take her pulse and test her blood, tap on her fillings, massage her pores, each dictating their intent on a tiny screen in block-lettered neon language, before she can be allowed through, onto the next, until, past one such juncture, just as she's feeling so lightheaded she can't lift her leg another step without a break, they emerge into a much larger space, one warehouse-sized and sturdy silver, lighted only by the distant glow of open sun allowed at last to shine in through the wide glass that spans the room's far end, so far off she can't imagine ever touching.

Her end of the room, as it remains, is bare of feature except for a small alcove installed into the wall behind her head, the glass that binds it small and frosted, behind one of which another person's obscured form appears to pose. It is unclear if this person is the same one she'd followed in, she realizes, who otherwise seems to have disappeared into thin air. A sign above the window, in very small, almost illegible, oddly stylish neon white font reads "processing"; just beneath that, in tiny glaring digits, appears what Alice can only guess by its format must be the current date and time, each so unmoored from her way of being that she can make nothing of them but that they're there.

The figure behind the glass seems to know already who Alice is, or, at least, why she appears. A mechanized voice in a speaker mounted in the glass between them repeats her assigned number, speaking quickly, and asks her to confirm it, which Alice does only by nodding, despite how she's unsure if the pronounced digits actually match those on her uniform or not. She can only sort of see the figure's stunted posture through the haze laid on the glass, the features blurred to plates and pockets, whorls where the eyes are, the open mouth. Then, suddenly, breaking her ogling, a steel drawer emerges from the gap right at her waist, like a bank teller in transaction, nearly hard and fast enough to knock her down had she been standing any closer. Inside the drawer she finds a silver stylus and a single piece of paper, blank except for a space upon which it appears she is meant to sign:

X _____

And though Alice's own throat burns with lurching questions—*what does this stand for, what am I agreeing to, how far have I come*—the words won't actually come; they buzz like insects around a flame, zapping out on contact with her tongue. Every word she might have ever chosen to speak holds hot and fumbling against the meat of her throat and larynx, on the inside, turning over and over as in nausea yet again; all syllable without an engine, nothing in her there where she would have expected her to be.

She is surprised, then, to see herself take up the stylus and calmly sign along the line in one quick, juicy stroke, even if what emerges looks nothing like her signature or anyone's; instead, she finds in horror, standing watching her own hand, she signs the same way she remembers immediately as the same she'd seen installed directly onto the gallery wall, by the dead artist, whose name she no longer recalls, some time so long ago it seems forever. Her writing arm begins trembling immediately thereafter, soon shaking so hard she has trouble standing up, centering herself again only after somehow managing to place the pen and paper back together into the drawer and push it in, though she immediately regrets doing so without clear reason besides knowing there is no way to take it back, nor any understanding of what making such a mark might mean to confirm. She waits and watches helplessly then for what to do next from the figure behind the glass, finding no breath left to push out any question, any demands, fearing nothing more than simply being left alone to her devices.

Again, at once, without a word, the drawer slides out. Inside it this time, Alice finds a black-wrapped package, marked with the same number as her own. It stinks of smoke so much that it makes her choke, blinking to try to see straight, to do as seems suggested, left unasked. She takes the package out and holds it up to her chest awkwardly but definitively, like a stranger's baby, then starts to unwrap it then and there, unsure what else she's meant to do; as what better time for anything than *now*.

Inside the package, under several layers of slick wrapping, she finds the clothes she must have been arrested in, as she remembers only upon contact: cropped white riding pants and a matching blouse, both of which seem salvaged from decades prior, the smell of her old perfume beneath the smoke stench somehow even more heavily familiar, as if soaked into the fabric. There's nothing in the pockets, no ID or credit card or anything with her name on it, besides a pair of twin black metal rings, which she does not remember ever owning or having wished to, though they seem to fit her just the same, slipping on with ease over her knuckle one after another, side by side, a perfect fit, and discovering only thereafter how she can't get them back off, the metal snagged obstinately against the flesh over the bone, digging in as if there'd never been another way. It doesn't hurt, though, Alice thinks, to have to wear it; it actually feels pleasant, even safe; something definitive for once, *something mine; a long time coming.*

All that's left in the box then is a cell phone, from which, she finds, upon turning it back on, that the memory has been erased; no contacts saved, no photos or history of calls; only the time appears set on the screen's default display of a flat white, neither it nor the current date beneath matching those above the processing window, in either second, minute, hour, day, month, or year. Even the design of the handset, too big and blotchy, heavy as granite, seems so outdated that she can't imagine having lived during a time when someone would have gone around with such a thing, why they would want to.

The rest of what she is meant to do, it seems, to complete her transaction, given what she knows, is all there is at hand. She struggles with unzipping the inmate jumpsuit she's been wearing for as long as she can remember, having to remember how to work it, suddenly lightheaded again, more so than last time, seeing double, before she steps out of the sticky cloth into the air. Her naked body underneath is pressed with powder, a thick white coat that keeps it dry, and beneath that the tingling wrinkles of her flesh seem even softer, like a child's. Through the lining she can see the networks of veins inside her mass, colored tendrils like lengths of wire whorled and interweaving, the sores and scars she has amassed as incalculable in their impression as any wind. She finds relief, at least, putting the old garments on over the body, covering herself over as in a costume, and how the hems still seem a perfect fit for every inch, despite her perceived weight loss, her heaving stomach; and yet in no way thereafter does she feel more familiar to herself, or more alive, and even less so, then, turning to face the far end of the room's buttressing glow that only widens as she approaches, unsure where else there is to head in freedom but toward the undetermined.

Outside, the daylight holds no warmth. All shade of sky above as Alice emerges underneath is flat as anyone with eyes ever might remember if they still could—not blue or gray but both, reflective. Below, the massive lot surrounding the facility stands equally barren, marked only by wires laced overhead coming and going from nowhere to nowhere else; and far in the distance, a high metal partition, for definition or protection, showing the open light back at itself. Beyond its presence nothing else is clear about the land beyond: an open world, each coordinate connecting into so many possible directions that nowhere seems to have a true place.

Nearer, Alice sees now as she her eyes go on adjusting to the glut: a long, white vehicle, with many windows, panels, wheels, idling along the curb; a limo, it appears, just like the one she'd driven herself around in some time that seems so long ago she can't remember where she'd gone. She's hardly even able to look at the thing directly in the high sunlight, its polished features tracing her vision with dizzy trailmarks, sticking at her eyes. She can't stop blinking, then, the plot between shots of seeing reeling for composure, as if being shaken, each breath only puffing up inside her, finding nowhere else to go.

In flashes, then, she sees the driver's door come open. A figure emerges from it, just far enough away to have no firm features, blurred but looming. And at once, blink by blink, he's so much closer then, and closer still each time she looks, the world around them seeming smaller too, shrinking in as he approaches.

The man is well dressed, so it appears, wearing a tailored suit of some expense, as well as fine gloves and reflective glasses that hide his hands and eyes. Alice finds her eyes drawn to his scar, once he is close enough to make it out, the jagged ridge running from his Adam's apple down beyond the neck of his starched shirt; the cut is rough, stitches still visible where he'd been sewn up. Again, he seems familiar, Alice thinks, if in a lost way, one she already knows she won't have back.

"Ms. Novak," the man says gallantly, once within arm's reach. "It's good to see you. You still look so much exactly like yourself." He seems to really mean it, Alice feels, despite his drab tone, and how she doesn't quite understand why he should know her. His eyes light, if for just a second, on the pair of black bands on her finger, together glinting oddly in the wide daylight; she even lets him take the hand then, slightly kneeling as if to examine the rings' condition close up, before gently pressing the back of her hand to his lips—a wet, hot point of impact, making her shudder—then again standing back up as he should, suddenly somehow taller by several feet than he had last seemed. She peers up at his face, looking for someone there she might have understood once, finding nothing as their air surrounding seems to broil, some unexpected pressure in their piecemeal interaction.

"Why would you call me by my mother's maiden name?" she blurts, only thereafter realizing the question as pertinent, true—*Ms. Ana Barbara Novak* being the name her mother had gone by only in the time before Alice's father's disappearance, having refused ever to take Knott but auto-flipping unto Smith thereafter overnight—isn't that right?—followed only by an ongoing denial it had ever been another way. Alice hadn't thought of it in so long, maybe forever, though now, upon address, she can remember having had the name taken from her just the same, forced to abandon her prior person just like that as the unfather installed his way into their life, giving her no choice eventually to begin living as if she'd been someone else the whole time. Still, the recognition strikes her funny, as if invented, something she's making up all on the spot, fixing premonitions to seem like revelations in the moment for better comfort. She can feel her face is at the same time beaming, calm, a far cry from how she feels inside—*miles of screaming*—as the two states refuse to correspond. She wants to raise her arms up in protest, to take this man by his lapels and shake him down, though her arms only hang limp, stuck at her sides.

"Of course you're right," the man says gently, raising his left hand to demonstrate abdication. He doesn't seem at all taken aback; if anything, he absorbs the beat of how she's feeling, purely professional. "I didn't mean to say it like that. You prefer Ms. Knott, of course. My sincerest of apologies; please accept them. It's just . . ." He pauses, scrolling inside himself after the correct words, "It was always so difficult to tell the two of you apart; and only more so as you grew older."

Alice feels the man's eyes moving back and forth across hers as he searches for her reaction, what else to say; meanwhile, the sky behind his head is shifting, suddenly muted, as if the sun has moved behind itself, eclipsing her desire to remain steadfast inside the moment, clinging to any kernel of larger certainty; like how the television felt some nights, the only exit any room might ever hold, wherein the longer she says nothing, the more the person nearest to her softens, settling back toward composure, in control.

"It's quite all right you don't quite recall me, you know," he says at last. "I was so often, in your experience, just out of scene. *More of an impossibility than a person,* as your father so often liked to say, though I never really understood quite what he meant until most recently, after having worked so closely hand in hand with your brother—I believe you call him Richard?—who in turn has sent me here today to operate on your behalf. Or, that is, to negotiate your *situation,* as it stands, which of course is still continuously developing, please remember, even as we speak."

He seems to study her thereafter, seeking reaction, some defining layer that might yet still come clear, the concurrent drift only widening by the second in their reserve, until suddenly he raises his right hand then, to remove his glasses, revealing pinpoint pupils surrounded by an intense, steely blue; *blue as the sky had been once,* Alice thinks, *yes, so everpresent,* and so *disarming,* if in a despondent manner, starkly contrasted by the sun-damaged color of his flesh. The impending clearer recognition drags her down, bunching together where she can't quite underline it, but can at last at least imagine a terrain fading into place.

"Are you . . . Smith?" Alice manages, still uncertain what she's saying as she says it. "*Something* Smith, I mean? Your name?" She finds she's fidgeting, a nervous habit, standing on one leg, then the other, unable to suppress an unintended smirk despite the flatness in his eyes. The inquiry sounds strange, she knows, and yet once uttered it seems to find harbor in some larger connotation. "Didn't you just come by at my house? Or was it that you lived there before us, for a while at least?"

Whoever he is, the man appears to consider her set of questions; he starts to form something back then, in response, before deciding against it at the last second, looking away. He puts his glasses back on, then, as if self-conscious, the dark curve of the lenses refracting malformed impressions of her façade bound up in the light's glare. "The last time I saw you," he says, leaning forward, as if to share a secret, "you'd just awakened from your coma, on your thirtieth birthday. That must have been twenty years ago by now." He's almost hissing now, his eyes in slits. "My god, where has all that time gone?" He starts to reach to touch her again, then, she senses, to offer connection, steady her shoulder; but again he stops himself, goes slack, letting his palms come to rest flat against his thighs. He stops and looks up at the sky directly, as if so that she might too, but therein only drawing further attention to his scar, the shoddy stitching, which she notices is more substantial even than she'd originally understood—his body seems to have been badly beaten, all under his clothing, she realizes, if so long ago that its damage seems incorporated into his person, healed away. She wishes she could just already understand him, absorb his purpose into her own path, as a parent should have long ago for her, out of instinct funded by some actual compassion, the kind that can't be manufactured beyond mere pheromones and chemicals. It's an oddly intimate feeling, she finds, particularly given her haziness of recognition, so little there to understand; and yet she feels it pulling at her, down around her, searching for handholds in her own mind; a mirror held up to a mirror, pressed together.

"I do remember you," Alice says, her tone convincing enough in its projection that it for once seems like her own voice—she seems to actually care about this person, she imagines, an impression perhaps spurred by his apparent familiarity with her life. She finds it feels good regardless to let the words out as confirmation, like scratching a rash knowing that when the scratching stops the itch will come back even worse. And so she repeats the phrase, covering their first urge over, and then again, and yet again—*I do remember, yes; I really do, even if I can't completely fathom why, or how it matters*—therein finding the cooling, coursing feeling of compliance redoubled with each repetition, as if she is not only saying it but really wants to.

If the man is pleased about her urge, though, he doesn't let on. If anything, his demeanor becomes at once again more guarded, polished with practice; he seems unwilling or unable to go any deeper into their relation, satisfied to have won her over to his side. Their interface from that point forward feels so certainly decided, as if now all other bets are off.

"It's getting late out here so quickly these days, wouldn't you say, dear?" she hears the man purr, while hooking his arm gently but firmly into hers. His body's oddly warm contour cleaves onto her completely, in such a way she can't remember how to lurch away, finding herself instead then leaning into him with all her weight. He leads her forward then, as tightly tucked, toward where the limo waits against the wider brightness, his remaining language filling in over all other signal in her head as might the refrain of an ad: "So little time left of all our time, yes, and still so much impending yet to parse."

Inside the vehicle, Alice finds herself surrounded by a similar disorienting sheen as on the outside, the many wide, interior windows only reflecting rather than allowing seeing out. Dozens of replications of her appear at once, captured at endless angles in the glass. Already she can't tell which of them is the most her, she thinks, which at the center, the self she might understand beyond all else.

The car's interior is so cold it seems angular, inflexible, bracing her on edge against the impending silhouette of her exhaustion, even clearer now that she is seated. It feels novel, in a way, to be alone in what resembles a state of luxury, if still in a way she doesn't quite feel fully adjusted to enjoy. The car's interior isn't the same one she'd arrived in before, she realizes, despite how alike it'd seemed when getting in; she already can't even detect where in the mirroring effect here there might still be a hatch to get back out. Nor does she hear an engine start, no sound of idling, though soon she feels the roll of motion underneath her lurching forward, without known destination; no concrete claim between her present state yet and what fate's future.

Suddenly, though, she's woozy then, as with motion sickness, generated in the shift between her expectation's states. She moves to press her forehead against the nearest window's mirror, into her own face, watching her eyes approach her eyes and disappear; then, through the edge of the reflection, held in its darkness, she finds that she can see the wider land beyond: a long, flattened contention scrolling out beyond beneath them, blank as blanched gravel, feeding on and on into itself, a mirror's match for all the still muted sky there just above, revealing nothing.

———

When the man's voice returns, it comes from somewhere through the air held underneath her, as if the shell of the car itself has learned to speak.

"It will be about a fifteen-hour drive," he says, his cadence clearly the same as of the man she'd met outside, though now removed of its familiarity by his face. The volume on the transmitting system is louder than need be; the syllables vibrate through her legs. "We would have flown you, but the board felt in this case, with so many elements yet unclear, it would be best to stay close to the center. Really we were fortunate you could still be accessed at all at this point, given the exposure."

"*Exposure*," Alice repeats. The word on her tongue feels fat in her mouth, too soft, something to swallow, projecting nothing else thereafter left to say.

As if to fill in the silence for her, a compartment in the back of the front seat slides open then at once, toward her face; through it a thick, black, leather-bound folio is passed, falling onto the seat before her as the compartment is again closed.

"You must be sure to correspond with Human Relations before any further media relations," the voice continues. "At this point, non-vital visibility is all but locked down, at least until the system has regained stability. Sadly, it's no longer clear how much of any source can be believed, what is known and not known, and under whose authority beyond our own."

The folio's front and back covers are unmarked, flat in a style Alice finds immediately repellent, though she can't say why. The volume feels heavier than it should for its size and smells like rotten soil when drawn open wide across her lap. The first page is blank, a glossy flyleaf, its sheen invasive, too much shine, and sticky where she touches. Its sheen is clammy, too, even warmer than the cover, an acidic quality to its enamel that itches at her skin in some dissolving way she can't quite feel. She can faintly make out the haze of her form's outline in its finish, there and not there.

The next page, as if to reinforce the flyleaf's reflective quality, reflects her visage also, though this time in the form of an actual photograph, taken some years younger, so it seems—a mug shot, by its context, staring head-on into the camera with her back against a wall, a sign bearing digits held up to her chest. Alice can barely recognize herself, despite her name there: so many dark platelets underlining her sickly skin—*so much like the driver's*, she imagines, if who she's been with then is really driving—and pores large enough to read like Braille; hair cut crudely, as if with safety scissors, by herself; her bloodshot eyes absent of light. *I look undead*, Alice thinks, *or outdated*, though it appears she's wearing the same clothes in the image still today, despite how her shape has changed so much beneath them from year to year, the skin regenerating, recompiling itself against her will. She wishes at once never to have to see herself that way again, and never to have to see any other one who she must be now, such that when she turns the page she knows it's for the last time.

The printed language on the following pages is brittle, pressed deep into the paper, as if stamped by a machine made long ago.

Deposition of Alice Knott

Below the title, blank lines for *Date, Place, Time* have been left incomplete.

The remaining text provides no context outside the transcribed statements.

> **—You understand why you are here?**

> *Because there could never be a format for our identities beyond everywhere we never were.*

Alice reads with her finger tracing along beneath each word, hearing the language of the response in her own voice, as if she were also saying it aloud.

> **—We're not talking about a "we," we're here because . . .**

> *. . . because the door has already been forced open, and now you're feeling extra fucked, yeah? You'd not felt fear like this before, had you, in all your lives, despite all you've seen of others' suffering, frequently even at your own hand—their ongoing trauma, their dementia, the all-consuming darkness. And yet you've already had so many extra chances to survive, so many warnings left*

unheeded. There's no answer I can give that satisfies the
question we've all been asked unending times, through
as many mouths as there are planets.

The dictation sounds familiar, Alice finds; not as if she'd spoken such before, but that she'd *read* it, long ago, so far back it predates any other memory in combination. She finds, then, as she continues, that she can hear the words already in her head before they appear, to the extent she can't tell if she is predicating their arrival, or vice versa.

—*Please state your name.*

My name is yes. My mask, like yours, was skin and organs, the hair and lips that made me desirable, capable of being used. I knew that every word I uttered wasn't mine, but more a code I used to fuse my spirit to the world, a collaboration with our eternal fate but ever-changing, impossible to apprehend. Of course this had been going on as long as there'd been bodies, a looming part of every person who believed they'd ever lived; and where the presence of our predecessors itched in us, it burned, and where it burned it begged for something else: to be let go—to be relieved of the very vocabulary we tried to use to identify ourselves with to one another, to understand, which in truth only made the faith of being so much worse, such that soon only by the destruction of what we thought defined our lives might we be actually allowed to live without a boundary, beyond fate.

In her reflections there surrounding, Alice sees herself seeing herself holding the pages up so she can read, alongside countless others of her in the same phase, on the same line, looking back up at her until again she looks away.

—When did you decide to start burning works of art?

Burned, sure. Or sometimes pummeled, shot to pieces. Sometimes I used sand or water to rip the lines away. In the end, all that mattered was that the transference had occurred; the object had been removed from existence, and so, in no time, from every history, any mind.

—Why?

All decisions were made inside my sleep. When I had a choice to make, I simply lay down and turned my mind off, and when I woke I found each time the damage had already been done. It was the world that did it for me; I was just a fulcrum, if one upon which all prior mechanisms of identity and control depended, unto, in its transition, a different form of bearing truth, one wherein the story we'd been telling ourselves all of this time could be supplanted, given soil in which it might one day actually thrive. But this is just the first step, out of billions, long past the point of turning back; my sole desire for what remains of here and now was simply to cut to the essence of our own image while we still can, to take control of what yet might come after, by any clock: that is, to merge the afterlife with the still living, the future dead; so that we might one day find something to believe in and understand without the heed of our creator, a reason to live long after we're no longer able.

Alice doesn't want to read what she is reading any longer; she wants to close her eyes and seal them shut, to not see the language on this or any page, forever; to instead, for once, find herself anywhere but exactly where she is, each impression interrupted only ever by the future, nothing past; wherein, between the pending words, as she moves through them, less and less space remains than just before, as if they're burning. The sentences, as such, no longer seem composed of only language, but lost mirages, tablature without a song.

—*I'm going to need you to be more specific.*

Of course you are; you who have been left without your own imagination, who have been split apart to hardly fragments despite all your preening. So how's this: My eye was your eye, and what we took on as vision became our bodies. The cells of all of us were whole as a world each, and just as void in hypothetical dimension as our false cosmos. In each direction, the walls of what we would become seized our world over and bound it up, to make it seem like it would disappear as soon as we did, no longer able to go on, which in our hearts we did not want to believe was true no matter how much we wanted to believe it; we could feel it pulsing in our cognition every second as our loved ones grew older, passed away, as the cells in our bodies grew harder and filled with tumors, each trauma slowly gnawing all ambition down to dust as we woke and carried on, trying to find anyone we recognized along the vast debris, desperate to feel belief; and still the longer we existed, the less about us we could still parse apart from any other, so loud did all the wailing come to rise, so numb at every urge were all our nightmares.

Something begins to scrape along the undercarriage of the car, then, Alice feels, metal on metal, only worse the more she attempts to read on through; then the sound is scraping the roof, too, and on either side, as if their passage through the world is turning narrow. The screeching spreads along the linings of her teeth and through her hair down to her skull, chafing her brain beneath the bone at points of spasm, at once then either ending or becoming so immense she can

no longer register the sense, a deafness forced into her diction made only worse by the fact that, still within her, the narration carries on.

—

Imagine there were only eight remaining artworks in the world, for instance. It doesn't matter who made them, though let's assume that whoever did by now had become dead. Let's also assume, which is no long shot, that no one living could remember how to make art, and all we had left were these eight creations built by the hands of people we had never heard speak or could even really imagine walking around on the same land. What would the work mean to us then? Would it seem impossible to understand how it could ever have been conceived? Would we want to make more in its image, or would we despise it?

Recall how when you are born, your mother is a stranger, and you a stranger just the same to her. You sleep at first in nearby rooms; then the rooms grow farther and farther apart; and between them there are other persons, rooms, languages, eyes. Because as our capabilities accrue, so does the need to establish further network: further bodies, memories, to feed the new space over into, and blank to fill it to keep it from its inevitable impossible conclusion. And so you learn to carry the blood you stole and copied from a body most like yours across locations it would have never, could not have ever. And in the make of every instant you become changed, a wholly different person with every second passing, and so each other life too in your wake, every instant of every hour, aggregating for every one of us alone until there is nowhere that is itself and never had been. The result is a greater dementia than already written in the blood of man; a more pure evil; as what is fearsome isn't actually the hole itself, but what lies at the bottom of that which has no actual bottom.

By now, the car is shaking so hard, Alice can't imagine how it could still be moving forward. Outside the glass, too, Alice discovers, pressing her head again against it, looking out, the world has shifted tense: there's nothing left there, not even sunlight, smudge, or concrete, only endless miles of thick white smoke, impenetrable to deeper vision, what could ever lie beyond; then nothing but smoke too where the car should be, or her body, the present page.

—

In the end, all our beauty has taken its toll. Every word we'd ever said had been the inverse of how we meant it, even when it sounded like words we felt we knew and carried on as true tradition, all the vows and prayers and wishes, every I love you, I will always love you, I am here. *And yet we believed each as our own, of course, as we knew no other way to know a reason for anything. From all our failures, the mud of being filled itself in through any space we could not hold, allowing the illusion of more freedom with each indication of our false prowess, so that everywhere we went the world seemed seamless, each instant touching each on either side. Every map we made in our own image was only as incorrect as our perception of the heavens, likewise the distance of dead stars, the depth of dreams. And though the function of our art, our reason for being, or so we thought, had been to try to nail down locations in this blather, provide points of significant recognition, lines of sight, this in turn served only to scourge the scene with more mirages, erroneous conclusions. In such fashion we lined our homes with errors, shit; and still we believed we recognized ourselves there in the onslaught. We slept with such creations hung above our bed, filling our houses, breeding only more amnesia, loss of faith; meanwhile, awestruck within the pretty colors, loops and lines, we were being trampled, filled with sickness, suffocated, killed in our sleep, over and over, high on the conglomerate of fiction, our skin soon nothing more than the grist the whorl of every era used to grease its viral contract: that once we'd lived, so must we pay the everlasting price.*

The longer Alice tries to see, the more it hurts her eyes to try to hold them open, till eventually she can't help but not; she finds the smoke is there behind her face too, inside her skull and through her body, and in all the feel of space around her anywhere she tries to move to pull apart; as if there's nothing different there to pull away to; the same absence alive at every side, each inch crammed in so close there's nowhere other.

—

In the end, the only way you will ever understand anything is to have never seen it; for there to no longer be this sentence or this book, if only in the context that the text of the book allows itself, by having said as much directly, to again become forgotten, or better yet never read and unremembered but by you and you alone; for there must be some difference between a mask and what it masks; all you couldn't even see or hear or feel held up against what remains at any point before your eyes.

What must be shaken loose in our remaining moment is the very mechanism of understanding, the site of the receptors, something more than God at last, the word of God, its whole conception; more than blood or hope or spirit after all; beyond retention, definition, for which we might not even need to live or die, but simply become.

Close your eyes, is what I'm saying. Close your eyes and turn the page.

But Alice's eyes are already closed, she finds; have been for some time. Instead, upon command, she makes them open, and as she does she hears a flash like fire bending through her living mind: a long, hot, rushing hissing, as if the cells and vessels in where her sight works are turning over, rising up.

Where she can feel her flesh, then, thereafter, she feels the pending world beyond it at her edges, pressing, as if to break her bones next, make a wish.

—

The next several hundred pages of the book are blank. Nothing fills the remaining space of the document, as if abandoned or left open for appending; nor then are the words still on the pages she's just read when she flips back through to find her place. The text is missing, absorbed into itself or never there.

—

"What's all this supposed to be?" Alice shouts, aiming her attention toward the partition between her and where the driver should be. She wants to continue the conversation, to deny participation in what the document contends, but instead she inhales and tastes no air, feels nothing flooding in to fill the space where her instinct might have been. Only the silence of the car in motion then remains, a high-end monotonic hum risen over all else, from the core of the machine.

She bangs her fists against the glass for the driver's attention, then her forearms, her whole chest; she buckles back against the seat, kicking with both feet at the same time, gased with adrenaline and rage. No, matter how or where she bashes at it, though, the partition hardly shudders, wholly stronger than it looks, made of more than sight can see.

Alice begins anew, frantic, determined. She pats her hands along the silver surface for a latch, any handle or button to a door or to a window she might access as an exit, and yet she finds only further featureless smoothness to the expanse: nothing clicking or upending, no way out. What is there actually outside where they are, she wonders, if she even could locate a way? Where are they headed, and how long has it already been? She can't remember any idea about where her family's house had been, her bed, her bleating screen; even the high walls of the prison seem better to have been held in than in here, where nothing seems to cohere but in terror.

She finds her phone stuffed in her pocket still, wiped of its memory as it remains, and tries to dial a number, any number, but can't remember who there had ever been to call, each entry ending only in malfunction or yet another open line, as if someone is there listening but not responding. No matter how she bangs around or what she shouts, the space won't change, nowhere else accessible beyond the mirrors' shaping at all sides, which she can see now has begun to go cloudy in her frenzy, her rising captive heat, as if to match the smoke-laced texture of the world beyond, the further queries rushing upward from her slowly drowning sense of any recognition, definition of the day. Where are there even air holes in the car, she wonders, her damp hands shaking as she tries to regain center, catch her breath. How much longer might she survive off of the air trapped in here with her? What else might be done thereafter with what remains?

Her life does not so much flash before her eyes then as thrash around inside her like a caught bird, her concentration all a sprawl and blood thinning out beneath her flesh, flushed up with rising fever in the space behind her face, dragging her down. She wants to scream but cannot, wants to explode but cannot; *there is nothing left that she can dream*, every inch of her is saying, all at the same time, so firmly and completely she can't remember then thereafter what else there had ever been to do but fester, flounder, writhe with fury so overwhelming she can't see straight.

"I can understand why you're disturbed," the man's voice throughout the car at last responds, calmer than ever, self-assured. "It's hard to remember anything at all, isn't it? Much less everything completely and in the proper context, day in, day out. If I may quote you here directly, from perhaps my favorite of all your writings, at least among the ones I've been opened yet to have read: 'Our only human history is a sieve made of innumerable eyes, in innumerable lifetimes, through which the face of hell floods forever.'"

The silence in the car thereafter spans unmeasured time, underscored by the clicking-dragging of the road beneath them, abrading any urge in her response with second thoughts. *The face of hell? All her writings? Human history?* She's no longer sure what she can parse apart from any grasp, nor which of her present feelings or sensations is actually hers, what logic might be connected to the driver's expectations in collaboration with her own; just as there were many rooms in every room all through her life, there were so many expressions in each expression, lives in each mind.

Somewhere there within that sprawl, she thinks, her present person lurks, waiting to discover what it might recover and carry on, bound up in error as it might be, growing only stronger in replication over time, until at long last there is no recognizable host left, only her mutation. And so the same must be true too with every other person, in the same breath—such that when someone begins to feel they recognize wherever she or any other felt they must be, they will at once be no longer in that place, nor had they ever been; the time had already long run past, covered over in its own wake by the pending signals of every other hour, every body; such that even now, when she tries to think of how this day, year, life began, she feels only the turning reels there, the shorting signals; it all just runs back over into itself, feeding data into data, over and over, until *there was never any fact; nothing there even in flashes, fragments of visions*, against which even this cognition framing awareness in her present thinking holds no authority outside its own realm, as the only source of open information.

"Or perhaps you know more than you let on," the voice suggests, in direct countermand, within. "Perhaps your first reaction is a false front, one your blood requires to keep pumping, and behind your face is someone else's, one pre-equipped with all the information of what's meant to happen, its application arriving not by fate, but by the fact of its true self: *what it commands*. As you yourself said, if you might remember, at our inauguration: 'As within every still image stands the place in time that its form had meant to embody, represent, therefore it also holds the forthcoming action it will harbor, what can be revealed only in our most haunted of all nightmares, through which we must learn to confront an otherwise impossible form of every future.' Is that not exactly what you wanted? The very reason that we are here? 'How every you in you is as much you as you are, so every past and every future, for every cell, until we discover how we might obliterate the barrier between emotions, between our very lives and minds and times; to force the signified back up against its signifier; every current second against all others already past and yet to come, forming a continuity at last no longer representable by plot.'"

As Alice hears the words uttered, she finds she can indeed begin to remember having said them; if not in this life, then in one of any of the many she could no longer use to correspond; a dream of monologue not even hers in having performed it countless times, having felt this very moment coming for her in the fit of all the other moments she'd felt she'd chosen her own way, but part of an inevitable conclusion she would have come to no matter how many different ways she tried to make the record skip, to turn away from what awaited and go elsewhere; not like a predetermined position, not quite, but one she accessed most directly in fear; the rub of all she really wanted welling up within the darkness of having had to go through it alone, to know the dire consequences of even living, as a performance, and still commit to going on, to rising and revising, in the name of doing what she must; which, already, in the wide tow of it, feels not at all like what she meant; the darker urges of collaboration with unwanted forces having infected her intentions with all their years of clawing, gnawing, bearing down, to the point that no matter what she might have ever wished would appear at last in her own life, she no longer wants anything to do with it at all; not here, not anywhere; not now, not ever. Each word she tries to stutter seems to mean something different from what it should; the gleam in the glass of the windows buzzing as if to shock her, slit her to ribbons; no beyond; the blood within her rolling over, coming up in nausea, filling her mouth, her lungs, her guts; no clear condition or idea to anything about her.

Alice holds her breath and closes her eyes. She tries to bear inside her mind the current second, then rewind it, to remember how she'd ever come into this day; how any string of passed hours could have ended as they have and placed her here, inside this car, this body. She can feel no entry point into her person, no particular dimension from which the person she'd turned into took its form. So much time had been spent exactly like this, forward and back; no path ahead from any point she could recall that might have led here, now, wherever that was, much less to find herself within an aspect shared in name by so many other lives desiring the same answers, in the same time. How could any second ever actually pass, then, and unto whose future?

She sees herself as from a remove then, as through her own face onto another face beyond, finding herself seated then not in a moving vehicle but in the padded chair inside her father's den, where he'd spent the last years of his life locked away, reading in silence, just like her now; a room familiar to her now in its dimensions and yet still disconnected given how she'd never been allowed inside it long enough to gain its trust. Still spread open in her lap is the black book, the same one he'd been reading on the night he died, she realizes, all those years, its binding loose and water-damaged, worn apart, in his edition, while in her own version the pages remain so sharp and unblemished, somehow brand new. She has been reading for some time like this, she knows, though she can't remember how long or what was said; she feels younger than she's ever been, unable to compare the present with the past; and yet she can still feel where the book's borrowed language assumes traction in her memory, every line briefly banging around inside her head until it is turned loose on by the next; the same way the days seem to have been full of glass; how there always seemed something hidden here that should not be hidden, something pressed beneath the letters in each line; and so something too beneath where they appear and scrawl inside her, taking hold.

The more she reads, too, the harder it is to remember she is reading, the networked pressure now surrounding her attention only compounding as she seeks to shake free of her impression of the present, a sudden, blank wall rising up inside her mind between her and any further information. Against her lap, the book feels so heavy, warm, as if it needs her, can imagine no other reader, no other way. She runs her fingertips along its spine and up around the unmarked cover, down the deckled edge, along the flaps, allows the slickened surface to slice into her fingerpads, slitting open tender flaps that then spew oily resin from their hollow, long tiny draughts of yellow smoke that dissipate at once across her face, making it almost impossible to breathe, much less go on reading.

▬

When Alice looks again, it's like rewinding. The world is overridden, mum, just out of reach. The condensation on the windows, as she can make them out from in the patchy blind, has turned to full wet, as has her hair and clothing, dark with sopping. She sees herself again in every pane, each of her younger than she still feels now, having seen nothing of their own she hasn't seen; on each of their fingers, one of the same rings she is wearing, no matter how she tries to pull them off, first tugging at her own fingers, then in her mind, through all the glass's fast impressions, the dark loops' tension growing only tighter on her hand, swelling as if to cut right down through to the bone. As she tries to push herself up out of herself, to force the grade of space another way, she sees that none of her innumerable reflections correspond, their bodies remaining motionless, all looking at her, held in place, each holding their own version of the leather-bound text spread open on their laps. And the same in her own lap, she finds; her eyes swim across the empty page, across which a scrolling line of live teleprompted language begins appearing, passing just slow enough for her to skim before again it disappears.

> *Major artworks in more than thirty countries are attacked in the broad daylight, bent up by men and women, young and old. When asked for comment, some refer directly to the name of Alice Knott; others remain purposeful in silence, or in derangement.*

She finds, too, within the reading, that what is described no longer pertains to who she is, what she has done, but a resolution culling from it; a kind of *future present*, perhaps, force-fed through aggregated news, transcribed in font both diminutive and garish, filling the space between them with its command.

> *The videos proliferate online, a discontinuous stream of shaky documentation of acts of vandalism. Museums both national and local close their doors and lock them, and some who don't are asked to do so by local police forces, until some more manageable solution can be reached.*

Alice can hear the others of her breathing, through the mirrors. They turn their pages as does she, each bringing the book closer and closer to her face as the print seems to grow smaller and smaller as she reads.

> *The uproar spills over into the outdoors, leaked like an overflow of water onto water, commingling temperatures apart, against the very ground we'd clasped for granted as it continued aging beneath our feet. The world is wide, full of its figments: A woman takes a sledgehammer to the Vietnam Memorial one clear and sunny day in Washington, state the reports. She's able to disfigure names across nearly two square feet of surface area before restraint, also injuring several*

officers and hero citizens in the process. A glinting froth
pours from her mouth, its bright white color captured
on camera as she barks and flails and blinks her eyes,
as if broadcasting a pattern. Later this same day, six
students throw themselves off the roof of the Whitney
Museum in New York, killing none, but causing brain
damage in four, paralyzing one from the waist down;
the sixth is fine, unscarred as if it had never happened;
she is placed under arrest and later successfully kills
herself banging her head against a wall.

Alice can no longer see the book there in her hands, so close to her
face now is the paper; nor can she see her hands or the arms connected
to her flesh, her body, what outside. The words are all there is, then all
there ever has been.

Within seventy-two hours, additional assaults have
been made inside America on the Lincoln Memorial,
the Washington Monument, and the Gateway Arch;
and on foreign soil against the Sphinx, the Great
Wall, the Eiffel Tower, the Parthenon, Easter Island,
as well as structures designed by Le Corbusier, Frank
Lloyd Wright, Rem Koolhaas, I. M. Pei. Armed guards
are assigned to other major monuments identified as
potential targets in continuous shifts, even as new
masses stand in lines to see the icons of a past they can't
remember, newly enthralling for their vulnerability,
the revived reminder that they one day might no longer
appear, regardless of what they might have meant to
stand for. By day's end, sectors of most major modern
cities have been regimented into gridlock, designed to
prevent unwanted action of any kind. From overhead,

the shots of enforced order look almost peaceful, silent from their distance, pocked with unnatural light, as upon the world there hangs a listening vigil. It would seem unreal were it not shown this way, like every unknown wish unfulfilled in transit from the heart of man, pushed in through the holes in all our senses, the fiber in our feelings, coming open.

There's nowhere else; no way to turn from here but toward what world might wait beyond the windows passing beyond sight. Each sentence seems to last a lifetime in its rendition, its transient texture spreading further wider and thinner against its own known definition until there's nothing left, including silence, its idea; no frame within which someone she once recognized or even loved could appear anywhere but buried in her, not even a name.

And on and on, the world over, still further works remain left out alone to bear their witness to any person who might come. In the night, unknown further creations are punched and stabbed and shot at and spit on and defaced, using screwdrivers, hammers, nails, scalpels, fingers, fists; sculptures are knocked off of their displays, the signals report, denting or chipping or becoming shattered on the hard floor into innumerable fragments, a finer dust that never could be gathered up and none alike; leaving only the understanding of what has been initiated in their undoing, in acts ranging from seething violence to an almost hypnotic glee, against works that had survived the multiplying means of nature and the want for preservation, through wars and riots, destitution and loss of mind; having been held captive even longer

in private quarters by collectors and historians and
restorers and hoarders and the investors and the rich
and bored; years of sunlight or electric fading all colors
as natural rot and erosion and friction faded the
shapes, even when restored time and again by minds
armed with science and good intentions, still resulting
in collaboration against the object's will; as whoever
touches any creation as well becomes part of it, and
who stands before it has existed in its field. In this
way, the unreal is made real, and the real is made
even more impossible to distinguish or identify,
much less to parse, passed as it has been through
so many sets of eyes and ragged instants bending
its premise beyond the grasp of recognition in our
bones, and still allowed somehow to spread its image
through space and time, against our will, until at
last we're left with what seems no choice but to lash
out; to stake our claim on our own minds through
some illusory version of new vengeance, in the name
of preservation of our own kind; and therein to
imagine we might be able yet to take back at least
a portion of the simulation of control, over the very
terms on which our spirit had been fomented and
transacted after all, against the unyielding panoply
of replications and inundations exercising their
authority on what still remains our lost faith, by
now spread so far and thin across our embodiment's
terrain that it becomes difficult to know if we are or
were ever actually alive, much less where and when
ever again we might stake a sense of hope or wonder
in any claim, left as we have been with so little sense
of recognition and even less still left to lose.

Alice turns to see herself again reflected and can make out only where there isn't what there was before she looked. *The air is ripping. The day is ripping. The world all overwritten. Nothing there.* Her neck is leaking fluid, a bright black oil slicking her shirt. Her arms aren't helping. She can't see anything; then she can see too much. *Infinite colors. Her unfather's voice.* He's reading to her as he would sometimes while her mother drove, the only time any of them were allowed to hear his stories. No one would tell her where they were going. They put a mask over her eyes. So many voices there alongside, then, multiplying, till it was like some infernal party she was not allowed to bear, one to which by the time they arrived she'd already fallen asleep, every time, the taste of metal in her mouth, unable to stand.

> *Notorious public figure Alice Knott, age fifty-nine, was executed today by lethal injection at federal facilities in A., less than eight days after being found guilty on all counts by a local jury of her peers.*

The unfather's breath against her neck, slurring his words again, this time in an infernal, cartoonish tone, like the occasional narrator of their favorite program, who through the screen would sell them dream vacations that never came; vitamins that claimed to cure all sickness and yet only made you tired, inconsolable; survival packs in case of plague, full of enough nonperishables to last a lifetime without leaving the house. Her mother cackling from the front seat, smoking out the window, strange rotten smoke; and her brother or unbrother there beside her, laughing right along, while at the same time squeezing her hand so hard she thought he'd pop it.

> *In a final statement, delivered flat on her back with eyes unblinking, Knott accepted blame for everything she'd done, as well as everything she'd failed to. She*

*expressed regret and a sincere wish for peace in the
lives of all those her actions had affected, both those
living and those no longer alive. Witnesses report that
she refused to close her eyes, staring straight on into the
two-way mirror behind which hundreds sat, come to
bear witness.*

Somewhere the wind beyond the car. The glass against her fists, thin
as a hiss, yet no less firm a place to bash her head in. Screaming for
a doorway, keys to the locks. Begging for someone at last to explain
to her the reasons, how to be. Feeling her brother's fingers then
constricting around her own, so tight she can no longer move; his
pulse so near to her own as he inhales in awe, sliding the metal band
off of her left hand and then at once onto his own; a matching ring
for each of them, just like their parents, as it had long been meant to
be, through all their lives. Then she can no longer feel the child there,
nor the seat's lines, the car's interior, any partition.

*Alice Knott is survived by no known kin. Memorial
services will be held in her hometown of X. tonight at
six o'clock and are open to the public.*

She finds that she can control her face again, then, at least a little. Her
arms are heavy and hard, like miles away, nearly impossible to hold up
long enough to claw at the hot cloth across her eyes until she's bleeding;
through veils of winding color. She is able, then, to see beyond the
light. Just above her, a breach has opened in the chrome, some kind of
sun roof. Somehow she can see it beyond all else; the sky above them all
a gore, full with a ripping wind beyond any further possible narration.

It takes all she can muster, gums clenched and breathing, seething
through the woozy pain that blurs her legs, for her to rise to press

against the long warm surface of the vehicle, pushing blind out on through its vibrant opening, head, shoulders, hands, into the rush at once so overwhelming it conforms around her body.

> *In lieu of flowers, interested parties are encouraged to send donations to the New International Preservation Effect, a mutual outreach initiative by ExxonMobil, Facebook, Void Corporation, and the Marines, fostering cross-cultural intersections in creative expression and innovation.*

The land sprawls out beneath her far and wide. She can no longer see the roof of the car so close against it, the muggy white metal becoming seamless with her skin, her arms somehow so long now she can almost reach beyond its breadth, feeling the cream-like whipping of the blur of land beyond as it blasts past—into more and more of the same remaining blank of solace; carried forward on against her will, toward anywhere she can't remember, her only mind remaining all full of platelets, a humming mold allowed at last to come alive.

There's nothing to see, finally, even with eyes open, no form of act or wish so clear as what is not—a thriving, waking cleft of broken, numbing air, so much like all that she remembers having swept across her life, binding all their hours held on in hope through entertainment, the unending anticipation of which had for so long been the only reason she survived, perpetually awaiting what could at last no longer be extended, day by day, pulled at last beyond the reach of any eye, all possible communication thereafter held indecipherable, impossible, part of a script without an actor, any lines.

Alice can't imagine what else there is to do then but to pull the rest of herself up through the opening. Her remaining flesh weighs nothing underneath, easy as feeding to hoist her lower half up through the hole behind the rest, the ongoing lines of lurch that form the world sculpting her engagement in it like a hand on arid clay. No sooner than she's through, she feels the space beneath her become closed up, at once again made seamless with the rest of all as it remains, the ground and sky beyond her overridden, splitting and smoothing itself over and over so fast it all seems at last to disappear: all her hours, all the language, the further silence flooding up and filling her there from within, absorbed into the very possibility of her own life. There isn't a story left to tell, then; nor any sensation or response; not a thought but to be carried forward, through the nothing.

All space coursing around her has become scrambled, full of heat. Corrupted flowmarks course the edges where every previous surface had once been. She can hear no sound of any life, no mutual presence in the present, rewound and pressed forward at the same time. All potential plot points now seem pressed together and held together, all at once, as if they'd never previously existed uncombined, smoke pouring out from the shape of any space drawn out from underneath and above her, from anywhere and anyone she'd ever been.

Alice claps her hands and holds her breath. She listens to the lines there spreading out within her, resolving into numbers without names—some kind of final prayer devised in her adrenaline as someone else's life flashes through her eyes.

She knows what she is meant to do before she does it, not because it has been written for her, but because it's all there is, all there ever had been, the only way; where as she throws herself headfirst into the blur of the world as it remains, all motion seizes, splits apart, having at last reached its source; the lost, fat vastness of all that she can remember how to feel now torn apart through its transference into fate.

0004

Alice is standing in the foyer of her home. She doesn't recognize the space at first, turning from facing the portrait mirror to look out into the front sitting room. She registers not what is there so much as what is off: no decorations on the walls now, no standing rust-colored wardrobe into which she and other guests could place their clothes, for so long full of countless strangers' forgotten garments, parts of costumes. Also missing is the way the room had always felt, a childish sense of private timelessness she'd been able to maintain most days within the space's forever-lurking smell of scorched sugar, a too-warm air until the dark came.

And where before there had been an exit from here to outside, now there's none; instead, only her clear awareness of where it'd been, pinned by the one small diamond-shaped window once installed at the missing door's center, for looking out, not in, and through which Alice can see—in place of where there'd once been a porch, a path, a stoop, trees, a street leading to more streets, houses, people—now only lawn, stretching out wide and far in all directions; and where in the sky above she sees no sun, no cloud or plane, but endless flatness, so sharp it's hard to look at.

Behind her, then, turning around, Alice finds Smith, the driver, who has followed her inside or must have. A spitting image of him, anyway, except for where the scar along his throat seems to have completely healed, the skin all smooth now and unbroken, and instead of a suit he's wearing white. He studies her wondering as if in awe, parsing his reaction to her reaction, which makes her only that much more aware of what is different in the space; yet her gait remains calm, her face vacant of remorse or consternation, for after all the house had always felt this way, had it not? Even before it hadn't?

How long have they been standing here, for instance? It seems forever, one of so many iterations of the same duration, identical but in small ways that only she could ever feel. In the next room, Alice finds the furniture gone missing, done away with: sofa and coffee table and rugs and chandeliers and lamps, leaving not even marks of wear from where they'd sat so long. The walls are blank as walls can be, not even bearing any signs of common use, pins or smears, cracks in the settling; nor are there windows, ways to let light in, even lamps, though she can see throughout the house clearly, each space's illumination somehow innate.

A corresponding absence spans all the house's other spaces, or so she finds, leading her companion forward through it, from room to room. Food and hardware are gone from the kitchen; beds gone from the guest bedrooms, and from her own, as if the evacuation that took place upon Richard's leaving has now been ultimately fulfilled, with nothing left. Some places where doors had once been now have none, the wall spread flat over its prior partition, scouring any passage into what had once been just behind.

Even her unbrother's bedroom, which she can't remember ever having entered, now stands with door left open for what seems to her the only time ever, its would-have-been contents likewise missing, the scuffed but freshly polished hardwood floors hardly bearing any remnant of how she would have once imagined the sick room's captured content, though it retains its haunted air. The room's layout is an exact copy of her own bedroom's, Alice realizes: the same placement of the closets and sharply sloping ceiling, a lone thin window above where there had always been a bed, too high to try to see out of from the floor; the only window remaining in the house, so it appears. She can sense the same strange lurking quality she felt about the wall between them all those years ago as she brushes her hand along it now, feeling for the first time what it would have been like to stand where he did, her unbrother, at least supposedly, in parallel to her own young self there on the far side, as if the wall were only a soundstage partition. She feels the urge to step up and pull it back, then, to reveal how their two rooms in fact had always been one, divided only for the illusion of privacy; such that all she'd ever had to do to see him there beside her was reach out, offer her hand.

Smith, having followed her in here, is staring at her even more intently now, face fixed with a strained grimace, as if he can't not smile or doesn't really wish to, its stricture stronger than whatever other urges might want his muscle. He seems to have to tell her something, to clarify why they are here, but as had she so many times prior, he can't make his body cooperate beyond ulterior designs. He looks so much thinner than when they'd first met, she decides, unsure now when that was, his skin pulled taut around the cheekbones, his hair more sparse and brittle, his pupils shrunk to almost nothing, the surrounding corneas all bloodshot, dry. She tries to find the words to draw him out, to ask him how they've ended up here, where her belongings are, what he even wants in following her around, but finds she too still can't quite remember how to speak or what to say. The air feels tense within her, or folded over, though she is not sure what that means; it's something her unbrother would have said, she imagines, air folded over, not quite her; the logic of his language now within her somehow, having at last allowed her into his room, a trace of underlying meaning transferred over in the rendition, perhaps, by just breathing his old air. When she tries to scroll her mind back through any prior perspective of who she is or how she's been, she finds only traces of a much more distant common past, all of it having already been invaded and revised by Richard, through and through her, connecting back to childhood hours spent together before he'd ever occurred to her, in her mind, coming unpressed: him and her, posing together in dress clothes pretending to be robots, without feelings; dreams of other planets they had shared in whispered secrets in their own language, untranslatable to any else; the gifts of glass beads, packs of magic powder, little knives they'd passed back and forth, each promising to keep them safe for when they would be needed; so many secrets laced day in, day out, in all the hours she'd used to cover over their ambitions and ideas; so much they had shared and weathered out together that she'd shuttered off or else erased.

Each of these phantasms, as she regards them, seems still more real to her than all the rest. She feels the pang of an awakening nostalgia resonating in the flattened absence of all else the house had held, despite how still in every one of those memories she can still feel the burning, itching underneath, how his face at all points remains blurred, sharing features with so many sorts of nearby passing faces; his person just off camera always, but without question really there, primary director of the production of his own meaning in her life, against her will; at the same time so strong and interlinked with all the rest of all there is—her house, her life, her mind—that she can no longer remember exactly how to explain what might have made her feel this forced distortion in her bloodlines, father or unfather, unbrother and no brother, death and life. That whole idea of something shifted in their balance—was it another of the ideas she and he had made up, *collaborated on*, she wonders, just then; some kind of system of bizarre games, one within which the longer she embraced it, the more completely any passing hour seemed to slip away, becoming written over, filled with ransom, until soon she could no longer tell the difference between feeling and believing, neither more true than any other, all the rest?

It's so easy, she thinks, suddenly, to see, to understand: the perception of so much change within her life, the sprawl, the warping, had been functions of life itself, each flaw a fact she must learn to include in her definition of what the world was at any moment. Had she begun to tell herself it was all not hers, but someone else's, a darker side of the same coin? How much hidden pleasure had she taken in letting her father be erased, while feigning horror, all time in tow thereafter all spent conditioning herself to be anybody but who she was? How much could have been so different for her if she'd only accepted her own life at once and without question, and so how different the world?

Smith, by now, is wholly beaming, his head so flush it seems his skin might come apart. He watches her as if he too can hear the words dictated in her head: how the same effect as she must feel now could be found as true of every other person, in their own distortions of their experience of life, bridging the gap between what they'd always wanted and what was, if only just to stay afloat, to be able to survive at all amid so much shock as must be required to even live. Such ongoing misapprehension formed the foundation of all life, she understands, the crumbling ground on which we wandered, the shifting light that filled the time between our eyes. Every inch of everything was and had been always teeming with what it wasn't, in congregation, over and over, on and on, such that only by becoming carried up within it, buried by it, would it ever sanctify her, let her be.

This observation is no less untrue than any else, Alice decides; only another part of her corrupted drive learning to re-create itself in its own image, an understanding—as manufactured as any—to illuminate how they've wound her down, turned her so hard and fast against her so many times, throughout so many lives, until she might at last completely acquiesce, on her own terms, which had been the whole point from the beginning, had it not? All her family had ever wanted for her, and all anybody ever, was to have the unnavigable immensity of being at last pulled down so tight around her that there was nothing more for her to do but let the others have their way; to make of her own life what most might suit them in the mirage of yet becoming entirely one's self, even while knowing that there would always be another lurch yet to come within the full collapse, how each would end up only yet another wrong beginning, and thereby made only stronger, more all-consuming, as we race forward along a fast unfolding present track that might only ever find a destination once in forfeit under one and all, at last, and whereby the living lines of any future could be found encoded only in her flesh, in the wake of which, with no way back and no beginning, we might begin to see what's yet to come.

They head back through the house the way they came, she and Smith, the only Smith she can remember. She can feel him right there beside her even with their arms linked, moving as she moves, eventually snaking his large, cold palm into her own, as would a child. As if triggered by this, she seems to take the lead, dragging them together forward into space; he seems now only able to follow along, waiting for her to make her own conclusions and decisions, which he must then go along with; *as if without her nothing else might ever be again, or ever have been at all.* She finds she wants him to understand her now, or her intentions: to see the house as she'd once seen it, decorated end to end with such fanciful nostalgia that he might relate to how different it is now, for better or for worse; though already knowing at the same time that nothing she could say might make him feel as she does.

And yet there's still one location he needs to see, Alice realizes, a location known in her mind as *the scene of the crime.* Most of the rest of the house bears nothing in her already any longer, not really, even in doting, each memory only more fodder for a hollow sort of heart, around which the true nature of the house had learned length by length to hide its face, somehow leaving only the occasion of intrusion and invasion as patent, real, amid the lacking texture of all else. Indeed, she finds the door down to the vault still right there as it had once been installed, the structure's metal rigging affixed into the surrounding brittle drywall of the remaining subject like a suture, out of place, and yet providing a sense of comfort to Alice in its definitive location, its persistence against all else.

Behind the door, as there had last been, are the stairs, fashioned of the same material as the door's smooth, silver metal, providing continuity to its frame; though now the steps seem shallower than before, Alice thinks, with barely enough room to put her foot down and not feel like falling. Nor are there handrails on either side, whereas before some days the rails were the only way she'd gotten down the stairs in the first place, inebriated beyond invention. Once they've started down, though, the descent begins to feel more usual, despite how the ongoing distance appears to span much longer than she remembers, begetting further lengths and lengths of such precarious balance, their manufacture now set in a spiral so as to shield the way forward and back both, eventually continuing so far that Alice imagines there might never be another checkpoint; as if either course might only go on and on forever in their way, beyond the necessary makeup of the physical landscape, where it ends and somewhere else entirely takes hold.

But then, like that, they're at the bottom, where again all looks the same as it once had been: the small metallic alcove, slick and featureless but for the flat vault's door and the panel requiring her passcode to proceed. As for the code, she'd typed it in so many times it had become a second nature, and yet for some reason Alice finds now, in midst of approach, that the muscle memory does not deliver; in the digits' place in her head, instead, she finds only other spooling strings of unrelated numbers bound together: her age, for instance, its ever-changing value, the days and dates all stuck together in her mind, each wanting its own significance in the fray where dates, phone numbers, page numbers bang around, mobbed beyond application. Suddenly there seem infinite possible combinations she might once have known. Any string of numbers now might be the one solution, all possible monikers ready for meaning in your context, claiming their own weight.

Amid her hesitation, Alice sees Smith move past her, his demeanor suddenly stirred to active, if still without expression, bearing no word. With all the fingers on both hands, then, as Alice watches, he starts to type at length into the pad, inputting hundreds of sequential characters as if typing out a sentence, a paragraph, a page. It might go on like this for the rest of their lives, Alice thinks; perhaps they could remain here on the far side of the vault door forever, stalled in the process of approach, remaining only ever in transition, not quite knowing what's to come; which is how it had always felt, as Alice lived it, never knowing at which stroke the falsely endless feed might at last be called complete, until it is, and they are in.

Beyond the door, the world around them opens up. They are in a lobby, or something like one, like the processing chamber from the prison but even larger, the walls farther apart and half translucent, rising high up to a glass ceiling that fills the room with artificial light. It's no longer certain which door in the wall behind them is the same they'd just come in through, already sealed shut and indistinguishable from the countless other doors on either side, lined up to fill the wall in both directions as far as the room goes.

Nor is it clear, yet, where they should stand. All directions seem the same direction, Alice senses, her eyes unfocused as the space around her seems to bloat, in search of traction, any firm feature. Not until she looks high above them, at the massive wall spanning the space's farther perimeter, do her eyes light on an image, so wide it's almost impossible to even really see. She strains to fix a context amid its overwhelming breadth, its hues glistening and shifting on reception, like gasoline. She finds the prospect can only be realized sector by sector, making the rest of the room there seem to disappear into it, hidden in plain sight.

The image is a portrait of a woman, Alice recognizes then, leering hard against the wide room's open glow. No, not only one woman, she resolves, but two, so much alike: twins, it seems, each young enough yet to grow up into something so much different; their faces thin, forbidding, at once ubiquitous and anonymous, open to drift. Their white bodysuits resemble matching horsehides, the flesh of either indistinguishable from the other in the frame, their limbs commingled as through one torso, sharing a blood. Each wears a metal band on her right hand, much like the one on Alice's own finger, she remembers, finding it suddenly tightening and burning in recognition against her flesh, though theirs are each mounted with a setting: the left figure's a garnet, the right's an aquamarine, the precious texture of each somehow an eyeful in its own right, overpowered only by the women's doubled, mesmerizing gaze. They appear to look right back at everything that might regard them, including Alice and her companion, as one and the same—a boundless, edgeless gaze, stern but without judgment—while also assuming some sort of reflection of any viewer's face, Alice's and Smith's alike, just exactly as they would appear to one another in the moment, in a way that any others also looking on must see their own faces rendered live, sculpted to appear to have existed forever on the massive canvas—*so as to each viewer, their own hope.* Behind them, in the portrait's background, a flood of cinder lines the world for miles, its boundless blackened landscape leading flat off into a silver sky that seems to extend into the very structure of the building, the very ground on which Alice herself stands.

▄▄▄

Where has she seen this scene before? Alice thinks, for some reason now in third person. *Why does it seem like something's about to rip straight through its shell?* She feels detained somehow in the image's presence, full of such overwhelming stillness that she can hear the liquid running through her veins, its emphasis so large and loose around her that it seems to run beneath her, through the floor, on and on somewhere far below the earth's curved surface. She might go on standing forever just like this, she then imagines, under the women's inert gaze, waiting to be granted an understanding previously impossible but through them and them alone. *And so you shall,* she hears them seethe, suddenly communicable beyond a need of tongue. *We had been alive there in every book you'd ever read, in every film and program you'd nodded off during, just out of frame until unseen; there in your sleep, too, tracing the locations between nightmares, which looking back from here spans your whole lifetime; until, at last now, at the center of only our attention, here you are.*

All motion, all other interaction, before this present second had been for Alice out of focus, or rather, out of frame; any questions she might have had, now or ever, about her life or how it went are done away with under their gaze, *gripped of an unscriptable logic,* so they are saying, *one made accessible only in having been at last relieved of the apparition of ourselves.* Such rationale, burst free from her prior forms of thinking, thereafter obscures all other fleeting sensory effect, shaping a feeling that thereafter retrofits itself through how it is, *all the rest bound up in false nostalgia, bought and sold to each as their own brand.* Which, at last, is not a pleasure, Alice understands, but endless pain; to know once and for all that, within what had once seemed one's own existence, they had only ever been playing along, not even for any present audience, but for themselves, in living misery at the ragged end of an era in which humans had imagined fertile purpose, exposed emotion, even pride, each even less their own than she'd imagined; that any person's life, in its ongoing manufacture, had been both the means by which they'd been tricked into signing off their only rights, in hopes of being retained in future seasons of a show that never aired, and also the precedent thereafter, preventing any further claim on what else they might have otherwise committed to, become.

The subsequent corresponding fissure—between Alice and herself, in collaboration with the women's faces overhead, the lengthless size behind their eyes—echoes in Alice's ears and all throughout her person, then and now, an instantaneous and overriding revision of the vocabulary of the present, such that suddenly *to not remember* is *to see*, and *to want to act* is *to feel time lurch out from underneath us, negating the very space where it had been*; and so too, at last, can she see each other self as she remembers it alike within the prior landscape of her life, each presence designed inside its own mind as the center of all experience, so desperate for traction that it would seize the world unto its end; each never dying in its own mind's understanding as it was never actually alive.

Above the image hangs a massive, shining title card, floating in its message made of curling neon, crimson and silver edged with every color underneath, welcoming the viewer to the room at last: VOID.

Something like centuries must pass then, so it feels; each hour in them absent of view, where the only measure of the time passed is time itself, not unlike how it might have felt to have her life remembered for her by someone else.

It is only Smith's voice, there just behind her, that breaks her thrall. His tone is lower, older than she remembers, nor is the effect quite even speech, suffused instead with clicks of tongue and heavy breathing. Smith himself, however, appears to understand exactly what he's saying, forcing the ongoing articulation despite how he can't seem to stop blinking his eyes, his skin so oily now it's like he's leaking, turning to mush. He looks even more memorable in such condition, Alice finds, like some actor in his most celebrated role, having wound his way into her life after decades of recurring appearance in the costume, if still always inherently *himself* just underneath, though no longer quite so free.

He raises his arm then, pointing above them at the looming image of the women. *This would be the last work of any living artist,* Alice can hear him impressing upon her then, a fact not carried through him as spoken, but by measuring his impression against the developing direction of her mind, within the nature of their scene's ongoing production. *It has been made for only you,* the script seems to hold, *both in your image and to end it, at last no longer needing to survive, such that when you turn away, it will be for the last time, and after which we cannot speak.*

Alice finds her head around her mind's eye already nodding, incorporating—*yes*—while beneath the lining of her flesh she feels the logic disseminating, binding her blood flow, her aging organs, all that she is with some necessary glue, like ambient music loosening within her where any prior understanding might have fried and come apart; it feels as if her very ability to feel is reformatting, given the new evidence now writhing in her linings like poison gas into a cave, taking with it too any sense of balance, any intention. Thereafter her vision feels divided into two: into who she had to have been to do what she'd done to get here, and who she is now as a result, even as each alike still go on changing even thereafter, no longer bound in their resolve. She can only go on seeing double, then, in trails of rubbled color, her arms suddenly so heavy that their connective tissues might soon rip, the glands along her neck bulging, full of cold, dark liquid, itching down the veins inside her hands, her buzzy knees. The room spins, somehow both around her and within her, as time itself elongates, becoming dragged.

Like the recurring glitch in the screenlight of the computer she'd so often slept with before the fire in their first house—which she could not remember until now—whose flames had taken over so much more than she could remember, in both her perception and her kind. How each day she'd always felt she'd already dreamt what was going to happen the night before, unable to shake the feeling not of simply already knowing what was coming, but of doing it all wrong, as if her performance of it meant more than any action, a feeling broken only upon the impact of her fainting every morning when trying to stand up from the bed, her head heavier than the rest of her, forever.

Alice can see herself only as from inside herself, she understands, watching as if she's already watched herself in this exact scene once before, somewhere, on a screen—*so many nights*, she thinks, *not just today; so many lifetimes*—though this time she can still feel where she might be alive inside the moment, given the ability, in *turning over*, to *actually perform*. She has never had a moment like this before, where she felt so directly linked to her own fate; until now so much of her life has felt like one long do-over, fanned through the wishes of so many others, their own faces forced into remand—for once this *now* has never had another, and never will, but rather something more like the reverse—as once she had experienced herself as such, she can't go back, a surface scraped so thin there's nothing left.

Around the edges of the room, then, Alice hears the sound of wider grinding against the fade inside her head, followed by an even lower bloat, like putty pressed into her ears from both sides, dropping the pressure. Her scope of vision follows, panning as might a camera toward the rows of stacking doors. Far down along the widened space, she sees, all pale fat bright and bare of detail, a door comes open from the outside. Another woman appears there in the cracked light, then: one dressed the same as Alice finds herself now, in the same white gown she had worn both day and night, her preferred costume throughout the years alone. On the woman's right hand's ring finger, a gemless band just like Alice's. Behind her, too, another man, dressed like Smith but with a slightly different face, familiar but of a different era. They both look back at Alice, seemingly not surprised to find her, but certain, steely, as if they'd known exactly how this would happen, had been waiting their whole lives to step into action, to replace her.

This man is wearing his own ring too—as is her own Smith, Alice realizes, turning toward him now, his own eyes closed against the appearance of their matching pair. The nearest man now seems unable to be able to stand the others' sudden presence, for some reason, bending at the knees there in a sudden pain that makes him ill, though Alice herself seems to feel nothing at all in their wake, only conceptually able to understand the way her flesh no longer has the will, or perhaps rather lacks the *utility*, her body's linings long since trained to undermine and then absorb any urge once seen as instinct, premonition, before it surfaces. Her body has at last reached its full exhaustion, beyond the point of all return—a fact she does not fear, at last, but fully embraces, leaning in to how the world thereafter seems to drown within itself, the once-surviving lifeforce felt even in strangers, in the inanimate, all run together, so flat as the horizon, all the land she'd never touch.

Alongside the door just opened, Alice sees then, another door follows likewise, and thereafter quickly yet another farther down; then countless more doors in the same way together, one by one or ten by ten, stacked and clustered, as through each doorway further versions of her enter—all different ages, sizes, brought in pairs, from endless iterations of her life; persons she might have even been once, in her imagination, while they in turn believed it was themselves who held her place; making Alice, then, the true stand-in in her own history, from their perspective, changed in and out so many times. Each is accompanied alike by strange companions, such as Smith: persons she had spent time with or passed by in rooms long elsewhere, through all the old scenes and landscapes she'd lived among and soon let go, here modeled to perform her, in reflection; a swift cast of innumerable selves, pouring forward for as long as she can see in the constrained space, door after door, life after life, dressed in the same clothes, rings on each finger, performing a lost expression in their eyes, and still more coming in through other entrances the room blossoms into, most so far away already she can hardly parse their bearing from the rest, obscured among her more intangible memories as they cohere, a fever screen of all the mislaid reflections of her life.

The tightness of the gauze around her neck and wrists, the cold wet swabs, as the men, the family's "doctors," had held her down and fixed her, still so young, certain there must be some way to connect her person to the kind of child that they'd always wanted. Her actual father's hands holding the book up as they read aloud together every night before they took him, at last having broken through the fine print on the pact that'd held our lives together all this time. Or the earsplitting sound the moon made when she watched it too long, the summer before the production crews began to block whole plots of land once called public; how much it hurt each time the clapper clicked, no matter how often she heard it or how far she might believe she'd gotten after walking offset. How some nights in the house it had seemed there was no door that didn't lead back to the room she had just come in through, no way out.

None of that had really happened, until it had, Alice understands; her every action surrounded by the fact of what was not. Each faded flash of prior timeline slides in upon her as through a spiral, searching for slits in which it might become installed, its software overwriting what had been previously expected; a life made up of cavities and rifts, all barely held together within her against the future possibility of pushing through, understanding herself as who she was, not who she wanted, much less anybody else. And still they can hear the others of her, in her image, sorting through her thinking, each emerged person's sense of self and life's desire pending in upon her from all directions; as to replace her, make her theirs; their own imagination of her overriding all else that she might be or ever wish to; and so too then every other person, dead or living, yet to live, each struck in their own way at a loss, capturing and dividing up inside themselves a workable representation of their nature, as it stands in evidence against each other's understanding of *the facts.*

Like how it felt once being underwater as a child, trying to hold her breath so long she had no breath left, and so had to breathe off something deeper, something else; where if she could only break her will and stay under just a bit longer, the realms of life and death would touch, she knew, move through her brain; and yet each time, as she had tried to drown herself so often, something in her anatomy had forced her up and out against her will. How the air would flood into her lungs again like fire, filling her body whether she wanted it or not. And still the world would feel no different having kept her among the living; she would no less know how to go on, to shape a hope. She had never found a way to discern between reality and desire, or even to remember which was which.

The mob of doubles appears to actually fear her, lurking and gawking like captured animals, waiting for her to disappear so that they might take her place—as they had with her true father, so she understands then, in a blink. Each face was activated only as a stand-in, desperate for connection back into the battery of its assigned role, more like a cursor than a person.

They regard her blankly, unable to act without command.

Alice finds she can no longer feel her flesh either; or rather at last she can't see what any inch of her is for, how she could go on being anything her own under such pressure, in the long, blown glow of the telescoping room, wherein still further bodies continue their ongoing onslaught of arrival, loud as an airport or a mall, through more doors than seem possible, swarming in around her and her nearest counterpart, still known in her ongoing register as Smith. When she turns to him for a reaction, some explanation, she finds he has begun to come apart: clusters of pigment foaming over where his outer façade won't hold together, with no real flesh or blood beneath outer façade won't hold together, with no real flesh or blood beneath the buzzing edges of his meat; all made only even hazier with her acknowledgment, as if where he is he really isn't.

Alice feels her own experience as if it's being collected and assessed. Her skin and sense all rubbery and buzzing, as every passing stab at making new memory becomes zapped upon contact, shattered to fragments no sooner than it appends its presence to the record of all time; and so again like that, every instant, so fast it's like it only really happens once, undoing any perceived familiarity on sight. The other bodies no longer seem to comprise what at first they appeared to embody in correlation to her person; the air itself between them takes on the texture of another mirror, encrypting bit by bit, until it has transformed the shape of where they are into a surface wider and deeper than the cumulative reflective light of all other mirrors, their surfaces melted down to form a single plane beyond the shape of this or any room; higher even than the sky, as we knew it ever, against a form of ground no longer ground, a form of flesh no longer aware.

How nothing ever felt the way she remembered until after she stopped being able to remember it at all, and then could never find a way to see it as it had been, amid the continuous threat of any second not actually continuing on into the next; how time might somehow not line up right in some small, unarticulated way and then veer off and not return, leaving her standing in a single, repeating day forever, someone else's, like one of countless colors of wire that fed back to the TV. How her father would close whatever book each time either one of them stepped into the room, foreclosing access to his marks in the margins, leaving her to access them through only her own imagination, none of it in any language she could identify, composed as if in commentary to itself, as if he had been the only author and only reader in the same flesh.

Amid such fractured recollections, Alice can sense that the prior persons living in her are hanging on only by coincidence, shadows of performances once new, now left adrift, searching through her for something undeniably true: not for an exit but for even deeper hold on what she needs, mashed together like vomit under mud, transforming their own meaning even as they shudder briefly once more into the spotlight of her imagination, felt still in the unseen wake of the massive image of the twin women before her. The surface of that image seems to glow, now, with an ineluctable incandescence, like miles of open sunlight filling in over the mass transmission of all else the world might want, seeming to grow only stronger, brighter, the more the remaining world spread out before them comes apart. She can hear their vibrant silence in her still, where her pulse had once been, her only voice, above the fray; no longer needing language or intention to apply their power to any fate, no threat or commandment to alter any divide between reality and will. They seem able to take hold in each partition of her as it loosens, slips apart, ripping up the archived climes inside her as their own, revealing underneath the surface of her person not flesh or bone, but something like a band of singing voices louder than all other input, embodying the idea of seeing, thinking, wanting, each as an extension of their eternal domain. For all this, the painting is but another mirror, a flimsy mask designed to draw her closer to what remained inhuman about the human: no longer God but God's marked absence, the wreck of logic and desire, the muddled fray of all we'd sworn over our faith in sight unseen, thereafter no longer granted harbor in our own mind's life but rather in shame. It's like the sound of everything she'd ever wished to say all at once; every word she'd wanted more than anything to command into meaning, bound up again in something never intended to be her own.

The sound—that is, their sound—will not stop rolling on, then, amid the mangling banging of her body crowded in so tight with all the others she can't feel; with all their output she takes in all words she had been hoarding in her mind in an attempt to maintain sanity, to carry on. The parts of her present life that she'd tried to hide for her and her alone now pushed into public access, no space for understanding in between. Suddenly she's shrieking, then, so hard it hurts; the sound is so prolonged in its effect that it takes a lifetime to push a breath out, every inch, and in such a way that once she's started letting it all out she can't stop, her malformed expression blasting out in lathering rapids across whatever else there might be to see, wiping out the world like an eraser in deluge, such that what remains thereafter in the wake of anywhere she looks or wants to is nothing more than bloated light, a bright and empty endless smoke spanning all sense of structure, order, information.

———

With her hands fumbling before her, then, feeling for surface within the living scene as it had last been, Alice finally turns. She faces Smith—his disrupted form hardly now more than crud and digits—and feels the fissure in her rushing up redoubled to override him, an overwhelming feeling of authority as simulated among the living even more complete in her control; as if at last there had been no other way that she could be, filled from end to end with centuries of shapeless screaming. It felt more now like majesty than pain, like a new purpose; or, rather, a purpose finally divulged after suffering so long in her own body, even if she finds no word within her quite to claim it, name its value. The flood of her vision shatters into his impression, his person at once rendered to clumps; all the lifelong fissures in his identity, his ideas, unbound upon direct contact with the power flowing through her, overriding; his flesh come apart as easily as any canvas, any page, the fluttering particles at once swallowed up and incorporated into the surrounding silver shine. Where any spirit might have once hidden somewhere inside him, she sees, the man is all but rub and bubble, nothing there to cling to in remand; and so too then, as Alice reads it, the loosened verve of the divulged man floods through her, its last impression dissolving everything about their location held between the pixels: everywhere there had ever been another person in any scene; any sense of definition without deception; any life and its desires-made-demands. The room at once around her runs together like putty, some kind of fledgling clay that won't meld or move no matter how she splatters, slips, finding no sure traction in the muddle, so far and wide apart it has nothing left to give, no architecture, as all the rest comes caving in around and throughout her. She feels a fire throttling through her fiber, dragging at her core, her intuition—all of it, at last—splitting open within her, until suddenly it's not only the sound and light of centuries of pain that's pouring through and through her, but all that she is: her blood, her love; the possibility of her presence interwoven with the marrow of words ever enlisted to describe to no one *who she was, why she is here.* Her body feels tugged taut to split, her sternum overwhelmed, not like a wound but like a sea, because *she wants this*, now more than anything: to see the world turned inside out, the air made smaller and thinner than all the walls in this space folding over and over on themselves, inverting their values. An older, sicker silence rushes through her—not *only* her, but every possibility of ever being; the mud of everything she ever was or dreamed of yet becoming gush from the imprint of her, gaining in nature, unto erasure, shaking her whole life loose to let it all through, all *right now*, until she needs more and more bandwidth to keep running. And so from her nostrils then and from her eardrums; from the tips of her fingers, busted of nailbeds, and the outline of her prints; from the lines along her palms and every pore, from her nipples and hair's ends and her navel, her vagina and her asshole; her beliefs; anywhere there's a hole or not a hole, all of it wanting at once in and out so badly, as if the very act of its excision creates only more yet in its wake. The stinging, clinging crud is all there is, all over the ground and unfurling fast and hot across the floor, gushing down the walls over the endless doors onto the absences of anybody else claimed to have existed, of past and future, none distinguishable from one another any longer but as more of the same grist, the grinding walls and long-clogged outlets of anywhere she can remember ever having been—or understood even only as a figment of her imagination—now opened and worn away. The wet, wide drive of every impossible world pours out from who she was, but also from the descending sky above, all of space, until it is dissolved in the elapsing contour of all proffered identity, until there's nowhere left for anything but the idea that at last here is an act that might last forever. As she tries to turn to see across the everlasting, crashing absence where all she'd once conceived had been her own, she finds the grade of space itself turns with her too, locked to her contour; she can discern at once the hidden line between what had once been and what remains, its cold equator showing exactly how and why the space had held together long as it already had. She'd needed to arrive here, she senses, not only to recognize it, but to see on through, beyond any idea of how it is now, unwinding and dissolving back into itself like ambient magma, split apart and redoubled so often that her participation in her own experience is no longer required; no frame for any sight and nowhere else left to be mapped; wherein so long as any light might wish to kindle, there's not a body or a structure or even land yet left to absorb it, only latent lobes that rise and then recede without demand; all space, all hours, rounded out in the same signal, no claim beyond the missing lay of open space under the only looming logo where a sun might once have reigned above us, simple and radiant:

Between the blinding bars within her mind, Alice can almost quite see out, homing in on the negation like a viewfinder at a glass eye. She can distinguish what appears to be her body, as it remains now, spread out beneath her, on her back, aged and naked, bearing scars; as if every bruise and wound she'd ever suffered, in all her prior hours, has been returned unhealed, set into place, the skin between them so thin and faded she can nearly see through her own self, then her reflection.

Her face is interlaced with wires, she understands then, tracing the air beneath her back to where her sight begins. Metallic tubing laces her perimeter at access points installed into her person, leading off into the walls and what behind. A bit has been fit in her jaw; she can taste its tangy metal between her teeth and in her brain too; can feel sharp flat heads scanning just beneath the inseam of her cerebrum, scraping, inserting. It doesn't hurt—or rather, she knows it *does* hurt, but not in a way that she can feel; nor can she remember how it ever felt to feel regardless; the light had always been like this, each room just like this, embedded floor to ceiling with a shining, depthless glow, like needing a mirror to see sunlight.

Amid the glut, as Alice sifts, appears the semblance of a face; an anonymous composite of impressions sourced from all the other faces she's ever seen, pressed together beyond any central semblance: a slur of pupils, nostrils, cheeks, hair; then, from those, lips around a mouth, teeth, a tongue, all of it at once so far away and still so near it's hard to know exactly how or where to aim the eyes.

The child looked so much like myself, Alice thinks, as if reading from plates carried lifelong somewhere inside her, to be accessed only now. *Or so much like someone I remembered and could not identify, myself a stranger, as if even I had forgotten how I was.*

And yet for all the ways she feels the face resembles hers, she also knows it could not be: the eras of their flesh are different, their formal definitions, what either wanted, what they are. These other eyes, so much like hers, held gore and order together, each definition epochs older than the rest of all there is, older than any other person who'd ever lived, and here before her filled up with incarnate texture much like gray, but graver, deeper, radiating.

The child forces a familiar smile, as if he can hear Alice thinking or already knows the story. The metal braces on his teeth are glinting silver, their metal chrome same as the tubing lacing Alice's flesh. Any other light inside the space cuts back whatever else might wish to look too long into it, and only more so as it might try to turn away.

The child's gaze spread out among my thoughts, my life, my fire, wedging into any open weakness in how I was. It crowded in around my mind, surrounding any dream or idea I'd hidden and did not even know, what I thought or felt or any else I'd ever been; all the hell and hope that I'd absorbed in prior time and could no longer distinguish from any else. Soon then I could recognize myself forgetting there could have ever been a place for who I was, that I might have ever thought back on some passed day and found myself there, still elapsing.

———

"You don't remember," the child states, its voice cutting at once through all other impression. The face's lips don't seem to need to move to make the question, nor does its expression ripple, yet Alice can hear the message just as clear; it feels like screws intruding in her linings, searching out her weakest points. The very presence of the speaking nudges open innumerable old sores, faintly detectable against the larger gnawing of her nature, held within her all entwined and interlocked. Alice feels as if there is nothing left within her that isn't the child's too, a common logic hanging over their shattered landscape of mutual memory.

Rooms where we'd stood together in no daylight, waiting for any other person to appear; how we always felt we were alone even in company; how nothing stuck but all the games we invented to pass time, like the one where the ground was lava and if you touched it you would disintegrate to nothing. Sometimes whole weeks would go by before the world revealed itself again as interactive, anywhere that we could touch. How we would take turns staying up late to watch the moon glow against darkness, in fear that if it went on too long unprotected it would fall out of the sky, which always ended in us each hard and fast asleep by morning, neither knowing what had happened in between, a state that soon became the only way we ever walked.

Each prompted memory unclasps another, like layers peeling off inside their common mind, none of which Alice really feels she recognizes upon contact and just as quickly can't deny. They seem all that remains to her, despite the sinking feeling of something slipping, simulated: parts of her perception rendered missing, left unlabeled; every hour in just some small way incomplete, regardless of how discreetly any user might wish to feed it faith.

"Of course I remember, Richard," Alice answers finally, her voice calm and clear, filling in over all else she might remember. "You are my blood. My brother. How could I not?" Where she'd felt the urge then to let the text out, she finds nothing underneath to follow; its meaning seems to peel off, feeding back into the face's expectant fiber, making it clearer with every dislocated surge. Soon the face is beaming brightly, fleshing its form out, showing its mouthful of vile teeth, hundreds of them, lining his throat and windpipe, each reflecting a nearly once-familiar world.

The stairwell in the house you'd found that led down to a checkered floor, which seemed to extend so far in all directions it had to be so much larger than the house; how you would get lost on it, you and he together, in the dim musk of all lost time, holding hands until you found your way back to somewhere real, thereafter traced for months, for years, under the sneaking suspicion that the world that you'd returned to wasn't ours, but had replaced one nearly like it, a fear that could be allayed only by your brother's ongoing persistence, his infectious calm. How the hands of your father, when you found him, in whatever version of your house this world contained, always seemed so large, so numb, fumbling to hold anything; how loud any signal had to be to make it through; thus the shaking, screaming din of the shows he would watch with you and Richard both so young there in the room, wrought with nauseating light, the volume up so loud you couldn't hear your own mind, allowing no thoughts of your own outside those provided by the screen; and somewhere, within that, held even nearer, the unremitting texture of your brother's voice, louder and clearer than all the rest, even your own feeling, right underneath you. How he had begun to seem to be able to read your thought, to know what you most wanted, how you were, what you feared and how it grew, no matter how completely you tried to hide inside it, like right now.

"Or 'unbrother,' as you always liked to call me," the child says, interrupting her apparent recognition, back to now. "Which would hurt my heart, I must admit, to the point of nearly dying, or wanting to die; until years later, when eventually I understood; when I could grasp what our blood was turning into, I mean; what all of any human blood was even for; how sometimes, in the ongoing mass of what you felt, I might be someone else; your brother, yes, but then your father, your unfather, your mother and unmother, your daughter, son; each all the same."

Alice's teeth sting; her eyes burn; her lips ache; her hips rip; her tender fire slowly dying out, sirens in her scraping; the sour muddle, full of friction, fiction; all of it wailing, waiting to be given pasture, any end, even as the present bending phrase only continues; awl to leather; heat to nowhere.

"Soon I could not keep control of what I was to you, latch onto it; which for years and hours scared me beyond death, how well you shook us off, myself as well as any other, the whole world handled each the same; how quickly anyone could be forgotten, blown into fragments, fault lines. For so long, all I wanted was to be understood, by you or any other, to become inculcated into satisfaction whether I had earned it yet or not; and still anything that happened, no matter what efforts I applied or what I gave up, only turned out the opposite of what I'd wished. In the end, it was your refusal, the depth of loss in that reality, that gave me something to push back on, to want to grow from, a living seed."

As in every memory, ever after, there he was, where for so long he had not been; no way back; he who had threaded his way into any mind where it took damage, in so many kinds of forms it populated its own world, something once flesh and phantom, found and lost. All the gaps in what you could remember, filled as if with plaster, comprising decades, years you had mostly already blacked out for yourself. And even where he wasn't, he still was, taking over anywhere left unattended, growing stronger. Years and years of correspondence from abroad; phones ringing in the evening without answer, while the rest of the world slept; his voice as close to your brain as it is now, even when silent; all laced together in a network that even as it whorls and clings under his gaze, you can't remember how so many years had passed already, or how many remained as yet to come; each day bleeding together so completely they might as well all be the same.

———

"I thought you died," Alice stutters, the words more slurred, forced out into the story between what might be actually allowed, pushed free from a warmth within her not quite felt. Nor is there any emotional force behind the words as she hears them, only an unsteady echo as at the tail end of long years spent in fade, clamoring to regain control over how even our language could fall out from underneath itself in becoming uttered. "Or I didn't know what to think," she goes on, feeling the cords inside her tighten, "in having lost you by losing control of my thinking, as if someone else was also in me; in every one of me . . . like right now."

Alice can see then how the face before her is still changing, from the prior incarnation she had recognized as Richard to something molten, somewhere else, each part of her overflowing as much with the flesh of those she'd shattered or run over as with any essence of herself. Nothing doesn't hurt that still feels familiar; she can feel nothing else but in its light, passed through every shade of future hour, days becoming decades. She can see among the unfurling lapses of impressions in his image taking familiar forms, just out of step—her family members, local leaders, pundits, spokespeople, anyone who might have passed before her eyes—each not quite who they were but still present in her software same as ever, turning over.

"I did die," the face says calmly. "And so did you. So did every person, every life, as we went on waiting for something that could never actually appear. The absence of any key to our creation made a coma of our dream lives, such that only within them might we live on, as in a state of total and ongoing subjugation to ourselves. The undeath of what remained possible in dreaming scalped our memory, caused our surest intentions to come caving in on all the rest. And throughout it all we each believed ourselves the center of not only ourselves but the whole world, through which someone else was always seeing and misconstruing, smearing its presence, unto end."

How some nights you would wake up so many times it was like the night could never happen, growing older the longer you lay awake and even longer until morning. Sometimes you would wake up so far from anywhere you knew, on piles of dirt along some shoreline, after Armageddon; or in a bed stuck inside someone else's life, alone. The only way you could find your way home was to lie down and go asleep again, praying that when you awakened it'd be fixed, and you'd forget it even happened, believing only that everybody else knew what was wrong, carrying on in spite of all you ever were, in the same way transferring their future absence into everything you touched or saw or even just imagined; any all.

▬

And yet none of this is true, Alice insists, her own voice still there alive, somewhere inside her. *None of these memories are mine.*

The words come in just beneath the others in her hearing, like subtitles on a film too near to see, a straining feeling welling over where any times touch. Nothing rings as quite actually there—little had, ever, but in perceived simulation—this time felt along the skin of the mirage not as her own error, some incalculable disease, but innate in all of us, the passed along as well as the future pending in the same stretch as her own.

The child's eyes are even wrong, she sees, looking not directly at her but just beyond, at anything that might be there beyond the living frame, more like a recording of someone wanting to appear alive, to really know you—the same sort of inherent interruption that had followed Alice her whole life, willing her to destroy the possibility of even existing in order to finally see something actual, the very sort of unresolved anticipation that gave each day its shape; though despite all else she had held on, depleted and scattered, yet still wanting to press past the active fault, the same way she had strained her way through every moment, looking forward while still wired to the past.

The child's face feels so close now, so integral to how she is, despite the vastness of their gap; as if without it, nothing of the world could ever be, an inherited feeling she feels enforced upon her even as its claim to any intimate proximity betrays its core. She sees faults now, in his complexion, breaks in the continuity of even a blur of possible familiarities, hints of another face behind the façade; not only the lasting impressions of the acne they had shared, but deeper damage—finer defects amid the rendering, derived not out of actual suffering, or even the evocation of it, but of a loss of resolution, lack of depth; inconsistencies created by the image's apparent failure to align with what it desires to portend.

The mutating face is more a mask than a memory, she understands then. The person the face represents is not even actually in there, Alice realizes, only what she might imagine it could be, modeled by Alice's own mind, through its confusion, using her own worst feelings against her as a mechanism of belief.

Still, the device cannot resist feeding off its own denial; the face's eyes continue changing even as her perception of him does, trying to shape its total image back toward a form that maintains an emotional effect. It seems that whatever the face of the child represents can sense what its audience is thinking, even beneath its disarray, suggesting there must still be limits to what it can access. Its reach can really extend only so far, then, Alice imagines, its presence determined as much by others' collaboration as by an infernal drive to overcome, control. How much cleaner to let the child's design fit as it wishes, she thinks, to let her mind slip and accept exactly what it projects itself to be, though the urge is undercut by the possibility that, upon concession, its desire might drive even deeper, more completely.

We had been constraining ourselves for so long without even meaning to, Alice feels the face behind the face reconfirming, as if in solidarity to her awareness, a new false flag, *that we've forgotten how to stop, nor do most of us have any kind of real desire to, much less a motive.* It's no longer quite a question asked only of Alice, then, but of anyone with whom she'd ever been brought into contact: those who'd seen her, felt her, in any form of broadcast, however far from truth its received impression might have been, however far out on the long lineage of adaptation she'd had to bend to make it fit into the timeline of her life.

All our days had always been aligned by someone else's want for setting, structure, she hears herself think, unsure by now which voice is thinking through her after all, *a mechanism by which some such overseer might transgress beyond human understanding,* and perhaps soon beyond a living face or need for voice at all, beyond flesh.

———

The mutating head is sweating, Alice notices, or leaking, the fluid different in how it glistens and distorts, freeing loose odd lodes of color inside each cell behind it. The image has begun consuming its own surface, it appears, distorting both the face and its speech: when the voice attempts to continue any narration, to direct her thought, its sound clips in and out around the edges, gumming up in passing places, full of lurch. It's as if the words no longer wish to stick together, clinging together where one's influence infects the other, becoming stung.

"And still you despised me for what I wasn't," the voice insists, taking on a plaintive tone amid its glitch, scrabbling to maintain its own integrity by blasting past it, "for where your own sense of reality diverged from what actually would happen, resulting in the ongoing enactment of a trauma by which our larger devastation might begin, wherein some would say such obfuscation would soon become our greatest gift, the very means by which we might transcend the necessity of human pain forever, once and for all."

Despite such consolation, slurring long and low into what might once have been soft, the guidance of the head is already turning stricter, more impenetrable, such that each word as it is considered by her system undoes itself at once, or at least rendered in some lost partition of herself still locked and combing for a key for any set of stimuli to come together, make the day click over into what it had always seemed it might best hold, toward the kind of life we might actually wish to live; in joy, in love, in aspiration. Despite it all, charged with such anguish, she would find a way to want to still believe in what could be, an urge made only more intense each time it splinters, over and over and again.

The face is glowing now, backlit with crumble like coals in fire. "Nowhere more could such a wound be carried on," it manages to mutter, the gears in the voice slowing and tangling, "but in every potential human action never permitted to eventually occur, in coexistence with our mythology's constantly remodeling emotional architecture, diverged in spirit from what we wanted to become given the opportunity to no longer have to want to strive—and so each act made equally redundant, thereby begetting actual liberty, for all."

For a moment, as the face falls deeper into its encoded manner of digression and justification, Alice watches as it transforms into the woman she had known as Alice Novak; then Smith, the president, her mother and her father and unfather; then Richard, through all his ages left unseen; and finally, behind that, the coagulating face of her own face replacing the previous completely, burned into fiber. Behind that, behind her, what outlasts isn't a face at all, has no complexion—more like a landmass, lost in time. The distinction between remaining flesh and what's behind it then collapses, leaving only lines of code, then smolder, then rubble.

"It would not take long before it was as if we never had existed even to the idea of ourselves," the last voice boils, no longer speech but infestation, a disease that rises up from underneath the crumbling words, "and then thereafter, in our absence, no such idea as fact or fiction—no true future, nor a past—no construct of self beyond where here we are now—not in a term but in a sentence being stuttered through its ending, and the silence after—"

The head is no longer there on the screen. The space where it had once been snows against its own suggested absence, in resolution, revealing coagulating patterns, forms of shape; each again then at once grown soft with blinding colors, flashing trails no sooner perceived than passed away.

Where at first there had been one head, now there are countless, their full projection ransacking the light; as many heads as had ever lived; billions upon billions of comprised shells, of past and future lives, each devoid of feature or persona; spanning more space than any sky.

They are all looking back up to the same point, toward a focus once represented as our Alice, by her own face, on the far side of the room; each spectator stunned by whatever it is they believe they feel they see of her or in her place, each seeming to possess knowledge far beyond the fact of where or who they are.

Their continuing image, from Alice's last perspective, extends further and further back across the erased faces, through endless open space the size of any ego; far beyond anything like Alice's conception, across all anybody might imagine, until we the audience, held just offscreen, no longer bear sufficient bandwidth to absorb the information, and so the system crashes, and the condition disappears.

And when I woke again the room was not the room as it had been, nor was it any of the rooms I'd ever passed through in my life; not a room really at all but a phantasm, full of air from fields of buried dead, their flesh disintegrated into soil and heat, with my own arms held as well there within it, soft as sound, and my lost skin within me struck with blooming, turning over, caressed wide open by the absence of the light.

Wherever I could sense myself, then, from in the absence, I knew at once the world was not the world as it had been, but more so a model of its last mirage, designed to fit around my mind, and simply by breathing in I understood how every other person had also had a similar process of understanding put to action at the same time. As well I knew the binding grease within my mind was every memory that hadn't happened yet, and now would never happen.

As I acknowledged this, through its intrusion, a larger blankness filled the air where I was not. It filled in fast and hard along the old lines of the prior world already far behind me, sealing me at once into its conception spreading forth, where within every breath I felt the present draft of human history disappearing as it stood, braced within that by the idea of my never having slept or ever awoken, in any life, nor seen or spoken, strung a thread. I kept finding my eyes were closed when I had believed them open, and as I tried to make them open again, the cells within the eyes would burn. The fact of burning firmed them, somehow; its heat enwrapped and wrapping still in fetid heat around my being, wearing it down by slowly poaching my own self-concept up from out of me and replacing it with its own unwritten code, without a key.

Therein, in the same breadth, I found I felt I knew at once that this condition loved me more than I had nature to believe. Its texture held no sickness, no intention beyond the winding of its whir; no further factor for identity beyond how, with any way I tried to move, I remained the only thing not already moving, spanned through all the different modes of narrative, without return; not a flesh but a sensation. Where had I ever really been? Why had I lived, or at least believed I had? To ask meant nothing, as in expecting any definition or description, my blank provided even less; every erased experience I'd once embodied having been already long turned into cinder, compressed as futures never glimpsed beyond their potential as passed plot.

What I saw as land then opening before me became like the act of seeing in and of itself; where even seeing as an action became like being pulled apart, revealed as nightmares draped throughout eternal night, each one larger than the universe's size, filling the indescribable space of our imagination as at last the frame of all creation had come alive, in place of us; a seeing, writhing state of being, from which there would no longer exist any exit, even death; no life to live but through what had already become accumulated as unnegotiable terrain, a scene shot without a lens into a darkness in which the lack of light itself had learned to think.

Where we were then was full of shining in the nothing. I saw that I had more eyes now than I could count, disguised inside the shades of flesh I carried in me all dismantled as every human memory, far and wide, only now throughout it, where all the air had once been, there was a hemisphere of blood, and we were all at once as close as skin upon it, each able to feel it changing just the same, a state within which I was not an I, nor any other, and where anywhere I'd ever been was so much smaller than itself; and yet still smaller every stitch, slipping only further still into negation where it could feel me begging for release; until, in no time at all so near, I could not feel anything at all, nor could I hear or taste or listen, pressed flat as I now was against the glass all in my heart, wider than even how dying felt in dreaming of it throughout all my living hours, so far apart within me now there was no longer anything to name.

0005

On the final video, in night vision, we see a massive glassy structure in the dark. It has no windows, no clear entrances or exits.

The complex is enormous; it fills the screen, taking up so much space that nothing else appears along the body of the land even as the camera pulls backward, revealing only more of the same. No sky, no sea, no other eye.

If there is sound in the video, it is the sound of nothing.

▬

Inside the complex, framing our perspective, another camera moves along a long white hall. Oblong mirrors installed at regular intervals along the passage disjointedly reflect the camera's path, showing it moving independent of any visible operator across a course of points at which some sense of recognition might occur, as one might have felt once in a museum. The camera appears to have no wires, to bear no logo, same as the soundtrack shares no sound.

▬

Eventually, somewhere along the hallway—we can no longer really tell how long—the camera comes to a stop. It turns to face the nearest mirror, identical to the others we have passed, then rolls forward to press against it, to see into it.

The mirror is transparent. Behind it appears a cubic chamber, four white walls, the same hue and texture as the others. At the center of the area, a body appears strapped down to a chrome table, its head laced with receptors, gauges, body braced with locks on the limbs and around the waist and neck and ankles. The body breathes, or so it seems from the gentle rising and falling of its frail chest. Otherwise, it is completely still, as if unconscious.

It takes a while to recognize the body's face: it is *Alice Knott*, a bygone name appearing in our mind as some echo of an icon of our memory, almost like a friend, or someone we'd wished to know in such a way, though really by now we are not sure who Alice Knott might be. She is so old it seems impossible; her skin a surgery of putty, puffy leather, lacing, colored veins. She has no hair, no teeth, no nails.

Why do we feel we understand? And why this strange impression of warmth in the recognition, despite its coarseness? It's not quite a wholehearted feeling, more a stinging in the places that love might have activated some years before. We find we wish that she could wake and look at us, or even rise, approach the window, a feeling complicated by our understanding that she does not know we are there.

▬

The video is interrupted by an ad for a memory medication, made by a brand that has no name. The ad depicts a single massive sky blue pill, large as an airfield, glistening in hard light against an incandescent background, absent of clear relation to any kind of environment in which we might have spent our life.

An insect flutters down from overhead; it is a grotesque thing, with many heads and wings, but also exaggeratedly juvenile, like an unlikable cartoon. The bug lands on the pill and begins to gnaw at its linings with all its mouths at once, sprawls of tendrils quivering in audible ecstasy.

Its pleasure attracts several other insects to the scene, all lighting down on the same pill, also taking up part in the feast; soon hundreds are gathered there, so thick you can no longer see the medication's pastel flesh beneath its living, buzzing coat. The POV pans back then to reveal a field of insects far as the eye can see, all fumbling and mangling at one another to reach the center.

Within the texture of the image, a tiny, sprawling text weaves its way, listing the product's side effects so fast no one could read them: nausea, vomiting, malaise, loss of appetite, weight loss, weakness, diarrhea, constipation, painful urination, bruising, tremors, increased blood pressure, chest pain, muscle cramps, headaches, fatigue, insomnia, drowsiness, dizziness, confusion, amnesia, hallucination, fainting, seizures, itching, swelling, difficulty breathing, blood clot, paralysis, sudden death.

After the ad, a flash of barcode, the same one we would remember seeing every time we blink, if only seeing the barcode didn't make you forget you've seen anything but what you're seeing next.

━━━

The video returns to Alice, on the bed. Our attention is tuned now to a small live monitor installed into the wall above her body, displaying its subject's current thoughts, fed from wires in her face into the network, for both maintenance and internal security. We know this because we already knew this. The feed is also being supplied into another form of serial entertainment, of which without realizing we have now become a part.

The screen reveals what Alice herself believes in the present moment: that she is lying in her childhood bed, looking up at the ceiling where she once designed a solar system on the plaster with glowing stickers, forming a mass of stars so crowded in and close that no inhabitable terrain among them could sustain human life. Staring into the constellation seems to make her happy, even now, content to be exactly where she is, though we, the viewer, do not feel the same; there is something missing from the moment, something inherent to it that might have made it feel true; as if we know something Alice does not, but we can't name it.

Through the cubicle's interior speakers, we hear the child Alice singing to herself, a made-up song with no clear melody or refrain, unknown lyrics displayed onscreen in an unrecognizable language. The song is the theme to the most popular TV program of all time, which we are not aware we've even heard.

━━

The camera moves back from the mirror and continues along the hall. Other mirrors blur on either side as it continues passing, an open color. It remains unclear if the camera is being operated by a remote presence, or if it is self-propelled.

Every so often, the camera stops again and approaches a different mirror, peers into a different room. Some of the bodies seem familiar, as had Alice, if still in a way we can't discern: persons we once knew who had since disappeared, leaving only fragments of impression, arcane sense. Others bear no connection at all, are only other bodies, people someone other than us must have once cared for; some seem sick, barely held together in their repose by artificial means.

The thoughts of many of these subjects are all but illegible: abstract wind-lanes of muddy color; wheels of fuzz. Others show pistons ramming into pistons on a wide field, or snow falling onto water and not melting but hissing and ejecting reams of colored smoke. None of the bodies ever moves more than in brief spasm, no correlation to anything onscreen, or to the camera, to us.

In many of the chambers, no one is there. The empty apparatuses remain unmanned, perhaps soon to be filled with someone or something else. The thought-screens above the empty beds exude an open glow, eclipsed of image, filling the chamber with a calm almost like daylight.

———

The video is interrupted now by an ad for drinking water, represented by a massive pool, wide as the sky, no land or other surface visible beyond. There's a soundtrack that sounds like way too many people have guitars. Somewhere far in the background, people are howling, as in great pain, pleading in the same wrecked language as from the song we already can't remember Alice singing, in her chamber, here heard as sickening, cringeworthy; a disease.

Suddenly the voices are cut off, choked into a matching silence, before a cloud rises through the waters; the blood; its muddy color fills in across the waters' shining surface, darkening the screen out, echo black.

In handwritten cursive font, then, the tagline: *Water Is a Privilege*, followed again by barcode.

Every so often, the camera passes a section on the wall that is not mirror but external window, allowing the viewer to see beyond the walls. None of the visible locations seems to match what we remember from the video's beginning: instead, the land is a flat, blotched gray. Fleeting stabs of electricity skirt across its stomach, spreading far out toward a sky absent of stars or planets, only matching panes of flatness, altogether more like a ceiling than a sky. Along the landscape, at various distances, we see the outline of other structures just like this one, with no wires strung between, no signage or definition to identify their nature. Corralling waves of light extend their command between more definitive patrols, a long, wide world of unseen lines of sight and sound spanning the complex's perimeter, designed to hold together no matter how far along them someone might wander if let loose, eventually circling any body straying across the continent back toward the center of the set, its outline pumped full of heavy air so hard and sharp it stings to breathe once activated by live commotion, any noise. So much better to remain within the parameters as defined, within which one's unique personal settings can be adjusted to fit one's preferences at any time, in collaboration, so long as those preferences are provided in writing three to six weeks in advance, so that we may be made aware you still have preferences.

Further off, too, beyond the ostensible horizon, at such a distance it blends in beneath the glut, a massive sprawl of metal bleachers lines the grounds, buried so brightly no one might ever make out a single face among the wall of watching bodies filling the tiers but left to stand, all their heads shaved and obscured in ways that make them impossible to tell apart; each struck open-mouthed in silence, silver-teethed, feeding, if still unclear at whose behest, or where else there might yet be that they might one day gather up and leave for, to return home.

The camera doesn't linger on the view; instead, it passes fast enough for one to imagine there was never any view at all.

———

This video will have no outside narration, we realize, hearing our own passing thoughts fill in whatever else does not; there is no sound to direct or manipulate our perspective, and no way to change the channel, though we remember how we used to sit before screens for hours upon hours imbibing custom content, every day.

Instead, there seems to be no space outside this one recording in our experience—only the video, nothing else—and though we have questions about context, infrastructure, how we're here, they must pass without real contemplation, for we can't seem to make the logic last. At times we become aware of what seems like someone breathing in the soundtrack, but this is only us, whoever we are.

———

And still we can't shake Alice from our mind. At each next mirror, we hope to see her again behind the glass, but it's always only someone else, a stranger or someone whose face we can't remember, one of an endless queue of bodies, none of whom appear to understand they're there. We recognize only the blank behind their look, the paling weight of endless pending in their unknown cooperation.

———

The last ad we remember is an ad for lard. It depicts the same model seen in other ads we can't remember seeing all our lives. In flashback we see her rubbing lard into her cheeks and lips and beaming, eating the lard alone off a chrome table, sleeping in a pile of the lard, cradling the lard in her arms and humming to it like a child. The house in the ad looks so much like the house you remember living in, though you can't remember anything about that life.

And yet, you know you want the lard. You want the lard so much you would pay any price they ask, but the ad gives no info on how to purchase. You can only wait.

Or perhaps you have the lard already. We know the ads we've seen must still repeat; that, or they are new ads that seem just like the old ones, presenting different things or the same things: an ad for holograms that fuck; an ad for fresh human hair, for feeding, and for caressing; an ad for a set of black leather-bound books, in a new edition of a once-popular series now reprinted in condensed form, all one volume, nearly the width of your own head.

Each time we see an ad we can't remember having seen it before, which seems true of the rest of the video as well, though we can't remember how or why.

———

Mirror after mirror, hall after hall; hour upon hour; all without timecode, any cut that's not an ad. What appears is what there is— and it is all there is. Chamber after chamber, body after body, screen after screen—no next direction to the world but what the world itself decides to see depicted on demand, dismissing all prior record wherein it might have never been the case without fanfare or relent, until at last, in the next chamber, strapped to a chrome table like all the others: There you are.

———

You don't recognize yourself at first, what with the wires and tubing obfuscating your features, the lines of age accrued in the shadow of your face amid the bone protruding through the flesh there worn away.

And yet, unlike the other bodies you have seen here, your eyes are open; you're staring out right back at where you are, through the mirror into the camera, though it's unclear if you are actually seeing, as any life behind your face there never flinches; nor does your expression change at all in being seen.

Still, yes, you feel, this must be you; how could you mistake your own two eyes, the same ones you've spent a life looking back into already, in mirrors, in pictures, the evidence of your surveillance? And so that must be the rest of your body there attached, you figure: the flesh and bones you'd lived inside for so long, the you you'd carried through sickness, pleasure, boredom, so many nights you can't recall beyond their dark. This face is your face, for certain; those arms are your arms; this condition all you know.

———

On the screen installed above your inert body, there you are too: an image of who you feel you must be in your present version, as you understand you, outside any other eye's description. You're sitting in a familiar room, wherever you happen to be now: perhaps your home, just barely breathing in the open, muted glow that fills our face.

In your hands is a book, held open near its ending, though you can't see any words marked on the page. You're grinning at yourself, showing your chrome teeth; your unblinking eyes like shining, so alive.

You see yourself seeing yourself, if only for a second, before the camera moves away.

MORE FROM ARCHWAY EDITIONS

Archways 1
    (edited by Chris Molnar and Nicodemus Nicoludis)
cokemachineglow: Writing Around Music 2005-2015
    (edited by Clayton Purdom)
Claire Donato – *Kind Mirrors, Ugly Ghosts*
John Farris – *Last Poems*
Gabriel Kruis – *Acid Virga*
Brantly Martin – *Highway B: Horrorfest*
NDA: An Autofiction Anthology
    (edited by Caitlin Forst)
Alice Notley – *Runes and Chords*
Ishmael Reed – *Life Among the Aryans*
Ishmael Reed – *The Haunting of Lin-Manuel Miranda*
Ishmael Reed – *The Slave Who Loved Caviar*
Mike Sacks – *Randy & Stinker Lets Loose*
Paul Schrader – *First Reformed*
Stacy Szymaszek – *Famous Hermits*
Erin Taylor – *Bimboland*
charles theonia – *Gay Heaven is a Dance Floor but I Can't Relax*
Unpublishable
    (edited by Chris Molnar and Etan Nechin)
Lindsey Webb – *Plat*

FORTHCOMING

Afsana Mousavi – *Love Story*
Christopher Coe – *Such Times*
Olivia Kan-Sperling – *Little Pink Book*
The Mystery of Perception
    (Lynne Tillman interviewed by Taylor Lewandowski)

Archway Editions can be found at your local bookstore
or ordered directly through Simon & Schuster

QUESTIONS? COMMENTS? CONCERNS? SEND CORRESPONDENCE TO:

       Archway Editions
       c/o powerHouse Books
       220 36th St., Building #2
       Brooklyn, NY 11232

ALSO BY BLAKE BUTLER

MOLLY

Blake Butler and Molly Brodak instantly connected, fell in love, married and built a life together. Both writers with deep roots in contemporary American literature, their union was an iconic joining of forces between two major and beloved talents.

Nearly three years into their marriage, grappling with mental illness and a lifetime of trauma, Molly took her own life. In the days and weeks after Molly's death, Blake discovered shocking secrets she had held back from the world, fundamentally altering his view of their relationship and who she was.

A masterpiece of autobiography, *Molly* is a riveting journey into the darkest and most unthinkable parts of the human heart, emerging with a hard-won, unsurpassedly beautiful understanding that expands the possibilities of language to comprehend and express true love.

Unrelentingly clear, honest and concise, *Molly* approaches the impossible directly, with a total empathy that has no parallel or precedent. A supremely important work that will be taught, loved, relied on and passed around for years to come, Blake Butler affirms now beyond question his position at the very top rank of writers.

Molly

Blake Butler

"The best book I've read this year."
—*LOS ANGELES TIMES*

"Terrifyingly intense and eerily spiritual...The best book I've read this year."
- *LOS ANGELES TIMES*

"These pages have a midnight sort of impact many novelists would kill to smuggle into their fiction."
- *NEW YORK TIMES*

"With *Molly*, Butler has created a towering tribute to Brodak, in all her complexities, and a harrowing document of unanswerable grief."
- *VANITY FAIR*

"[5 stars]...Extraordinary and raw...the triumph of his book lies in its compassion."
- *THE TELEGRAPH*

"A powerfully sad book...Writers are often praised as 'fearless,' but Butler is not. In *Molly*, he makes fear his companion. That is the only way to write, and to live."
- *THE NEW YORKER*

"I'm not sure I've ever been so totally consumed by any book the way I was by *Molly*."
- *INTERVIEW*

BLAKE BUTLER is the author of twelve book-length works, including *Molly* (Archway Editions), *300,000,000* (Harper Perennial), *There is No Year* (Harper Perennial), and *Scorch Atlas* (Featherproof Books). His short fiction, interviews, reviews, and essays have appeared widely, including in *The New York Times*, *Harper's*, *The Paris Review*, *Fence*, *BOMB*, *Bookforum*, and as an ongoing column at *Vice*. In 2021, he was longlisted for the Joyce Carol Oates Prize. He is a founding editor of HTMLGIANT.